Perceivers

#3

MIND EVOLUTION

by

Jane Killick

Elly Books

Mind Evolution
Perceivers #3

by

Jane Killick

Published by Elly Books

ISBN: 978-1-908340-23-8

Copyright © Jane Killick 2016

ellybooks.com

ONE

THE terror from the hostages seeped through the wall, filling Michael's mind with their desperation to remain alive. Like a colony of bees trapped in a jar, their fear buzzed as a collective, screaming their bottled up cry for help.

There was nothing he could do for them, not on the other side of the wall of the boardroom where they were imprisoned. The only thing he could do, was his job. He pressed his cheek and hands against the cool plaster of the wall and filtered out the thoughts of the armed police officers who hid in strategic places in the office building. He concentrated only on the thoughts and feelings of the hostages, breaking through their collective terror to perceive the individuals inside.

A woman hoped the table she was crouched under would protect her enough for her to stay alive for her children. A man tried to block out the pain radiating from the bullet wound in his leg. Another man repeated The Lord's Prayer silently in his head: *Our Father, who art in heaven, give us …* Michael didn't stop to listen, he lingered only enough to acknowledge each presence before moving onto the next. To linger would be to care and to care would be to lose objectivity.

A tap on Michael's shoulder in the physical world broke him out of his trance and he opened his eyes to see Inspector Anthony Patterson mouthing a question at him. "How many?"

The newly promoted police officer looked just as dishevelled as he had done when he was a sergeant. He'd thrown a bulletproof police vest over his crumpled brown suit and put on a communications headset in such a hurry that a tuft of wiry ginger hair stuck out from behind his ear.

"How many hostages?" Patterson whispered.

"Seven," said Michael as quiet as he could, wishing Patterson wasn't a norm so he could have transmitted his words in a simple thought.

Patterson relayed the information over his headset.

If seven were alive, it meant three were dead.

"What about Farron?"

Farron was his target, the man who had pulled a gun from his briefcase and filled the boardroom with flying bullets, turning him from an apparently ordinary businessman into a terrorist. Michael needed to pull information from his head to help the police negotiator — even though Farron had already resisted any attempt at negotiation — and to help the armed response unit should they need to storm the room.

Michael closed his eyes and sent his mind back through the wall to find him. He felt guilty for turning his back on the thoughts of the hostages clamouring for attention, but pushing them aside allowed him to detect the singular quiet presence that had to be Farron. "Found him."

Whatever anger, political fervour or madness had caused Farron to do what he did, it had faded to a dull anxiety. The ringing in Farron's ears from the gunshots had helped block out the whimpers of the people he had fired at, but as it diminished he was coming to realise that he was just as trapped as they were. His only comfort was the heaviness of the gun on his lap. He stroked his fingers along the barrel, knowing it was the one thing that still gave him control.

"Where is he?" said Patterson in Michael's ear, breaking his concentration for a moment.

Michael tried to lock on to the visual cortex of Farron's brain, but it was like grasping for air. He caught flashes of what Farron could see: his finger clasped around the trigger of the gun, a splash of someone else's blood on his shoe, but nothing of the room or where he was standing. "Not sure. Can't see." Perceiving a person hidden behind a wall was a stretch, even for his ability.

One word echoed in Farron's mind: *Elaine.* His lovely Elaine. It brought up an image of a woman, her face framed by blonde hair and defined by precise make-up. None of this was her fault, Farron thought. She shouldn't have to watch him being led out of the building in handcuffs or suffer the trauma of a trial. He remembered her from another happier time: this time her face was pale, tired but content as she sat up in a hospital bed cradling a tiny baby. His little Lilly was the most innocent of them all. He couldn't leave her with the legacy of a father whose crimes were repeated on the news for weeks and weeks. *I can't let it end like that.*

Michael pulled himself out of Farron's mind. Like the rush of forcing himself to wake up from a nightmare, he was suddenly in the reality of the corridor. He reached forward and grasped the sleeve of Patterson's scratchy wool jacket. "I don't think he intends to come out of this alive."

The realisation fell across Patterson's face as he turned his back and spoke into the radio.

A movement of black against the white corridor walls alerted Michael to the figure behind Patterson. An armed policeman, dressed from helmet to boot in black armour, padded forward in a semi-crouched position, clutching his rifle.

"Wh—?" Michael's half-spoken word was cut by Patterson slapping his hand across his mouth. In a rush, he opened his perception and the flood of thoughts of armed officers entered his mind, all concentrating on orders to storm the boardroom.

Michael's body was propelled backwards by Patterson half-dragging him down the corridor. Michael stumbled, then caught his step and shook himself free as they ran together. To the end of the corridor where it turned into another passageway and the door to a fire escape offered a way out. Michael stopped. Patterson tugged at his sleeve. *We need to get out*, came Patterson's thoughts. Michael shook his head: he hadn't yet got the information he wanted from Farron's mind.

Two black-armoured firearms officers passed them, running near-silent on the carpet. The first continued down the corridor, but the second paused and looked at them with intense blue eyes. "Stay down and keep down," she said, just loud enough to hear.

They crouched at the corner, the wall their only barrier, with Michael peering out from behind it and Patterson keeping him pulled back.

The first shot cracked the air like a lightning bolt, igniting screams from the hostages. A crash as the door was broken down. Other people's adrenaline flooded into Michael's perception. A stab of pain shot into him. Instinctively, he clutched his side where he felt a bullet burn through his flesh.

But the pain wasn't real, it belonged to someone else.

He shut down his perception, expunging every whisper of thought and feeling from other people and took refuge inside his own head. He curled up his body — like he curled up his mind — as tightly as he could while wearing his stiff bulletproof jacket. He closed his eyes, but he couldn't block out the sounds. Like a fireworks display gone wrong, he listened to the terror of the crowd as gunfire exploded around them.

Then, the explosions stopped. Leaving only the crying and whimpering of those who had survived.

Michael opened his eyes to see Patterson beside him as he put his fingers to the earpiece of his headset and listened to what was being said over the radio. Michael couldn't hear the radio transmission, but if he eavesdropped lightly at the edge of Patterson's thoughts, he could get an understanding of what was going on.

The siege was over. Farron had been shot in the chest, and although he was still breathing, his prospects didn't look good.

Michael stood up, realising he didn't have long. He started back down the corridor the way they had come.

"Where are you going? Patterson called out.

"He's going to die," said Michael. He broke into a run.

At the entrance to the boardroom, two black-armoured officers stood in his way, just inside the wooden splintered remains of the door. The gap formed by the silhouettes of their bodies allowed him to see inside to where the bloodied corpse of an office worker lay on the floor where she had fallen: her arms splayed out unnaturally at her sides and her white blouse stained with red. Every so often, the wailing of one of the survivors cut through the eerie silence. Michael kept his perception tightly closed. Seeing and hearing evidence of the carnage was enough.

He darted through the gap between the officers.

"Hey!"

Michael stopped abruptly on the other side. Not because the officer had called after him, but because of what he could see.

He hadn't thought of what it would be like to step into the middle of a massacre until the singed smell of gunpowder was in his nostrils and he tasted the saltiness of freshly splattered blood in the air.

Three bodies lay among the upturned chairs and bullet-holed table. A man in a suit and tie sat slumped on his chair with the bloody mass of what was left of his brain exposed at the point half his skull had been blown away. Another was face down in a pool of red by the door: shot, perhaps, as she ran for her life. Six remained: two being comforted by firearms officers, one literally shaking as he sat under the table clinging to a corner leg, and the remaining three staring with glassy eyes as they staggered towards the door.

A hand touched Michael's shoulder. "Excuse me, sir. You must leave." It was one of the firearms officers.

"It's okay. He's with me," said Inspector Patterson, as he came through the door.

Michael smiled at him. It was a relief to have Patterson at his back.

Michael turned to the room and that's when he saw the huddle of black-clad firearms officers in one corner. As one of them stepped aside to speak into his headset and call for paramedics, he revealed the body of a man on the floor. At first, it looked like another bloodied corpse, until Michael saw the slow rise and fall of the man's chest.

Carefully, Michael opened his perception just enough to let in the man's thoughts. He was hit with a dizzying rush of pain and fear that sent him staggering backwards. He put his hand out and felt the steadying presence of Patterson at his side.

"Are you all right?"

Michael didn't acknowledge Patterson's question, he was too absorbed filtering out Farron's reaction to the fatal gunshot so he could get to the thoughts underneath. The thoughts whirled like pieces of debris picked up by a tornado. They lifted into the air where they were twisted and broken before being discarded. *Is this the end?… Elaine, I… I have to… God, are you there?…*

Michael stepped closer, he needed to make a connection with Farron's eyes to get deep into his mind. The hands of a firearms officer pushed him back and there was the sound of Patterson's familiar voice telling him to let Michael through.

Kneeling down beside him, Michael saw how Farron's skin had grown translucent on his face and sunk onto the framework of his skull. He pushed aside the man's surface thoughts and delved deeper.

Farron gasped as Michael reached the centre of his brain.

Normally, he would carefully weave his way through the pathways to the heart of a person's memory, but with Farron there was no time.

Confused images bounced back at Michael. Like a frantic search through a room, he opened every door and cupboard, but found only useless trinkets.

An image of two elderly people standing in a sunny garden — Farron's parents?

A memory of clicking a magazine of bullets into place and hiding a gun in his briefcase.

A stray thought that he should have updated his will.

"Why did you do it? Why?" Michael asked him out loud, desperate to provoke a response.

Farron looked at him with glassy, terrified eyes. His hand grabbed at Michael's fingers. Michael felt their weak, cold and sweaty grip. "Tell," Farron spluttered through the blood that had gathered in his mouth.

An image of a woman's face, framed by blonde hair, took over his thoughts. "Tell Elaine I …" But his breath died before he could say he was sorry. The image faded to nothing. Michael lingered where Farron's mind had been for a moment, but there was nothing left to perceive.

He sat back and let Farron's dead hand slip from his fingers. Around him, the noise and movement of paramedics rushing into the room brought relief so loud from the surviving hostages, that Michael could feel it. One of them came to the corner to treat Farron.

"He's dead," said Michael.

The paramedic ignored him, checking Farron for a pulse. He started chest compressions, but all that did was force more blood out of the wound. After a moment, the paramedic gave up and went to treat one of the survivors.

The officers in black armour had also drifted away and even Patterson was on the other side of the room helping one of the wounded.

Suddenly hot in his bulletproof vest, Michael ripped open the Velcro, pulled it off and tossed it in front of him. "Shit!"

All of it had been for nothing. He should have looked into Farron's mind and understood why an ordinary businessman had staged a massacre in the boardroom. He should have been able to give police the answers that no one else could see. But he had no answers. All he had learnt was that Farron wanted to tell his wife he was sorry.

TWO

THE mug of coffee levitated into the air until it was level with Michael's eyes. There was nothing else in his consciousness except the plain white ceramic mug floating on a cloud of his thoughts. Steam rose from the hot liquid inside. This was easy for Michael now, to wrap his mind around an object and move it through sheer force of will. As long as the object was no bigger than a coffee mug and he didn't lift it too high.

The door to his room opened, breaking his concentration. The mug plummeted to the floor. It landed hard on its base, vomiting hot coffee across the carpet in a steaming brown river.

Pauline stood in his doorway, her lithe figure and long black hair lit from behind by the corridor lights. He perceived an apologetic aura from her. "Sorry," she said, just to underline it.

"Don't you knock?"

"Sorry," she said again.

Michael looked at the mess on his carpet. Even though the carpet was brown to start with, the coffee would leave a nasty stain. Norm the Norm was going to kill him. He swore.

Uninvited, Pauline walked in and pulled the flannel from on top of his wash bag which he had left on the chest of drawers that morning. She threw it across to him and he caught it by reflex. He gave her a stern look and made sure his feelings leaked out so she perceived he wasn't happy.

"I thought you were a strong perceiver who doesn't need people to knock," she said.

He sensed her sarcasm and decided to ignore it. All the perceivers in Galen House knew that keeping their perception open enough to sense people in the corridor was tantamount to letting in madness. Like the rest of them, when Michael shut himself off in his room, he cut off his access to all other minds.

"I was busy," he said.

"Evidently," she said, looking down at the mess at their feet. She ripped the flannel back from his hands. "Give me that if you're not going to use it."

Pauline threw it on the floor on top of the spillage and stood on it, trampling her feet over every piece until its white towelling fluffiness turned to brown soddenness. She picked it up by the corner and dumped it next to the wash bag where it continued to steam away like a pile of poo.

"Got any more?" she said.

"Coffee?" said Michael.

"Flannels!" she said. "Or a towel would be better."

"Um …" Michael pulled a spare towel from the bottom drawer. This time, he was the one who threw it on the stain and trampled on it. Every so often he stepped on a patch untouched by the flannel and felt the damp soak through to his bare feet. When he had finished, he picked up the towel and he saw the spillage was less noticeable.

Pauline examined it, placing her hand on the carpet and feeling all around. "Use water and soap on it, soak it up with a few more towels and you might get rid of it," she said. "What were you doing? I thought you were levitating empty Coke cans."

"I'm trying to improve," said Michael. "A full mug is heavier."

"What's wrong with a glass of water?"

"I didn't have a glass of water, I had a mug of coffee."

He'd got back from work and made it for himself out of force of habit. But he didn't feel like drinking it. The bodies in the boardroom still haunted him. If somehow he could have used his telekinetic ability to stop the bullets or take the gun out of Farron's hand, he might have been able to save them. But all his telekinesis was good for was levitating mugs of coffee — and not very good at that, it seemed.

He hadn't let any of those thoughts escape his mind, but Pauline would still be able to perceive his contemplative mood.

"Anyway," she said. "I came to say if you don't come soon, you'll miss dinner."

He didn't care, he wasn't hungry. Being in a man's mind as he lay dying does that to an appetite. "If it's that ghastly steak and kidney pie again, I'm not interested," he said, trying to make light of it.

"If you won't come for the food, come for Alex," she said. "He's got a secret and I can't get it out of him."

"You want me to read his mind?" He could if he had to, but it was part of the perceivers' code not to pry into each other's thoughts, especially those of friends.

"No!" said Pauline. "I mean he won't tell me. I think it's because I'm a girl. He'll tell you."

"I don't want company tonight, I had a really shit day."

She grabbed his hand. "All the more reason to come to dinner. Finding out Alex's secret will take your mind off things."

She tugged him out of his room. He followed. It seemed he didn't have any choice.

THE smell of gravy and boiled vegetables hung in the communal area. With the warm bodies of thirty or more perceivers breathing alongside the steam of hot dinners, the air conditioning struggled to cope.

The teenagers in regulation grey T-shirts and trousers were more or less Michael's only family now. It was the same for all of them. Even those with a mother, father and siblings at home. Once they had been taken away and given a role in the Perceiver Corps, their connections to their old lives were virtually severed.

The ones in the Corps were the strong ones, the ones who could perceive more than surface thoughts, the ones the authorities decided to train to be part of an elite team with access to people's minds. A few were as old as Michael — now eighteen and officially an adult — while some were as young as thirteen and, he knew, still cried themselves to sleep at night. Better than being left to fend for themselves as a hated perceiver in the wider community. Or worse, having their power taken away by the cure.

Standing watching over them in khaki army dress uniform was Sergeant Norman Macaulay, the man they called Norm the Norm. Sometimes, Michael allowed himself to feel sorry for him, stuck between his army superior officers and the perceiver kids he was charged with looking after.

Norm had not been in Galen House as much since he was diagnosed with a heart condition. It had been good for his young charges, as he had not had the time or energy to control them as much as he once had, but Michael perceived it was tough for Norm. He said that allowing them more freedom to come and go from the base was part of the process of trusting them more as they got older. In truth, it was a way of managing his workload without having to bring in younger and fitter army officers who might undermine his authority.

Norm nodded at Michael as he passed. "I think there's some chicken left if you're quick," he said. In his thoughts, Michael perceived his concern for what he had witnessed that day in the office block. Norm had been briefed, of course. Both of them knew it and neither of them said anything. Norm had come from a traditional soldier background where nobody spoke about the bad things that happened because, in the wars he fought in, the troops on the ground had to go out and fight even when they knew it could kill them.

Pauline nudged Michael in the ribs and pointed at Alex. He was sat at the back, flanked by two empty chairs, and staring silently at something on his phone.

"See you in a bit," said Michael and went to find the aforementioned chicken.

He returned with an unappetising plate with mushroom gravy slopping towards the edges, soaking his mound of potato and every vegetable in its path. Pauline was already sitting next to Alex and gave him a welcoming smile, but Alex didn't look up from his phone until Michael sat down opposite.

"You should've got here sooner," said Alex. "The fish was much nicer, which was why we ate it all."

"I was busy," said Michael, poking at his mound of mashed potato like it was an old ants' nest and he was seeing if there was anything left alive in there.

"Busy doing what?" said Alex.

Michael didn't fancy eating any of his mashed potato, but he put a forkful in his mouth anyway to stop himself having to answer. It was salty and a bit cold around the edges.

Pauline picked up the pepper pot in front of her and raised it up and down, mimicking Michael's telekinetic power.

Alex understood immediately. "You should teach me to do that sometime."

"I did," said Michael. "The only time you lifted the can was when you got angry with it and threw it across the room. Then you stamped on it until it was a squashed lump of metal."

"Then you should teach me better."

"Hmm." Michael could barely teach himself. Lifting coffee mugs was a great party trick, but in terms of achieving anything, all he'd managed to do was stain the carpet. "I promise I'll try to teach you again if you tell me your secret."

"Secret?" said Alex. He pretended to be all innocent, but such subterfuge among perceivers was never going to work.

"Pauline tells me you have a secret."

"Does she now?" Alex glared at her.

Pauline smiled back.

"Pauline shouldn't stick her nose in where it's not wanted," said Alex.

"Hey!" she said, affronted. "You were the one that said go check on Michael after what happened to him today."

"How did you know …?" Michael began. And then he realised. They had read Norm's mind. It was an easy trick and the sergeant, being a norm, was all too vulnerable a target. "That man's a bloody security risk."

"We were worried about you," said Pauline.

"Well, thank you for your concern, but it's not warranted. Which you would have found out for yourself if you'd asked me."

"Sorry, Michael," said Alex. Michael perceived his regret was genuine.

"Okay, so you know mine," Michael said, dropping his fork on the plate and giving Alex his full attention. "Now it's time for you to tell me yours."

"I don't have a secret, Pauline's making it all up."

Pauline allowed her mouth to fall open in exaggerated shock. Michael just looked back at Alex, his friend should've known better than to lie to a fellow perceiver.

"Is it something to do with what you've been staring at on your phone?" Michael reached across the table to grab the phone from Alex's hands, but he whipped it away.

"If you must know, I met a girl," said Alex. Michael perceived his embarrassment, even though he tried to screen it from him. It was one of the more difficult emotions to mask from perceivers. It didn't help that his face had flushed at the same time.

Michael pushed his dinner aside — the smell of the mushroom sauce had started to make him feel queasy anyway — and leant right across the table to get closer to Alex. "Tell me more."

"There's nothing to tell."

Michael did not move from his position and kept up his gaze without blinking. Pauline leant over too, placing her elbow on the table and resting her chin on her hand.

Alex visibly squirmed and then relented. "We met at court, okay? She was waiting to be called as a witness to some other case and I was sent out for legal argument in the case I was supposed to be perceiving, so we got chatting. Then we went for lunch. That's it."

"So what was that you were doing on your phone?" said Michael. He guessed it had something to do with the girl, probably a photo or a message from her.

"She asked if I might be around for lunch tomorrow," Alex said. "Satisfied?" He secreted his phone in his pocket, out of Michael's reach.

"Tell us more," said Pauline, her curiosity bubbling. "What's she like? Is she a norm?"

"She's a perceiver, if you must know," said Alex. "She lives on the outside under Perceivers' Law."

"There's actually people like that?" said Pauline. "I thought that was a myth."

"Sarah says there's lots of low-level perceivers living out there now," said Alex. "She says there's whole online communities, if you know where to look. That's how she learnt how to control her perception, like how to pick up on thoughts without staring at someone with crazy eyes and how to block thoughts and emotions from other perceivers."

Pauline chuckled. "Online communities. I had to come here to learn that stuff."

"That's because you're special," said Michael.

"Thank you, Michael," she said.

He felt the heat of embarrassment rush to his face. He wasn't sure why. "I meant you're a strong perceiver, like we all are."

"Anyway," said Alex. "We had lunch. It's not a big secret like Pauline made out."

Michael could perceive his friend's excitement about the girl. It was in his body language and the way he talked, as well as in his emotions. "Just be careful," he said.

"It's lunch, Michael, we're not getting married."

"All the same, people out there aren't supposed to know about us in here."

"It's all right for you, Michael. You have a thing going on with Pauline. It's not that easy for the rest of us." He stood up from the table, so quick that his chair scraped back against the floor. "I'm going back to my room where no one is going to pry into my private life."

"Alex!" Michael started after him, but his friend wasn't listening and was already halfway towards the accommodation block.

"Leave him," said Pauline. "He's upset that you don't think this girl is necessarily as wonderful as he thinks she is."

"I can perceive that," said Michael. "I was just saying ..."

"I know."

"What did he mean about you and me having a 'thing'?"

She laughed. "Nothing."

The sound of clunking cutlery and plates around them caused Michael to look up. Some of the other perceivers were clearing up.

Peter was suddenly at their table. Despite being short, Peter's muscular frame was wide enough to cast a sizeable shadow. "You finished with that?" he said, pointing to Michael's barely touched chicken in mushroom sauce.

"Yes," said Michael.

"No," said Pauline.

Peter grimaced. "Well, hurry up, me and Kev want to get this place cleaned up for the rugby." He turned and went off to hassle another table. Sometimes, when there was a big sporting event on, they set up a TV in the common area of Galen House and everyone watched it together. It was actually quite fun.

"I'm going to go back to my room, then," said Pauline, standing. "Try to eat some chicken."

With that, Pauline left him sitting at the table with his unappetising meal while perceivers cleaned up around him. He watched her go, her shapely hips swaying with each step and her long black hair bouncing down the back of her grey T-shirt, and wondered what sort of 'thing' they had.

THREE

THE reception area at Power Grid UK looked like a bomb had hit it. The dusty footprints of police officers and paramedics were trampled into the purple carpet, turning it into a mottled grey. The matching fabric-covered sofa, which was supposed to offer guests a calming place to sit, had been pulled out from the wall for some unknown reason and left at an angle. Objects dropped by office workers fleeing the building were strewn across the floor: bits of paper, supermarket receipts, a pen. Someone had even dropped their mobile phone and it had been kicked over to the sofa where it lay with a red 'battery-low' warning light blinking on and off.

No one sat at the reception desk to welcome visitors. Even the company logo on the front, a yellow lightning bolt striking against black, had been dulled by a layer of dust. Behind the desk, two lift doors opened and a forensic officer in full white bodysuit stepped out carrying a case of scientific instruments. Behind her, hidden in a dark corner, was a tall man with his right arm in a sling. Michael recognised him as one of the survivors from the boardroom.

The man took a more hesitant step out into reception, saw Patterson waiting for him and found a confidence from somewhere as he stepped out to greet him. "Inspector?"

"You must be David Etchin," said Patterson.

"I won't shake your hand, if that's all right," said Etchin, patting his harnessed arm with his other hand. "I was involved in a bit of an incident yesterday, you might have heard."

Etchin was doing that British thing of trying to make a joke out of something that wasn't funny to try to put everyone at ease.

"I'm surprised you're back at work at all," said Patterson.

"The wheels of commerce will continue to turn whether I'm here or not. Better to be here, I think."

Patterson looked around at the mess in the reception area as a police officer arrived with a tray of takeaway coffees for his colleagues. "Is there somewhere where we can talk?"

"Of course," said Etchin. He turned to the lift, which had closed its doors, and pressed the button to call it back again. "I would take you to my office, but it's full of your police colleagues at the moment. Goodness knows what they expect to find in there. Unless they are after the lunch I didn't eat yesterday. I got a meal deal with a bag of crisps and a drink for three pounds — good value, I thought."

Etchin's nervous chattering stopped as the lift doors opened. The three of them stepped inside. Etchin reached past Michael and pressed the button for the third floor. "Are you the Inspector's sidekick?" he asked.

"Michael Sanderson," said Michael.

"It's right what they say about policemen looking younger," said Etchin.

"Yes," said Michael. He'd thought that turning eighteen would have stopped older people looking at him like he was a child, but he had been wrong. Perhaps he should consider growing a beard.

"I suppose you've heard that before," said Etchin.

"A few times."

The lift took them to the third floor as requested. It was the floor where the boardroom was situated and, as they stepped out into the corridor, Michael noticed a smear of blood on the wall. If the others had seen it, they said nothing, as Etchin took a left turn.

They passed by the corridor which led to the boardroom, cordoned off with police tape, and Michael couldn't stop himself glancing down it. Outside the remnants of the room's smashed up doors were two more forensic officers dressed in white overalls and a plain clothes police officer pacing up and down while talking on her phone.

Only a few paces further on, they stopped at an ordinary brown wooden door.

"We can use this office," said Etchin.

Etchin led them into an unremarkable room containing a desk, two chairs and a computer. A coffee mug, a plate with crumbs on it and a half-eaten packet of chewy mints were the only signs that a real person had ever used it. Etchin went behind the desk and sat down. "This is Michelle's office," he said by way of explanation. "She won't mind, she's off today." *A lot of people are off today*, said his thoughts.

Patterson stopped, uncertainly, beside the guest chair and looked across at Michael.

"It's all right, I'll stand," said Michael.

Patterson made no hesitation in taking advantage and dropped his untidy body onto the chair. He pulled out his phone along with a stylo which allowed his handwritten notes to be turned into readable type.

"I can't believe what an idiot I was," said Etchin, without being prompted. "I knew Nigel was having a tough time, I *knew* it, but I did nothing."

"Nigel Farron was a troubled man?" said Patterson.

"His mother died last year, then his wife had a baby a couple of months back, so I figured that was it. We've all been there, do you know what I mean? Being woken up in the middle of the night, spending all your spare money on nappies and clothes they instantly grow out of. I mean, I love my kids, the little scallywags, but those first few months…"

While Patterson listened to Etchin's answers and made notes, Michael perceived him. Etchin was thinking of his children, two boys and a girl who were — going by the fuzzy images in his memory — pre-teens. He was thinking how lucky he was to still be there for them. If the bullet had been just a little bit over to the left…

"He was stressed?" prompted Patterson.

"We all were. Well, *are*, really. We're heavily into renewables here at Power Grid UK. I know everyone says it was over-hyped by the environmentalists, but I seriously believe it's the future. Coal and oil won't last forever, and if you consider the amount of money it costs to build and de-commission a nuclear power station…" He paused. "You don't want to know about renewable energy, do you?"

"Not really."

"Suffice to say, we had a lot going on in the business and Nigel was feeling the stress. But, honest to God, if I'd known he was going to get hold of a gun and…" His words could no longer hold back his feelings. Guilt washed over him, bringing with it memory flashes of the blood-splattered bodies of his dead colleagues.

"Can you take me through what happened?" said Patterson.

Etchin let out a long, slow breath. The soft light of the room caught the excess of liquid in his eyes, but he maintained enough self-control to stop it turning into tears. Michael felt Etchin's pain as he accessed the memory, trying and failing to disentangle the facts from the emotion. "It was an ordinary meeting. We discussed a project we have on the go, one we're having difficulty with. There was a lot of discussion, but people barely raised their voices." In his mind, he remembered a man in a suit — not Farron, a man called Tim — shouting at the others, getting red in the face. Around the table, ten people in business suits sat calmly as if nothing was wrong, chewing on the end of a pencil, making notes on a tablet, leaning back in their chair. As he remembered them, he also remembered how they looked moments later, with dead eyes staring out of their bloodied corpses or dragging their bleeding bodies under the table for some kind of cover. He closed his eyes to push the horror away.

"And then …?" asked Patterson.

"Nigel picked up his briefcase from beside his chair and put it on his lap. I didn't take any notice. I thought he was getting out a file, or a pen or a bottle of water."

"But it was a gun," Patterson suggested.

The image was clear in Etchin's mind, the steel grey of the weapon, heavy in Farron's hand as he pulled back the slide and the first bullet clicked into place. "I'd never seen a gun before, except on TV and, I know it sounds stupid, but we just sat and watched him do it. He might as well have brought some home-made cakes for us to try. Then the shooting started." It was the noise that he remembered, the ear-splitting explosions and the screaming, still resonating in his skull.

"Who was he shooting at?"

"Nobody. Everybody. It was chaos."

"It wasn't a targeted attack, then?" said Patterson.

"I should have known. I should have stopped him."

"You can't blame yourself."

"I should have suspended him or sacked him when I had the chance. But he had a new baby, how could I?"

Patterson looked up from the scrawled writing he'd styloed on his phone. "Sack him? For being stressed?"

"Perhaps I wasn't clear," said Etchin. "I employed a private detective to follow him."

Patterson's surprise was so sudden that Michael felt it, even as he was perceiving Etchin. Patterson almost dropped his stylo. "A private detective?"

"You don't know anything about the energy business, Inspector, but it can be cut-throat. Espionage has been known to be a major problem."

"You think Farron was a spy?"

"I thought he was a stressed father with a new baby. But I had to be sure, you know? Multi-billion-dollar contracts have been lost because someone inside Company A sold information to Company B."

"This private detective … what did he or she say?"

"That's the thing, I never got around to reading the report. It arrived a couple of days before and I was so busy with back-to-back meetings that I didn't have time. I was going to schedule some time — well, today as it happens." He paused and dropped his voice to a confessional whisper. "Perhaps I was afraid of what I would read."

"I would like a copy of that report," said Patterson.

"It's in my office. When your colleagues finish confiscating my lunch, I'll get it couriered over."

"Email might be easier. If you could log in from your phone from here? Or another company computer, perhaps?"

Etchin smiled, an expression without joy or humour. "Computer espionage is what we fear the most. Hackers are clever people. The report is in hard copy, but I have a courier I can trust. You'll have to wait, I'm afraid, Inspector."

Patterson nodded. "Why do you think Farron did it, Mr Etchin?"

Michael's perception revealed that he genuinely didn't know. "The TV was saying last night it was some kind of terrorist attack," said Etchin. "This morning, they think Nigel was mad. It's all speculation."

"I wasn't asking what journalists think, I want to know what you think," said Patterson.

"I think Nigel was my colleague and my friend. The man I knew would never have done this."

The interview was over. Michael stepped out in the corridor while Patterson stayed inside and gave Etchin an address for him to send the private detective's report.

Down the corridor, a woman in a trouser suit with a mass of wavy black hair, which bounced as she walked, ducked out from under the police tape. Behind her, a smaller younger figure did the same.

It was Pauline.

She must have perceived his presence, as she turned her head to look at him.

What are you doing here? thought Michael.

I'm working with CID on this case, came her thoughts in reply.

The lift doors must have opened because Pauline followed the wavy-haired woman into a hole in the wall and disappeared.

Patterson emerged from the office.

"Do you need me to show you out?" said Etchin from behind.

"No need," said Patterson. "Come on, Michael."

FOUR

ALEX threw the Coke can against the wall with such force that a dribble of leftover drink burped out of the top and sprayed a brown watery splash over the paintwork.

Five seconds before, the innocent Coke can had been sitting happily on the floor of Michael's room while Alex glared at it and tried to move it with his mind. He'd also tried shouting at it, then swearing at it, but in the end, the only thing that would lift the can off the floor was picking it up.

"I can't do it! I can't do it!"

"You can't do it *yet*," said Michael, still sitting on the second-hand rug he'd bought to cover up the coffee stain on the carpet.

"I can't do it at all," Alex insisted. He stormed over to where the can had dropped to the floor and stood on it. The thin metal collapsed easily under his shoe. Then he jumped up and down on it until it was squashed flat. He kicked it and it clattered against the door and fell back to the floor.

"It's not the can's fault," said Michael. He looked at the squashed aluminium, its colourful branding now unreadable after its encounter with Alex's foot.

Michael extended his mind towards it, perceiving its crumpled contours. When he was sure he had its whole surface within his thoughts, he imagined how easy it would be to lift the object into the air. The squashed can obeyed, levitating until it was level with his eyes and floating on air. He brought its effortless weight towards him until it hovered over the rubbish bin. He let go with his thoughts and gravity took the can. It dropped into the bucket with a clang.

"How do you *do* that?" said Alex, mesmerised by the display of telekinetic power once again, still not quite believing there wasn't a secret wire hidden somewhere.

"You *know* how I do it," said Michael. "I keep telling you."

"I keep doing what you tell me — so why can't I lift as much as a speck of dust?" Alex took two long strides across Michael's rug and propelled himself onto Michael's bed. The mattress creaked under his body weight. Michael turned to see his friend taking up the entirety of his single bed.

Michael stood, picked up Alex's legs and dropped them on the far side of the bed so it freed up space for him to sit. "You need to keep practising," he told him.

Alex took no notice. "Do you know what I think?" he said.

"Do I *want* to know what you think?"

"I think it's something to do with your messed up brain."

Michael recoiled. "I'm not messed up."

"They took your perception away, then gave it back to you," said Alex. "Sounds messed up to me."

Michael lowered his voice, he didn't want to take the chance that someone would overhear. "I had the cure, like thousands of kids. It was reversed, that's all it was. I've got the same perception powers now that I had when I hit puberty."

"Except it destroyed your memories in the process."

Michael suddenly hated Alex. He hated him for being in his room, he hated him for jumping on his bed, he hated him for suggesting he was some sort of weirdo. Like being a perceiver in a world of norms didn't make him outcast enough. "I'm trying to remember why I was ever stupid enough to tell you about this in the first place."

"Because I'm your friend," said Alex. "Because every time I asked you about your past, you ignored the question and put up your perceiver blocks like you were afraid I was going to force my way through them. Or you lied, or you repeated something about yourself that you read in your file."

"I wish I hadn't told you," said Michael.

"Have you told Pauline?"

"No." His voice almost a whisper.

"You need to tell her," said Alex. "Especially if you and her have a thing going."

"We haven't got 'a thing'. Why do you keep saying that?"

"Because I look at you two when you're together and I perceive you. It's not something to be ashamed of."

Michael looked away from his friend. He picked a piece of dirt off the duvet which must have fallen off Alex's shoe and chucked it in the bin. It made a quiet metallic ding as it hit the squashed Coke can. "Yeah, well, I don't know what the army would say about it."

"The army can go f—" Alex was aware he was shouting again and stopped mid-sentence. "Norm the Norm and his cronies aren't going to stop me getting to know the girl that I've met. I've got a whole body full of hormones and I have every intention of obeying their chemical messages when I get the chance. You're a year older than me, you must get it worse. Unless all that messing about in your head damaged that bit of your brain too."

"I'm not brain damaged," said Michael.

"What would you call it?"

Michael called it amnesia. It sounded less dramatic.

And anyway, he had hormones. He just lived in an army base where having girls in your room after lights out could get you put on toilet-cleaning duty for a week.

Alex could be right about the telekinesis, though. As far as they knew, no other perceiver had ever been able to move objects with their mind. "What if it's not something special about my brain," said Michael. "What if it's something special about my body?"

Alex looked him up and down as he perched on the edge of the bed. "There's nothing special about your body, Mike."

Michael whacked him across the ankles for being facetious. "What I went through physically. The first time my power emerged…"

Alex propped himself up on his elbows. "That kid tried to set you on fire," he said, clearly sensing where Michael's thoughts were going. "You used telekinesis to undo the wires that tied you to the chair."

"And the second time—"

"You hurled that knife across the room into the chest of the boy in Russia."

"I thought I was going to die," said Michael. "I wasn't sitting in my room trying to get a Coke can to float in the air, I was desperate to find a way to save my life."

"You think the power might have been triggered by extreme stress?" said Alex.

"It's a theory," said Michael.

"How do we test it?"

Michael grinned as a plan began to form in his head. "How do you fancy nearly dying?"

FIVE

THE sound of Patterson's voice booming out from his office caused Michael to stop in the corridor outside. A woman's voice could also be heard in stern counterpoint to him. It sounded like an argument that Michael didn't want to get involved in and so he hovered on the other side of the closed door.

He thought about opening his perception just enough to understand what the row was about, but he didn't want Patterson's angry emotions rattling around in his head, so he opted for listening instead.

"… not what I'm paid for!" Patterson shouted. "Have you any idea how many …" something inaudible "… I've got on my desk?"

The woman's voice was quieter and even more difficult to make out: "… understand … resources. Just until … finished."

Sod it, Michael thought. If he was going to spend the rest of the day with Patterson's residual anger, he might as well perceive it now. He leant closer into the door and carefully opened his perception.

He got a blast of Patterson's fury, immediately followed by a blast of air across his face as the door flew open, centimetres from his nose.

He stepped backwards as the woman with the mass of wavy black hair from the Power Grid UK offices strode out and into the corridor. "Excuse me," she said pointedly.

Michael virtually flattened himself against the wall to stop himself being run down as she walked off with the determination of someone desperate to get as far away as possible from Patterson.

Michael figured he should make his presence known before Patterson caught him loitering. He took a breath and stepped towards the door.

He nearly got his nose knocked off again as Patterson came storming out, holding his jacket with one hand, causing it to flap about behind him like a bullfighter's cape. He saw Michael, didn't seem surprised, and kept walking without missing a beat.

"Come on," he snapped.

Michael trotted after him. "Where are we going?"

"To interview the widow," said Patterson.

Michael was going to ask 'what widow?', but decided better of it.

"First, I'm going to have a crap," said Patterson as they passed the door to the gents. "Meet you in the car park." He banged the door with his hand, which opened at his bidding, and disappeared inside, taking his aura of anger with him.

PATTERSON'S anger joined them in the car. It seemed to pulsate with the rhythm of the windscreen wipers as they swiped away scatters of raindrops. He had Radio 5 Live turned up loud — louder than either of them needed to hear it — as two football pundits argued over whether Arsenal should sack their manager or not.

Patterson occasionally joined in. "Give the guy a break! It's not his fault half the squad are injured." But it wasn't the football pundits he was angry with, it was the woman with the black wavy hair.

Her name was DCI Elizabeth Mulgrew and she was in charge of the investigation into the Farron case. Michael could have got this information by reading someone's mind, but in this instance he had simply asked the desk sergeant. She was part of the Criminal Investigation Department (CID), and Patterson was part of the Metropolitan Police Counter Terrorism Unit and this, apparently, was what all the fuss was about.

Patterson was trying to forget about his argument with her, but it still festered. Eventually, he swore at the radio and turned it off.

It left an empty ugliness in the car, quickly filled by the sound of rain falling from the grey sky onto the windscreen and being swiped away. Patterson's anger rumbled, like the wheels of the cars around them on the wet road, until he could hold it in no more.

"What am I doing here?"

It sounded like a rhetorical question, but Patterson left a space which suggested it should be answered. "Driving to interview the widow?" Michael suggested.

"It's a stressed businessman with a screw loose. It's not a terrorist inquiry. I should be back catching violent maniacs, not driving out to bloody Surrey to interview some bloody woman that I know damn well has already been interviewed by that bloody Mulgrew woman."

"He did hold the boardroom of a major British company hostage at gunpoint," said Michael, trying to placate him.

"I told her," Patterson continued. "At first it may have looked like a terrorist incident and they were absolutely right to call us in. But now I should be getting back to catching the real bad guys, not tying up the loose ends of one of CID's inquiries."

"Maybe you can interview the widow, write your report and pass the inquiry back to them."

"Arse!" Patterson muttered to himself.

He wasn't swearing at Michael, he was swearing at the road. *Is that the Woking turn?* his thoughts grumbled. *I can't see a thing in this sodding rain.* He hit the indicators to say he was turning left as he looked in the rear-view mirror to find a space to cut across traffic to the inside lane. He swerved and put up a hand to thank a driver behind who was more or less forced to let him in to avoid a nasty collision. The driver sounded his horn in response.

Somehow they made the turn to Woking unscathed and ended up on another grey road under grey skies with rain being swiped periodically off the windscreen.

"Sometimes it makes me think they're trying to get rid of me," said Patterson.

Michael felt a chill as he sensed that wasn't exactly what Patterson meant. "Or they're trying to get rid of *me*," said Michael.

"What rubbish," said Patterson. "Where did you get that idea?"

"I can read minds, remember."

Patterson shot him a glance, taking his eyes off the road for a second. "Not mine, I hope."

"The other people in the unit know what I am. They're detectives, they were bound to figure it out sooner or later. I'm younger than all of them, half the age of most of them, with no official rank and yet I've been hanging around offices where a lot of classified stuff is going on. It wasn't a secret that was going to be kept for long."

"Then they must realise that some of the breaks we had, we wouldn't have had without you. The extremist bastards are getting clever now, it's not always easy to trace the people they're working with through their internet contacts. You've pulled a lot of names out of reluctant heads."

Michael had done, it was true. His contribution to the unit should have been obvious. Maybe it was too obvious. "If they're not worried about me looking into their heads, perhaps they're worried about their jobs. Who needs a detective when you have a mind reader?"

"There will always be a need for detectives," said Patterson.

Michael believed him, but he also believed Patterson's unspoken suspicion that someone in Counter Terrorism wanted to see less of Michael and more of traditional police work. "You should ask for me to be transferred," he told Patterson. "I don't mind. I'm used to people not wanting me around when they find out what I am. It's not something you should have to put up with."

But Patterson didn't seem to be listening. "Can you check what the address is of this widow woman again?" he said. "Then stick it in the satnav?"

"I thought you said you hated the way the satnav gives you orders," said Michael. "You said it interrupts the radio when you're trying to listen to the football."

"It appears I say a lot of sensible things," said Patterson. "Sometimes you have to choose the lesser of two evils — and listening to the smug satnav is better than getting lost."

Michael silently acknowledged his logic and did as he was told.

THE house was an ordinary house. Expensive, detached from its neighbours with enough windows to suggest at least four bedrooms and fronted by a trimmed patch of lawn alongside a block-paved driveway. It was easy to imagine that, on an ordinary day, it would have been quiet in the cul-de-sac where Nigel Farron used to live. But two days since he had massacred three colleagues was not an ordinary day. Two police cars and a forensic van were parked outside. Beyond them a line of police tape kept out the reporters and the curious passers-by, all looking bedraggled from the rain which had now turned into light drizzle. Beyond them, the modern journalist's paraphernalia of satellite trucks and broadcast vehicles showed how the world was still fascinated by what the media was calling, The Boardroom Massacre.

Patterson did up his tie as he walked up the drive, expunging from his mind all the thoughts that had plagued him on the journey over. Michael followed, pulling his police identification from his pocket as they approached the man in uniform guarding the door. Patterson fumbled for his own ID and was still fumbling when they reached the doorstep. Patterson's pockets were as disorganised as his mind. With two pockets in his trousers, two on the outside of his suit jacket and another one inside, he could never remember where he put anything.

"It's okay, Inspector Patterson," said the uniformed officer. "I know who you are."

At that moment, Patterson found his ID in his inside jacket pocket and showed the officer anyway.

The officer nodded him through. "She's in the living room, sir."

"Thank you," said Patterson. He paused for a moment. Michael perceived he was trying to remember the officer's name, but he had obviously packed that information in a forgotten pocket of his mind and so he gave up and stepped inside.

Someone had laid plastic sheeting in the hallway of the house to protect the hardwood flooring underneath from all the detectives who had been traipsing over it all morning. It hadn't been that successful as it had bunched up in places, exposing bits of the floor underneath which now had at least one damp and muddy footprint on it.

The plastic crinkled underfoot as they stepped inside. They were only just over the threshold when the sound of boots on the stairs ahead of them caused Michael to look up. Two detectives in white forensic coveralls were coming down with plastic crates of stuff piled so high that they could barely see over the top of them. Patterson and Michael stepped aside to allow them past. When the detectives reached the bottom of the stairs, Michael saw the corner of a laptop computer sticking out of the top of one of the crates.

Once the way was clear, Patterson and Michael were able to get to a door to the left of the hallway which, logic dictated, led into the living room.

Logic was correct, but the room didn't feel like a welcoming place to live in. It was morbidly dark, the curtains having been drawn to keep out the outside world. A female police officer in uniform sat on the sofa, with a cluster of half-drunk mugs of tea and coffee in front of her. Standing, was a woman Michael instantly recognised as Elaine, the woman from Farron's mind. Just like his memory, she had blonde hair which framed a face defined by precise make-up.

Holding herself with arms folded across her chest, she was shaking ever so slightly like a smoker waiting to be let outside for a cigarette. Michael opened his perception and allowed her feelings to touch him. She was numb. The anger and grief inside of her had been worn out and simmered behind a blank tiredness.

"Mrs Farron," said Inspector Patterson. He showed her his identification. "I'm Inspector Patterson, and this is my assistant Michael Sanderson."

She shrugged. Like he could have said he was the Pope and Michael was the Devil.

"I know this is difficult, but I have a few questions."

"What a surprise," said Elaine. She shook a little more.

Michael perceived anger was growing at the back of her mind.

"Would you like to sit down?" Patterson asked.

"No, I would not like to sit down," said Elaine. "I would not like a cup of tea, I would not like a cup of coffee, I would not like to pop out for some air, I would not like a cigarette, I would not like to try to eat something. I would like you all to *get the hell out of my house!*" She paused. Took a breath. "But I know you won't, so ask your bloody questions. I don't actually know anything, but it's not like that's going to stop you."

Patterson glanced at the police officer on the sofa as if for some assistance. She raised her eyebrows. He turned to his phone which he had pulled from his pocket and opened the app he used for taking notes.

"Did your husband have any problems at work?" Patterson asked.

"Sometimes," Elaine replied.

"Such as ...?"

"He had to go away on business sometimes and he hated being away from home. He said he couldn't sleep in a strange bed."

"So he had trouble sleeping?"

"Not at home, no."

"He was away a lot then?"

"Not really."

"You said he didn't like business trips away."

"When he went on them, which wasn't very often, he didn't."

"I see. Were there other problems?"

"It was a job," said Elaine. "It was like any job. Sometimes he liked it, sometimes he hated it. Sometimes things drove him crazy, sometimes everything was fine. It was normal, Nigel was normal. If he had problems at work, they weren't the sort to make him take a gun and shoot people."

Inside her mind, Elaine thought back over her life with Farron, trying to remember times where he hinted he wasn't happy or had shown signs of being homicidal. But she only remembered the nice things, of spending his whole weekend decorating the bedroom to save them some money, of him getting up in the middle of the night to tend to Baby Lilly, of laughing over some silly joke in the kitchen.

"Had he seemed different lately?" said Patterson. "Agitated or distracted or secretive?"

She thought of him again. The last few weeks, coming home late from work, being too tired to talk to her — or *saying* he was too tired to talk to her — taking phone calls on his mobile and making out it was 'no one'. "Maybe."

Patterson waited for her to fill the silence. He smiled. She didn't elaborate. He pretended to write something on his phone with his stylo, then looked up at her again. "How would you describe his mood over the last couple of weeks?"

"He was distant. I thought it was because it was coming up to our tenth wedding anniv…" Her grief came to the surface, cracking through her words, threatening to form a tear in her watery eyes.

"Distant?" said Patterson. "Do you think he could have been planning something?"

"*Yes!*" she screamed, unfolding her arms and throwing them above her head. "A romantic weekend away! A candlelit dinner! Not getting a gun and shooting a load of innocent people. Not my Nigel. *No*. No way! Something made him do it, someone…"

The sound of a baby crying rose from the corner of the room.

It didn't sound real. It was distorted, and Michael couldn't perceive anyone else in the room. He'd only perceived a baby once before and it was weird, with a presence like a person but thoughts that barely coalesced. This baby didn't even have that.

He turned to look at the source of the noise and saw it was a baby monitor. The cries of a real child were being relayed through a speaker on the front of a white egg-shaped plastic box with green lights that flashed with each sound.

Elaine closed her eyes and let her tiredness overcome her for a moment.

"I'll go," said the police officer, getting up from the sofa.

Elaine opened her eyes and glared at the woman. "You leave my baby alone." Finding some energy from somewhere, she headed for the door. Her footsteps could soon be heard thumping up the stairs.

All three of them exchanged looks.

"I'm going to follow her," said Michael.

"I don't think that's wise," said the police officer, who'd sat back down on the sofa after being snapped at by Elaine.

"I'm not going to talk to her," said Michael. "Just—" he gave Patterson a knowing look "—see if she's all right."

Patterson nodded and Michael took this as his cue to leave the room.

Walking up the stairs, he got a strange stereo effect of the baby crying, as the sound from the baby monitor got quieter and the crying of the real child got louder.

He reached out to understand the dynamics of the people upstairs and perceived there to be three police officers, as well as Elaine and the strange unthinking mind which had to belong to Baby Lilly. There was also something else, a familiar presence which, for a moment, he didn't understand. But, as he got closer and filtered it out from the others, he realised it was Pauline.

Following her aura, he stepped into the nearest room at the back of the house and found himself in Nigel and Elaine Farron's bedroom. He imagined it had been a neat and tidy room before the police had got there. But now the bedclothes were screwed up in a ball on the floor and the bare mattress was standing up on its side, leaning against the wall and exposing the base underneath. One of the police officers Michael had perceived was kneeling behind the bed in white forensic coveralls with the hood up so only her face was visible. She had pulled up a section of the carpet and was wrestling with one of the floorboards underneath.

Pauline stood just inside the doorway. Rather than wear her perceiver greys or her usual black street clothes, she had made a compromise for work with a pair of black trousers and a black shirt. Only the floppy black cardigan she wore over the top, clutching it around her slim body like she was cold, reflected any of her personality.

"What are you doing here?" said Michael as he stepped inside.

"I'm attached to CID," she said.

"I meant in the house."

"I think they were trying to get me out of the office." She laughed, but she wasn't being ironic. She allowed her real thoughts to slip from her mind: *I thought they wanted me to perceive criminals to find out their secrets, but now I'm here perceiving a mattress.*

I know the feeling, Michael thought back. Then he reverted to speaking out loud, knowing that mind-speaking made norms feel uncomfortable. "Found anything interesting?"

"I think they've got a bit of a moth problem, judging by the state of some of Farron's shirts," said Pauline.

Michael frowned. "So nothing interesting, then."

"Depends if you're interested in moths or not."

Both of them perceived a moment of surprise from the officer behind the bed. They turned to look as she emerged holding up a clear plastic bag with a collection of syringes inside. "Well, well, well," she said.

"He was taking drugs?" said Pauline. She rushed round to the other side of the bed. Michael followed.

There, they saw the officer kneeling beside a hole in the floor, with the loose floorboard she had removed resting on her knee. Between the joists was a dark and dusty hole where the syringes must have been hidden.

"Looks like someone didn't want these to be found by accident," said the officer. She put the bag of syringes inside an evidence bag and put it into the bottom of a plastic crate beside her.

The woman put her gloved hand in the space under the floor and rooted around. After a moment, she pulled out another bag. This time, it contained two small vials of clear liquid. "Interesting."

"Doesn't heroin and all that stuff come in powder?" said Pauline.

"Usually," said the officer. "It has to be put into liquid form to inject, obviously. But most of the time an addict will do that just before they shoot up. It's rare to find it in liquid form." She sealed the vials in an evidence bag and chucked that in the crate too. "One for the lab, I think."

"That supports Patterson's theory he was a stressed businessman," said Michael. "If he'd resorted to using drugs."

Michael felt a wave of aggravation pass by at the edge of his perception and saw, through the open bedroom door, that Elaine was heading back towards the stairs, cradling her baby who had now stopped crying. "I'd best get back," he said.

"Yeah," said Pauline.

"I'll see you back at the base." He put his hand on her shoulder as a friendly gesture and felt the warmth of her body through her soft cardigan. It gave him a tingly feeling he wasn't expecting. Embarrassed, he turned and went out onto the landing.

Michael was slightly annoyed with himself for not secretly perceiving Farron's widow as he had planned, and he quickened his step to get close enough to her to eavesdrop on her thoughts as she went back into the living room.

Instances of her husband's behaviour over the past few weeks were still churning through her mind. Every time Farron got a phone call, he went into the other room to take it. Every time he came home late from work, he looked stressed out. Every time she asked him what was wrong, or who it was on the telephone, he would answer with the words 'nothing' or 'no one'. She had believed him then. She hated herself for believing him now.

"What a beautiful baby," said Patterson, as Elaine entered the living room.

Michael perceived something strange come over the rough-and-ready inspector. As Patterson looked at the little girl, being cuddled in her bereaved mother's arms, he softened. It was odd to see how such a shrewd policeman could be disarmed by someone so small and helpless.

"How old?" asked Patterson.

"Lilly's almost six months now." Michael perceived how Elaine felt the little girl's weight so much more now that she had grown, and couldn't hold her for as long as she used to. "Shame she has to grow up without a father."

The little girl made a gurgling sound and pulled at the blanket she was wrapped in, bringing a corner of it down to her mouth to suck.

"I'm sorry about your husband," said Patterson.

"I don't want your sympathy, I want to know what happened."

Patterson squirmed. "I'm afraid, it seems there is little doubt he—"

"Don't tell me Nigel did it on his own," she interrupted. "Because I know my Nigel, and he would never, *never* do something like this unless he was coerced." Her voice wavered as she tried to suppress her emotions. "You have to prove it because … I just found out this morning that our insurance won't pay out if the police decide he did it to himself. You have to prove it wasn't him, Inspector."

Michael perceived that Patterson wanted to tell her that everything would be all right for her and the baby, but he didn't believe it. He had sympathy for Elaine and Lilly, but his mind was flashing back to the other dead bodies in the boardroom and he knew that each of them had families who would mourn for them just as much. All those families had every right to blame Farron for destroying their lives.

So Patterson said nothing. He had many questions in his head, but as he thought of them, he vetoed them all.

Michael took his chance. "Was your husband using drugs?" he asked.

The blast of anger thrown back at him by Elaine almost knocked him backwards. She turned to him, her tired eyes wide with accusation. "What are you saying?"

"We found some syringes and vials hidden under the floorboards in your bedroom," he said.

He caught a whiff of Patterson's surprise, but he kept his perception focussed on Elaine.

"Drugs? Nigel? You're insane!"

"Are they *your* drugs?"

Elaine's emotions told him everything she knew about the drugs stash. She knew nothing. They weren't hers and if they were her husband's, then he had kept them hidden from her. "No! You've got a nerve coming in here and suggesting my husband was a drug addict and a murderer. *A fucking nerve!*"

Baby Lilly started crying again. A loud, frightened cry that filled the room.

Elaine jiggled her up and down in her arms, but Elaine's movements were desperate, not soothing and Lilly wouldn't be calmed.

The other adults went stiff, not knowing quite what to do with themselves.

The uniformed officer got up from the sofa. "Why don't you sit down," she said.

"I don't want to sit down," Elaine snapped back.

The officer smiled. "I'll make you a cup of tea."

"I *don't* want a cup of tea."

"I'll bring some biscuits for you," the officer continued. "Some sugar will do you good. And I'll get little Lilly a nice bottle."

The officer left the living room.

Elaine, reluctantly, sat on the sofa, resting the weight of her child on her lap.

Lilly's cries quietened, but didn't stop.

"Well, um," said Patterson. "I think those are enough questions for now."

"Good," said Elaine.

He closed the note app on his phone and put it in his pocket. "We'll be in touch."

Elaine looked up from cradling her baby. "When will your people be out of my house?"

"By the end of the day, I hope," he said.

"Good."

"We'll show ourselves out," said Patterson. He retreated to the door.

Michael half followed, but something nagging at his mind made him turn back to her. "I was there when he died," he said.

Elaine regarded him with weary eyes.

"I think you should know that the last thing he thought of was you," he said.

"Don't patronise me by lying to make me feel better." Her weariness showed in her voice.

He couldn't tell her it was true. He couldn't tell her he knew what was in Farron's mind because he had perceived it, so he pretended Farron's last thoughts were Farron's last words. "The last thing he said was, 'tell Elaine'. I think he was trying to say he was sorry."

"Sorry's not good enough," she said. "I need to know why. Nigel was a *nice* person, he wouldn't do what people say he did. That wasn't Nigel, that wasn't Nigel at all."

"We're going to try to find that out, I promise."

As Michael left the room, he perceived Elaine didn't believe him. She had been Farron's wife for almost ten years. If she didn't know why he pulled a gun on his colleagues, then she believed a group of policemen with meaningless platitudes would never know.

SIX

THE swell of worried minds was palpable at the gatehouse of Ethical Energy Engineers Plc. Michael could not see them yet, but he knew they were there: as many as two hundred people standing out in the cold as chaos erupted around them. All he could see was a plume of smoke rising from an office building and the red and blue flashing lights of emergency services. As they drove closer, Michael saw the evacuated office workers huddled together in the flat car park next to the building.

He also saw the origin of the smoke, pouring in a black plume from an office window ten floors up. There were only a handful of firefighters on the ground below, the rest presumably having gone inside the building.

Patterson dumped the car on the grass verge and he led Michael closer to the building where they were intercepted by DCI Mulgrew, her black wavy hair tied back from her face in a ponytail.

"What's going on?" said Patterson.

"One of the workers went crazy," said Mulgrew. "Started smashing up everyone's computer with a cricket bat and locked himself in his office. His colleagues tried talking to him through the locked door, then they saw smoke and hit the fire alarm."

Patterson wiped a strand of wiry ginger hair from his forehead. "He set his own office on fire?"

"We think so," said Mulgrew.

"You seriously believe this could be connected to the boardroom massacre?"

She shrugged. "It's a theory."

"Two bonkers businessmen does not a summer make."

Michael was in the midst of untangling Patterson's perverted proverb when a gasp rose from the evacuated office workers in the car park. En masse, they looked up at the building.

Michael looked up too and saw the unmistakable figure of a man standing on a window ledge, the white of his hands and face visible against the black of the smoke and the charcoal colour of his suit.

"Jesus," said Mulgrew. "He's not going to jump?"

"Maybe he's desperate for air," said Patterson. "It's the suffocation that kills most people in a fire, not the flames."

A short wail of an emergency siren caused all three of them to turn. An ambulance was trying to get through. They stepped onto the grass and it trundled past them, its red and blue lights whirring on its roof.

Michael barely took his eyes off the man, teetering on the edge of the window, clutching onto the wall to keep himself from falling.

"Michael?" asked Patterson.

He realised the inspector was asking him if he could perceive the man. He shook his head. "He's too far away and there's too many other people. I need to get closer."

"Closer for what?" said Mulgrew. So she hadn't figured out he was a perceiver and he was not about to tell her. He stepped away, then broke into a run, bypassing them both and heading for the burning building.

"Michael!" Patterson called after him, but Michael ignored his cry. He was smaller, younger and faster than the inspector, and easily slalomed his way past the other observers.

Until he ran — literally — into the chest of a fireman who stepped into his path.

"Where do you think you're going?" The man was as big and burly as firefighters traditionally are, but his voice was thin as if years of working with smoke had reduced his lung capacity.

"I have to get inside," said Michael. He looked up to the business-man who was still on the ledge.

"The building is on fire," said the firefighter. "You have to stay back."

Patterson was suddenly at his side, puffing after running the few steps to catch up with him. "Is there any way my colleague can get close to the man?" He fumbled for his ID, finding it in the third pocket he searched.

"Let us do our job, Inspector, then you can do yours." He folded his arms across his ample chest and made it plain that he wasn't going to let either of them past.

Patterson tugged at Michael's sleeve and pulled him back a few steps so the firefighter couldn't hear. "When they rescue him, you can perceive him all you want," he whispered. "He's right, it's too dangerous to get close to him now."

"Like the armed police 'rescued' Farron?"

"That was different," Patterson assured him.

But Michael was already looking around for another way. One of the fire engines was moving slowly towards the building, the ladder on its roof gradually extending with a firefighter standing on the end. He saw his chance.

Michael headed towards the fire engine, walking this time so as not to draw attention to himself. Fortunately most people were watching the man hanging out of the window and he was able to make his way round the back without being noticed.

He climbed up onto the top of the fire engine.

The firefighter standing on the ladder shouted up to the burning window. "Stay there! We'll get you down."

Michael dropped the blocks around his perception to see if he could find the mind of the man on the windowsill, but the thoughts and feelings from people on the ground crowded in. The clamour of people's fear and excitement was too much and he closed his perception down again.

The ladder opened its jaws as it extended further, carrying the lone firefighter higher and higher towards the stricken man.

Michael clambered along the top of the fire engine to the base of the ladder and started climbing up.

"Oi!" he heard someone shout from the ground. Someone, it appeared, who had just realised what he was up to. "Get down from there!"

He ignored their words and kept climbing, feeling unsteady like a mountaineer who had foolishly embarked on an expedition without a rope. Every time he picked up his foot and put it onto the next rung, he was aware that the angle of the ladder was getting steeper.

The firefighter was almost a metre from the window, but Michael was only halfway along the ladder. The trail of black smoke, which he had seen rising from the window when he was on the ground, was now thicker and blacker. Maybe Michael was close enough. He stopped climbing and clung on tight. He concentrated, lifting his blocks slowly to find the man's mind without letting in background noise from the crowd below.

He found the firefighter first. The professional could feel heat on his face which told him he had barely minutes before the flames were licking at the window. *Just a little bit closer, just a little bit closer*, said the fireman's thoughts.

Michael rejected them and searched harder. As soon as he touched the businessman's mind, he knew it belonged to him. The fear was there, more tangible than those on the ground, but it was overwhelmed by a sense of panic and desperation. There was heat at his back. Soon, the businessman feared, it would set fire to the jacket of his suit. He wanted to take it off, but he daren't let go of the wall.

The man took in a mouthful of what he expected to be clean air, but it was unexpectedly contaminated by smoke. He coughed violently, wobbling on the edge. Below, the crowd gasped.

"Hold on, I've nearly got you," said the firefighter.

That scared the man even more. *Out of the frying pan…* he thought, as he leant further out of the window and looked down at the hard, black road beneath.

"Don't look down, look at *me*," said the firefighter, reaching out his hand.

The man did neither. He closed his eyes. Michael perceived how the businessman welcomed the dark of the inside of his own eyelids. All he wanted was for the darkness to take him. To step back inside the office was to endure the torture of being burned alive. Stepping outside the window would allow it all to be over in a second.

Michael suddenly realised what he was going to do and shouted: "No! Don't!"

It caused the firefighter to look behind him. "Get off the ladder!"

"You need to rescue him before it's too late!" Michael answered, scrambling up the rungs desperately trying to reach the man.

But it was futile.

The man let go of the wall, his eyes still shut. Michael perceived the whirl of his mind settle as he stood calmly for the briefest moment, listening to the whistle of the wind and ignoring the cries of the people below.

The firefighter looked back to the window. "Hold on just a moment, sir. I've nearly got you."

The ladder edged closer. But not close enough.

The man clutched onto memories of sleepless nights, of guilt, of the many many days where life was like being locked in a cage as wolves with snarling teeth clawed at the bars. He decided to step away from it in the only way he could.

He stepped onto air.

The window was suddenly empty.

The man plummeted, his jacket flapping behind him like a torn, useless parachute.

The surge of horror from the minds on the ground filled Michael's perception in the split second before he closed it down. Before he experienced the man's death.

He only heard it. The body landed with a dull thud below.

An unceremonious end to an adult life.

MICHAEL stood behind the line of police tape and looked at the place where the man had fallen to his death. All that was left was the stain of his six-foot-tall body, written in blood on the asphalt surface. The blobs had begun to turn maroon as they reacted with the oxygen in the air and congealed onto the road. An ugly memorial.

He felt a familiar presence at his side. It was Pauline. He turned to see her face, smiling with an expression that was more condolence than happiness. She wore the same black trousers and blouse as she had at the widow's house, but this time with a long black coat over the top. Strands of hair blew into her face and she pulled them back behind her ear. The breeze also carried the faint perfume of her deodorant which Michael found somehow comforting.

"Benjamin Conte," said Pauline.

"What?" said Michael.

"That was his name."

"Sounds like an ordinary name."

"The witnesses said he was an ordinary bloke," said Pauline. "I perceived them, they were telling the truth."

"I should have stopped him," said Michael. "I perceived he was going to commit suicide and I did nothing."

"I was told you were too far away to reach him. You shouted a warning, but not even the firefighter was close enough."

"You don't understand, you weren't there," he said.

"Then allow me to understand," she said. She put a delicate finger on his cheek and turned him to face her.

He knew what she was suggesting, but he turned away and stared back at the bloody stain in front of him.

"Michael, we can talk about it forever, or you can let me in."

"It's not something you want to experience."

"I'm working with the police now, pretend it's part of the job."

She turned his face to look at her again and this time he let her. She put her hands to his cheeks to hold him still and he felt the welcome coolness of her fingertips.

Then he felt her perception pushing at the edge of his blocks. "Let me in," she said.

Steadily, he lowered his blocks and cast his mind back to the moments before the man fell.

Pauline experienced it through his memories, just as he had experienced it. The man's desperation, his guilt, and the longing for silence.

Having another perceiver in your mind is an uncomfortable feeling, like standing naked in front of them. He became self-conscious, stepped back from her hands and pulled up his barriers again.

"He'd made the decision to die long before you were there," said Pauline.

"But I could have changed his mind, I could have—"

"You could have done nothing. He didn't want to be rescued, he wanted it to end."

"But why? I don't understand it. I wanted to see deeper into his mind, but there wasn't enough time."

"The witnesses say he flipped," said Pauline. "One moment he was your average stressed businessman, the next he was smashing their computers with a cricket bat. He played cricket for a local team, apparently, and did practice on a Wednesday night, so he kept a cricket bat at work. After that, he locked himself in his office and set fire to it. No one who's planning to live locks themselves in a room and sets it on fire."

"It doesn't make any sense. It's like Farron. Normal one minute, suicidal the next."

"Do you think they're linked?" said Pauline.

Michael shrugged. "It was why we were called in, I think. Two stressed businessmen going mental, both worked in the energy industry. Then again, it could all be a coincidence. Farron's boss made some comment about there being a lot of stress around the renewable energy industry. Out of the number of people who work in that area, I suppose it's not out of the question for two of them to go off the rails."

"Except people who go off the rails usually they get drunk, have an affair or go to their doctor for anti-depressants," said Pauline.

Michael nodded and tried a half-smile. "Yeah."

The sound of a woman calling her name made Pauline look behind her. Michael looked too. It was Mulgrew, walking towards them with her ponytail bobbing behind her and a clear plastic bag in her latex-gloved hand.

"Look what I've found," she said with a beaming smile.

Michael looked closer at the bag as she neared them. Inside were two hypodermic needles sealed into sterile packaging and a couple of small vials filled with clear liquid.

Mulgrew came to a stop in front of them and held up the bag to Pauline's eye level. "Look familiar?" she said.

"It's like the drugs we found in Farron's house," said Pauline.

"This little stash," said Mulgrew, "was found locked up in Conte's desk drawer. Lucky for us, it was protected from the fire."

"So this case *is* linked to Farron," said Michael.

"They were both apparently on drugs," said Mulgrew. "Although what that has to do with going crazy on your work colleagues, I really don't know."

"Can we find out what the drugs are?" said Pauline.

"Farron's stash is at the lab, but I'll put a rush on it," said Mulgrew. "I hope it doesn't turn out to be insulin and they're both diabetics, because I'm going to look a right dipstick."

SEVEN

MICHAEL emerged from the shade of the trees into the autumn sunshine and took a moment to catch his breath. Feeling the weight of the rucksack of equipment on his back, he let the straps slip from his shoulders and lowered it to his feet. The breeze ruffled through the material of his jacket, cooling his hot back and drying his sweat.

Pauline stopped next to him. "You should have let me carry that part of the way," she said.

"It was fine," said Michael. He had had to do much worse in the days when he first joined the Perceiver Corps and the army had taken him walking for miles with a burden on his back. Although he hated it then, he had built up enough stamina to mean that a walk at his own pace, and without Norm the Norm shouting at him, was easy.

She dropped her much smaller backpack next to his. "What a view," she said.

Michael had to agree. The pictures he had seen on the internet of the Victoria Bridge had done little to convey its true magnificence. Arching with red-painted steel over the River Severn, it effortlessly spanned the sixty metres to the bank on the other side. The train tracks it carried ran straight across the bridge, bordered by two sets of easy climbable railings, before the tracks curved off into fields in the distance.

He had inadvertently chosen a beautiful day to make the long journey to Worcestershire. The sky was the sort of blue that not even an English summer could produce, a deep colour that made the sun appear even more golden. Below them, the shallow river flowed steadily downstream. If Michael kept still, he could hear its whispering ripples.

Pauline rifled around in her bag and pulled out two bottles of water, one of which she handed to Michael. He unscrewed the top and sipped until his mouth felt as clean as the air.

"There's Alex," said Pauline, pointing to where a narrow path of dried mud marked out an alternative route to the bridge.

Michael turned too and saw movement among the trees which he soon realised was Alex's green camouflage jacket. As Alex emerged from behind the branch of a tree, he saw he was being observed, and waved.

At his side was a girl of about his age. At first Michael assumed it must be some random person out for a walk, but as she caught up with Alex and they walked side by side, it became obvious they were together.

"Who's that?" said Pauline.

"Don't know," said Michael. "Must be that girlfriend he's been going on about."

She was noticeably shorter than Alex with a spindly frame and was picking her way over the uneven ground in inappropriate high-heeled boots. Her short-cropped blonde hair was like a match head on her stick-like body, and was obviously an unnatural colour as it was yellowy at the ends and darker near the roots. But what he noticed most about her was that she had her perception blocks raised at full strength. There was no perceiving anything from her, other than the strain it took her to maintain those blocks. Unlike him and the others, for whom blocking was a natural part of living with perceivers, her lesser ability made it difficult for her.

"What did he bring her for?" said Pauline.

"I don't know," said Michael. Although he had some theories. Top of the list was that Alex wanted to impress her.

He felt Pauline's resentment for just a moment before she increased the strength of her blocks to match that of the approaching girl.

"Been waiting long?" said Alex as he joined them.

"We just got here," said Michael. He was replying to Alex, but he was looking at the girl.

"This is Sarah," said Alex, taking the hint. "Sarah, this is Michael and Pauline."

The girl managed a shy smile and awkwardly offered out a hand to shake. It felt strangely formal, but both Michael and Pauline shook her hand, for lack of another option. Her fingers were bony and cold to the touch.

"This is a surprise, Sarah," said Pauline. "Alex didn't mention you were coming."

"It was a last minute thing," said Alex. "She suggested we meet up this weekend, I said I had this other thing on and it seemed a good idea to combine the two."

"Did it?" said Pauline.

Michael kicked her toe, hoping she would get the message through the thick leather of her sensible walking boots. He would have used his thoughts to tell her to keep her mouth shut if there wasn't a chance that Sarah could have perceived them. "So," said Michael out loud. "According to the rail timetable, we've got about an hour. We better get going."

Pauline set off first, her walking boots clomping across the dried earth beneath and then onto the bridge, stepping from sleeper to sleeper with large strides. Sarah followed, reaching out for the railings as she wobbled on her high heels.

Michael pulled at Alex's sleeve to hold him back from the others. "You shouldn't have brought her," he said.

"I didn't think it would be a problem."

"Well, it is."

"She's cool, Mike, I'm telling you."

"Only the three of us know about my telekinetic ability. I haven't dared tell anyone else, but you think it's okay to mention it to your girlfriend who you've known for only five minutes."

"It's not like she's going to tell anybody else," said Alex.

"She better not," said Michael.

"Hey!" shouted Sarah. She had made it about a quarter of the way across the bridge and was standing in the middle of the train tracks waving back at them. "Are you boys coming or what?"

"Be right there!" said Alex. He broke into a jog and soon caught up with her.

Michael picked up his rucksack and put his arms through the straps.

He was the last to arrive at the centre of the bridge, where the apex of the arch meant there was very little steel between their feet and the air above the river. The stretch of water running beneath them was even more impressive when standing directly above it. It looked almost inviting, its dark waters reflecting some of the blue of the sky as it flowed down past the gold and red of trees getting ready to shed their leaves for the winter.

Michael took off his rucksack, unzipped it and turned it upside down so all the equipment tumbled out onto the railway tracks in a mass of harness straps and safety lines. One final shake produced the scrunched up orange plastic of an inflatable life raft.

"I always wanted to try bungee jumping," said Sarah.

Pauline gave her a hard stare, but as it was from behind her head, Sarah didn't notice. And, as she had her perceiver blocks on full, she didn't feel it either.

"It's not for you, love," said Alex.

If Alex was going to spend all day calling her *love*, thought Michael, he might be inclined to allow Sarah to try bungee jumping — without a rope.

Alex put his hands on the railings and leant out to look down at the water. It was a long way to fall. "Are you sure this is safe?" he asked Michael.

"I've gone over the instructions a million times forwards, backwards and sideways," he said. "It's perfectly safe as long as the harness is secured properly."

"And you know how to secure it, right?" said Alex.

"Oh no," said Michael, feigning ignorance. "I forgot to ask about that bit."

Pauline laughed behind him.

"It's a good job I can perceive you're lying," said Alex. Even so, his face had gone as white as the knuckles of his hands gripping tightly to the railings.

"It was you who said you wanted to do this, remember?" said Michael.

"Yeah," said Alex. "But that was back in my room with my feet on the ground. Now that I'm here, it looks a horribly long way to fall." He peered out over the railing.

"We'll test it first, don't worry," said Michael.

The equipment had come through army stores, via a soldier on the base who he had befriended (or 'bribed' as it was also known). Bungee jumping wasn't part of military training for enlisted personnel, but it was used as a team-building exercise for cadets, which meant there were resources which could be borrowed if you talked to the right person.

Michael took Pauline's backpack, which was already reasonably heavy with the bottles of water, and filled it with as much heavy stuff as they could find. Which included some of the larger rocky pebbles on the track, Alex's jacket and even Michael's own boots. The bag made a poor substitute for a human body, and the harness — which was designed to go over arms and legs — had to be tied to the bag with one of the spare ropes he had brought with him.

He clipped the other end of the harness to the top railing and sat Pauline's bag next to it.

"Ready?" said Michael, looking round at the others.

They either nodded or said that they were ready.

He pushed the bag off the top of the bridge and it plummeted straight down, straps flapping in the wind, the bungee cord unfurling behind it, until it was nearly a body's length from the water. The cord tightened and stretched as the elastic slowed its fall, reaching the limits of the line just above the river before it bounced back up again. It bobbed up and down for a few more bounces and settled to dangling above the river. The bag twisted on the end of the line, but stayed secure in its harness.

"It works!" cried Sarah.

"I'm just glad your boots are safe and I won't have to carry you back to the train," said Pauline.

Michael was inwardly relieved. Alex looked like he was about to be sick.

Michael hauled back the bag, released it from the harness and returned everybody's property, including his own boots which he put back on his feet.

He untangled the harness and squatted to the ground, holding out the strongly woven straps for Alex to step into.

"Are you sure about this, Michael?" he said, not lifting either foot anywhere closer to the harness.

"You saw the test," said Michael.

"A bag with boots in is hardly the same thing as me."

"Oh, stop being such a big girl's blouse," Pauline shouted. "If you're not going to do it, I will." She pushed at his shoulder as if to shove him aside. He stumbled a little, but held his ground.

"No, I can do it," said Alex. "I'm the one who's been practising with the Coke can, after all."

She held up her hands as if surrendering and stepped back again.

"Pauline," said Michael, "take the life raft down to the bank and get ready, will you?"

"And miss all the fun?" she said.

"Pauline, we agreed," said Michael. He had no time for games.

"Okay, okay, I'm going." She swiped up the inflatable raft from where it was lying on the ground and walked back along the bridge the way they had come in order to get to the water in the more conventional way by walking down the bank.

Alex stepped gingerly into the straps of his harness. Michael pulled it up so two padded sections were secure around his bum. He helped Alex put his arms through the two remaining straps and ensured the clips were fastened at the front. He grabbed hold of the harness and yanked it, pulling Alex forward.

"That's secure," said Michael and clipped on the bungee cord.

"Don't you clip it to my feet?" said Alex.

"Not with railing jumps. You need to be able to climb over the railings and a foot harness secures your feet together so you can't do that."

"Oh," said Alex. "You really have researched this, haven't you?"

Michael slapped him on the back. "It's up to you now."

Alex put his two hands on the railings and put his weight against them, trying to shake the metal to see how sturdy it was. Despite having been there since 1861, the railings didn't move.

Michael leant over to see Pauline down below on the bank side, holding the large orange life raft which she must have inflated using the ripcord.

Alex perched on top of the railings with one leg either side.

"Remember," said Michael, "this is about you triggering your power. When Pauline puts the raft on the water, that's your cue to jump. As you're falling, act like your life depends on that raft being there to break your fall. If you really have a telekinetic power locked inside you, and if we're right about fear and adrenaline triggering it, this should work."

Alex nodded rapidly and nervously. "Right," he said. He swung his second leg over the railing and clung onto the rail behind, his feet teetering on the ledge of the bridge, as he looked into the water below.

Sarah put a comforting hand on his shoulder and kissed him on the cheek. "Good luck."

Below, Pauline took a step down to the water's edge and pushed the raft out.

"One last thing," said Michael, stepping close enough to whisper into Alex's ear. "I haven't attached the harness."

He pushed Alex hard in the back.

"Wh—? *Arrrrggggghhhh!*"

Alex's word turned to a scream as his hands slipped from the railing and he fell.

The bungee cord unravelled out behind him.

So quickly, Michael hoped, that Alex wouldn't have perceived he was lying.

The raft drifted gently downstream as Alex plummeted, his arms and legs flailing desperately, until the cord tightened. His descent slowed — his weight still pulling him down to the water — until his hands slapped at the surface, sending spray up into his face, and he bounced back up again on the elastic.

Michael perceived the whole thing. The moment of fear and betrayal, overwhelmed by adrenaline, turning to exhilaration as he realised the cord was secure after all.

"*Woo hoo!*" Alex cried as he dangled on the line. "*Woo-woo-woo hoooo!*"

Beside the bank, too far for him to reach, the life raft bobbed uselessly down the river, unmoved by any power that wasn't the buoyancy of the water and the motion of the river.

Michael shut off his perception and enclosed himself in his own disappointment. The fall hadn't been long enough for Alex to face the real prospect of death and he'd known the safety equipment was going to save him. It hadn't worked.

PAULINE came back from the bank and helped the other two haul Alex back up to the bridge.

"That was amazing!" he said, as he grabbed hold of the railings. "Can I do it again?"

"This was an experiment, not a joyride," said Michael.

Alex clambered back over the railings and began unclipping himself from the harness.

"Honestly, Michael," said Alex. "You should have a go. It's great fun." The adrenaline had to be still in his system because it was making him talk more than he might otherwise have done.

"I'll have a go," said Sarah.

"If she's doing it," said Pauline, "I'm doing it too."

"Nobody else is doing it," said Michael, getting angry at them now. "We need to pack up and go."

Alex dropped his safety harness to the ground and it landed on the train tracks with a clatter of safety buckles. He stepped out of it and came over to Michael where he was leaning against the top rail trying to calm his disappointment. "Sorry, I tried to move the raft, but everything happened so fast and it was such a rush."

"No, it was a stupid idea," said Michael. "I probably couldn't simulate the real fear of death unless I actually tried to kill you. You can be annoying sometimes, Alex, but I don't think I'd ever go that far."

"Thanks," said Alex. "I think."

To Michael's surprise, it was Sarah who squatted down to gather up all the harness equipment and put it into the rucksack. She must have tidied it all up as she went because she was down there for a while making a thorough job of it.

Pauline ignored them all while she thumbed through a series of pages on her phone. "There's a couple of nice places we could go to for lunch, if you like."

"Not yet! I want to take a picture of Alex on the bridge," said Sarah. She put her hand on his shoulder. "Stay right there. Don't move a muscle."

Michael raised his eyebrows, annoyed all over again about Alex bringing his girlfriend without asking. He lifted the rucksack onto his back and began walking the thirty or so metres back across the bridge.

"We can stop off for lunch somewhere, can't we?" said Pauline. "At least make it a nice day out."

"I suppose," said Michael. Behind them, Sarah was telling Alex to smile as she backed away to get a better angle for her photograph.

Michael and Pauline were almost at the edge of the bridge.

"What's that?" said Pauline, who was following behind him.

"What's what?" said Michael.

"Can't you feel it?" She bent down and touched the bare train track with her hand. "It's vibrating."

"The train!" said Michael, realising. "There's a heritage steam train comes down here. I said we only had an hour."

He and Pauline stepped off the tracks at the end of the bridge. Michael turned to see white smoke puffing above the trees on the other side. Alex still stood in the middle of the bridge maintaining a smile while Sarah backed away holding her phone in front of her face.

"Alex, come on!" Michael shouted. "The train's coming."

"No, wait!" said Sarah. "I've nearly got the picture."

It was now possible to hear the puffing steam and the rattle of the tracks as the train got closer.

A whistle pierced the sky.

"Got it!" said Sarah, and scampered back down the tracks to join Michael and Pauline.

Alex turned to look just as the train emerged from the trees, its black face staring them down as it chugged towards the bridge. He went to run, but his foot hit an invisible barrier and he fell forward. He reached out his hands to save himself and went crashing to the ground.

"Alex!" shouted Michael.

Alex struggled to get up, but his feet scratched uselessly at the ground like tiny little rat claws.

Sarah reached Michael and Pauline. "I tied his shoelaces together," she said, quietly and coldly.

"What?!" He faced her, not quite believing what she was saying, at the same time perceiving it was true.

"You want him to think he's going to die, don't you?" said Sarah.

"Not if it's actually going to get him killed, you crazy bitch!"

Back on the bridge, Alex had realised what had happened and he was crouched on the ground, frantically picking at the laces on his boots.

"Alex!" cried Michael as the train entered the other side of the bridge, speeding towards them with all the energy of a Victorian steam engine.

Michael surged forward, ready to run and rescue his friend, but Pauline grabbed his arm and pulled him back hard. "You'll never make it there in time," she said.

Standing helplessly on the dried earth, he watched Alex getting more panicky as the train's impersonal face got closer, fired by angry steam blowing out of its head. "Forget the laces, kick them off, kick them off!"

He didn't know if Alex had heard him or if he had figured it out for himself, but suddenly his boots were off his feet and he was running down the track, his socks desperately kicking up a scattering of stones. Still the train closed in on him.

Alex glanced back, the train almost at his heels. Michael saw the terror on his face for just a moment before he launched himself at the railings. Even with his body pressed against the steel, he was still in the train's path. He climbed over them, like he had done in preparation for the bungee jump, clutching onto the top rail as his legs dangled high above the river.

The train steamed past, blasting air into Alex's face, blowing out his hair and the loose material of his jacket. Still he clung on, the weakening strength of his hands the only thing that stopped him plummeting into the water below, this time with no harness or bungee cord to save him.

Michael stood helpless beside the bridge as the train continued to puff across the last thirty metres, the engine pulling carriage after carriage and preventing him from running onto the tracks to help his friend.

"He can't hang on much longer," said Pauline.

Michael saw that she was right, but hearing it out loud didn't help them find a solution.

"The safety line is still attached to the bridge," said Sarah.

Alex's annoying girlfriend was right. Clipped to the top railing, about a metre from where Alex was hanging, was the metal safety clasp of a rope.

"I missed it when I was clearing up," said Sarah.

Michael didn't know if he believed she forgot it or if she left it there on purpose, but he had no time to care. "Alex, can you reach the safety line?!" Michael shouted, his words lost in the fiery roar of the steam engine.

"Send him our thoughts," said Pauline, clasping his hand. He felt the comforting warmth of her fingers around his. "And hope to hell he's got his perception wide open."

Together they thought: *Safety line to your right. Can you reach it?*

Maybe Alex heard them in his head, maybe he just saw the rope on his own as he looked around in desperation. Either way, he reached out a hand. But as soon as he let go of the railing with his right hand, his left hand began to slip. He grabbed the railing again with both hands and held on tight as his legs swung underneath him.

"He can always drop into the river," said Sarah. "Like jumping off a diving board into a swimming pool."

"The water's not deep enough," said Michael. "He'll kill himself."

The last carriage thundered past them and the train blew a triumphant whistle as it continued on its journey, oblivious to the horror it had narrowly avoided.

Michael jumped onto the tracks — followed by the two girls — and ran. But he was still thirty metres away from Alex. "Hold on!" he cried.

Alex was barely holding on.

Michael saw his terrified look as he realised he wasn't going to make it. He turned from his friend back to the rope which hung tantalisingly close and yet frustratingly far from his grasp. He made one last stretch for it, reaching with all his strength, sacrificing even the muscles in his left hand. As Alex's fingers slipped from the rail, Michael heard Pauline scream.

He stopped running and watched Alex fall.

The rope, barely swaying in the breeze under the bridge, suddenly swung an impossible arc towards Alex. Alex caught it and clutched it tight to his chest. The rope pulled taut and his body jolted to a halt, putting a sudden end to his deathly plunge.

"Michael!" he screamed, as he dangled above the river. "I did it!"

Michael, Pauline and Sarah made it to the centre of the bridge where the rope was fixed securely to the rail. Michael looked down at his friend, swinging in the open air. "Bring me up, please," was all his exhausted voice could say.

For the second time that morning, they hauled him to safety. He was still shaking from the experience and they had to help him over the rails.

To Michael's dismay, Alex fell into Sarah's arms. He squeezed her thin body so tight that she could barely breathe under the weight of his gratitude at still being alive.

"Did you see what I did, Michael?" said Alex as he emerged from the embrace. "I made the rope move towards me."

"You reached for it," said Michael.

"No," said Alex. "I couldn't reach it. I tried, but it was too far. As I felt myself falling, I *willed* it to come closer to me — and it did! The power that you were trying to teach me with the Coke can saved my life."

Silence fell across the bridge. Only the sound of the water flowing beneath made any comment.

So, Michael thought, you didn't have to be brain damaged to make telekinesis work. You just had to be desperate.

"What about that lunch I was talking about?" said Pauline, breaking everyone's contemplation.

"Yeah," said Alex, squeezing his girlfriend again and kissing the top of her head. "Hell, yeah."

EIGHT

IT looked like it had snowed paper on Inspector Patterson's desk. White A4 sheets were spread over his keyboard, on top of his mouse, arching over his desk phone and flattened under his cold cup of coffee. If they had been put into any sort of order or sifted into any sort of pile, then it was one of Patterson's own devising, incomprehensible to the outside world.

Patterson was the only person in a room of desks usually staffed by other detectives. It made the place seem unusually quiet and timeless. Patterson had taken his tie off and slung it over the top of the computer monitor, while his jacket hung over the back of his chair. His hair looked even more like a mass of unbrushed wiry ginger than normal and the air smelled like it had been recycled through a pair of human lungs at least four times.

Patterson looked up from the snowy landscape and peered over the top of his glasses as Michael walked in. "Oh, it's you," he said.

"Who did you expect it to be?" said Michael.

"If it was the cleaner, I was going to tell him not to bother." He rifled under the papers where he eventually found his phone. He hit the screen and nothing happened. "Bloody thing needs charging. What's the time?"

"Morning," said Michael.

Patterson leant back in his chair, stretching out his body with the cracking of joints which had been hunched up for too long. "I thought so."

"What are you reading?"

"Etchin finally sent over that private detective report on Farron."

"Interesting?" said Michael.

"A lot of boring stuff about when he goes to the supermarket, what time he gets up, what route he drives to work. I should pin this up in my bedroom and read it every time I'm tempted to jack in police work for a cushy nine-to-five."

"Not interesting, then."

Patterson grinned at that, sending a frisson of excitement through the room. "Not until you read it in conjunction with Farron's financial reports."

Michael pulled up a chair from the desk behind and sat down. He waited for Patterson to tell him, but moments passed and he did not. "What financial reports?"

Patterson picked up his coffee mug. As he raised it to his lips, the mug brought with it a sheet of paper stuck to the bottom. Patterson peeled it off and stopped before drinking it. He peered at the contents of the mug and wrinkled his nose. "Get me a fresh one of these, could you?"

Michael sighed and got off his chair again. He grabbed the mug and returned ten minutes later with a clean one of steaming coffee. Patterson took it gratefully and blew over the surface to try to make it cool enough to drink.

"The report on Farron," Michael prompted.

"Right," said Patterson, clearing a space on his desk, finding a coaster underneath the papers and putting his mug on it. "The private detective followed him for about a week, doing all the usual stuff like going to work and the supermarket and all that. But he also followed him on two occasions where he met *this* man." Patterson rummaged through his snow of papers until he found a printed photograph showing the face of a white chubby balding man in a brown bomber jacket.

Michael didn't recognise him. "Who's that?"

"According to my friend in the drugs squad, Arnold Rebecki," said Patterson. "Low-level drug dealer with several convictions for possession with intent to supply both Class A and Class B."

"So, Farron was using drugs," said Michael. "He took too much heroin, went bonkers and shot his colleagues."

"So it looks at first sight, but not when you look a little closer. When you're a junkie, what's the one thing you need?" said Patterson. "And don't go looking into my head trying to find the answer."

"I promise I won't," said Michael, agreeing to play along with Patterson's game which, according to the grin on his face, he was enjoying. "Um … so junkies need … a supplier?"

"Which is Rebecki. And what do drug dealers require you to give them in order to supply you with drugs?"

"Money," said Michael, suddenly realising the obvious.

"Bingo," said Patterson. "And what does Farron's financial records show he has?"

"Money?" ventured Michael.

"Bingo again. Which he shouldn't have if he's got a serious drug habit. Users may start off with money, but once they become addicts, money is usually what they don't have because they spend all of it on whatever it is they're shooting into their arm or snorting up their nose."

"You're confusing me," said Michael.

"Look at this." Patterson searched through his papers again. "Oh, hang on, those files are digital." He shook his head with his own stupidity, unburied his mouse and waggled it to wake his computer.

Michael abandoned his chair and came round to look at the screen. It was alight with a credit card statement that had Nigel M. Farron's name across the top. Like most credit card statements, it was a long list of transactions with a hefty negative balance that required to be paid off.

"This is Farron's credit card from about a year ago," said Patterson. "All looks normal, he goes to the supermarket once or twice a week, buys petrol, there's the odd online purchase from a clothing store, that sort of thing."

"Okay," said Michael, not yet seeing what Patterson was getting at.

"Now, this is last month's credit card statement." With a few clicks of the mouse, Patterson brought up a similar document. The heading was the same, but the list of transactions had shrunk to almost nothing, just one purchase from Marks and Spencer, a deposit labelled 'thank you' by the credit card company and a zero balance.

"So, he stopped using this card and started to use a different one. People do that all the time."

Patterson turned away from the screen, his face lit by both its brightness and his excitement at the discovery. "He stopped using *any* credit card."

"Maybe his wife started doing all the shopping after they had the baby."

"Nope," said Patterson. "The private detective followed him going to the supermarket as normal. He even noted how many shopping bags he brought out with him — some people can take 'thorough' to an obsessive level."

"So …?"

"So, I think he was paying for everything in cash." Patterson leant back in his chair with self-satisfaction.

"Why is that important?" said Michael.

"*Because*, my young friend, if you're moving money around illegally, cash is the best way to hide it. It doesn't show up on things like financial reports that the police might persuade banks to hand over."

"So, he wasn't a drug user, he was a drug dealer?"

Patterson nodded. "I thought so too. But then I went back to the thorough report from our friend the private detective and there's no evidence of Farron dealing drugs. He goes to work, goes to the supermarket and meets up with that Rebecki man. Unless people are tunnelling into his house to buy their drugs, or he's selling them at work — which, even then, could only be to a few people — I don't think he was dealing."

"You think he was being *paid* to do something."

"Now you're getting it," said Patterson. "Farron was clever. On the face of it, there's nothing in his bank account to arouse suspicion. He had a lot of money, but he was a high-paid executive of a big energy firm, so why not? His salary is paid in, his mortgage is paid out, a couple of direct debits for council tax and stuff, and regular deposits from his mother."

"Didn't Farron's boss say his mother had died last year?"

"Yeah, I checked. More or less a year before Farron's baby arrived. His bank statements show she had always given him money when she was alive: twenty quid here, a hundred quid there. But after she died, that went up to five hundred quid at a time. I can't prove it yet — I would have to subpoena her bank records — but I bet Farron was paying cash into *her* account and using *that* to launder the money before it reached his bank. To the casual observer, it looks like his mother is helping out with the new baby. Except she can't have been because she was dead."

"Okay, so we know he was being paid. What do we do now?" said Michael.

"We talk to this guy." Patterson tapped the top of his paper-strewn desk where he had tossed the surveillance photograph of Farron's suspected drugs supplier. "Arnold Rebecki."

ARNOLD Rebecki looked different to his picture. Perhaps it was the lighting in the interrogation room, so harsh compared to the shadows of the place he had been photographed meeting Farron. Perhaps it was the stubble that he had failed to shave off his chin that morning, or the fact he was wearing a smart tweed jacket as opposed to the brown bomber jacket in the picture. More likely, it was the confidence that grew the longer he sat opposite Patterson, as he realised the police had no evidence against him. "No comment," he said for the umpteenth time.

Patterson referred back to the notes he had in front of him. "We know you supplied drugs to Nigel Farron," said Patterson.

Michael watched Rebecki from his position sitting at the table next to Patterson and perceived him as he answered. "You don't know nothing. You claim I was seen with this man and you know that I have a conviction for drug dealing, but you've added two and two together to make five."

"If you weren't dealing drugs," said Patterson, "what were you doing meeting Farron?"

"I didn't say I met him," said Rebecki. "You said I met him. I don't remember the guy. You say you have a photograph of me meeting him, so he might have stopped me to ask the time or something. I don't remember."

Michael perceived he was lying.

"Then how did Farron come to be in possession of the drugs we found at his house?" said Patterson.

"I wouldn't know," said Rebecki. "I don't move in those circles anymore. I did my time, I learnt my lesson, I am rehabilitated." The memory of prison was still raw inside him. Michael experienced his memories of rooms of men in blue and white striped shirts, a place where counting down the days to his release was the only thing that kept him sane. The only things he learnt during his months inside were the tricks other inmates told him about how to conduct himself during police questioning.

"What were the drugs you supplied to Nigel Farron?"

"I didn't ..." He was suddenly tired of repeating himself, so he reverted to the easiest answer. "No comment." But, in his head, he remembered the same question occurring to him. *Take the money and don't ask*, he had told himself, as a stack of twenty pound notes was pressed into his hands at the same time as he was given a plastic bag of syringes and vials of liquid.

"Did you supply Benjamin Conte with drugs?" said Patterson.

The name triggered the image of Conte's picture staring out at him from the television news. The same face he remembered meeting in the semi-dark of a bus stop at night. "I didn't supply anyone with drugs," said Rebecki.

Michael scribbled a note on the pad in front of him and passed it to Patterson. 'Was he paid to supply drugs to Farron and Conte?'

Patterson read the note. Despite his confused expression, he asked the question. "Were you paid to supply drugs to Farron and Conte?"

Rebecki's confidence slipped. "What do you mean?"

"Were you paid to supply drugs to Farron and Conte?" Patterson repeated.

Rebecki didn't think about the answer, instead he thought about the man in a blue and white striped shirt who had told him that bursting into tears during an interrogation could throw a copper off the scent.

Rebecki knew he couldn't cry on demand, so he laughed. "Inspector, I don't know if you're new to this game," he said, still chuckling. "But the way the drug business works is that the addict pays the dealer for the gear. The dealer doesn't get paid to do the supplying. Unless the whole thing has turned upside down since I last played the game."

"Who paid for the drugs, Mr Rebecki?" said Patterson.

"I don't know anything about drugs. I spent time in prison, I didn't like it. I'm not going back there." The sound of the guard turning the key in the lock of his cell rose from his memory. He could still hear the echo of the metal bolts clicking into place and see the inside of a door with no door handle.

Rebecki stood up. "You're not going to arrest me, are you, Inspector?"

"Not today," said Patterson.

"Then I am free to go."

Patterson closed his file and leant back in his chair. "You are free to go."

Michael felt that desperate feeling of something slipping away from him.

Rebecki approached the door.

"You'll need to be escorted out," said Patterson.

"I'll do it," said Michael. Rebecki may have been finished answering Patterson's questions, but Michael hadn't finished perceiving him.

They walked in silence down the corridor, Rebecki trying to think of anything other than drugs and prison. He thought of fish and chips. *I deserve fish and chips, there's not that much cholesterol in one portion anyway*, he told himself. It was depressingly not what Michael wanted to perceive.

They were coming up to the security door that marked the threshold between the interior of the police station and the public reception area. Michael realised he was running out of time.

"It's a shame you won't tell us who supplied you with the drugs," said Michael, casually, monitoring Rebecki's mind for anything he might subconsciously reveal. "It would really help us out with our investigation."

"Nice try," said Rebecki. "But you're not allowed to question me outside of the room."

Michael walked on ahead. When he got to the door, he turned and stared Rebecki right in the face. "We know someone paid you to deliver the drugs to Farron and Conte — who was it?"

Rebecki had no intention of telling Michael, but his subconscious mind couldn't help but answer such a direct question. An image of a memory flashed involuntarily: a man with dark hair swept in a fringe across his face. Michael searched for a name to go with the face, but the buzz of the opening security door destroyed the moment. The image disintegrated almost as soon as it appeared.

The person who had opened the door from the other side — a police officer in uniform of black tie and bright white shirt — walked through. "Excuse me," he said.

Michael was forced to get out of the way.

His movement gave Rebecki a clear path and, as soon as the police officer had passed, the drug dealer was out of the door.

Michael perceived him as he left, but it was clear he would get nothing more out of Rebecki's mind that day. Rebecki — thinking about fish and chips again — hurried past the members of the public in reception and out through the glass revolving door into the street, taking his knowledge with him.

NINE

THE bubbles in Michael's ginger beer shandy clung to the inside of the glass until the air inside them could no longer hold on and they drifted through the browny yellow sea to the surface and popped in a gentle fizz. He could watch the bubbles all night until his drink went flat, blocking out the rest of the world as he allowed his own thoughts to rise to the surface. But, that night, he had others with him and his thoughts were not something he was going to keep to himself.

The pub was a couple of miles from the base and popular with the soldiers stationed there because they could get a skinful and stagger back to their beds without having to worry about driving. For that reason, and because the publican was strict about underage kids being in there, it was largely avoided by perceivers. Which made it a good place to meet. It was also early evening and quiet, other than a single table of soldiers sitting at the other side of the bar, talking loudly and paying no attention to anyone else.

Michael had chosen a round table in a dark corner at the back of the pub for the meeting. He and Pauline sat on two chairs facing the wall. Alex sat on a bench-seat on the other side of the table with his arm around Sarah's shoulders. Pauline wasn't doing a very good job at masking her resentment at Sarah being there, but maybe that was on purpose.

Michael sipped his drink. The tiny splashes of bursting bubbles tickled his nose before the hit of ginger tingled in his mouth and flowed down his throat, leaving an after-hint of alcohol. The weak mix of beer with non-alcoholic ginger pop was about as much as he dared drink without clouding his perception. He was, after all, the only one drinking, as the others were underage, so he had bought them soft drinks to avoid the ire of the publican. Sarah sat with a glass of orange juice in front of her, while Alex and Pauline had chosen to have Coke. Like her blonde hair and the strain it took to keep up her perceiver blocks, the bright orange of Sarah's glass set her apart.

"So, Alex," said Michael. "I think you know what I'm going to ask."

Alex didn't say anything. He picked up his glass of Coke, but rather than drink it, he set it aside. He concentrated on the beer mat where a ring of condensation had soaked into the cardboard. The beer mat lifted from the table. Gently at first, then higher until it hovered parallel to the top of Alex's glass.

"Put it down!" Michael whispered insistently.

But Alex ignored him and the beer mat rose still higher, levitating until it was at eye level.

Michael reached out and snatched it from the air. "Not in here!" he said, putting the beer mat under his own drink so Alex couldn't get at it.

"I thought it was easier to show you than tell you," said Alex.

"But not in public," said Michael, glancing behind him at the barman who was emptying glasses from a dishwasher behind the bar, and the soldiers who were laughing at some joke he hadn't heard.

"I don't know why we're not meeting back at the base, anyway," said Pauline.

"Because Sarah isn't allowed in," said Alex.

"I don't see that as a problem," said Pauline.

"Pauline!" Michael warned her. He didn't like Sarah being there either, but rowing about it wasn't going to help.

"I was only saying, that this thing—" She stopped short at saying the words out loud. *This telekinesis thing is ours, not hers.*

"She was there at the railway bridge," said Alex. "In a way, it was her who made it happen."

Sarah was looking increasingly uncomfortable, even though she was being cuddled by her boyfriend. "I can speak up for myself, you know!" she said.

"Okay, okay," said Michael, waving his hands in a calming action. "Sarah was there then and she's here now. Alex trusts her, so it's fine for her to stay. Isn't it, Pauline?"

"I suppose," she said.

"I know you don't think I'm like you," said Sarah. "But I'm more like you than a norm."

"Of course you are," said Alex. He gave her a hug and kissed the top her head.

Michael found the public display of affection uncomfortable, but made sure he blocked his emotions from the others.

"The point is," said Michael, keeping his voice low. "The experiment was a success. Alex has the power, like me."

"I've been practising like you showed me with the Coke can," said Alex. "It gets easier every time. But before the train, there was nothing — it's like the ability has been switched on."

"So, what do we do about it?" said Michael.

"Nothing," said Pauline.

"Do we have that right to keep this to ourselves?" said Michael. "If it can happen to me, a natural born, and it can happen to Alex, it means it can happen to all of us."

"Only if we're willing to nearly get run over by a train," said Pauline. "Speaking personally, that's not something I want to do any time soon."

"I'd do it," said Sarah.

"Would it work with you?" said Pauline. "Not being, you know, as strong as us."

"I'd like to find out," she said.

"You don't need to prove anything to me," said Alex. "I love you just the way you are."

Sarah went a little red and kissed him on the cheek, but kept her embarrassment locked up behind those perceiver blocks of hers.

Michael tried to ignore them. "I think we should tell Norm the Norm," said Michael.

"No!" said Pauline.

"Are you serious?" said Alex.

"Norm's only going to tell Agent Cooper," said Pauline. "And he's going to tell the people who run the perceiver programme and before long they'll be tying us all to train tracks and sending a steam locomotive to run us over."

"Don't be ridiculous," said Michael.

"It's not ridiculous, not when you think of what they've done to us already," said Pauline.

Sarah leant forward. "What have they done?" she asked.

The others were ready to ignore her question, but not Pauline. "It's all right for you," she told Sarah. "You're not strong enough to get noticed, you're able to live out there in the real world under Perceivers' Law. But if you're strong like us, you get taken away from your families and made to live out here."

"Keep your voice down," said Michael.

"What do you know about it?" said Pauline. "You didn't have a family to be taken away from."

Her words stung far sharper than he was going to allow her to perceive. He hadn't been taken away from his family, *they* had been taken from *him*. When his memories were destroyed, his mother and father effectively went with them. He still had a mother, living alone somewhere, but he never went to see her because he knew it would be like meeting a stranger. Perhaps he had loved her once, but he didn't remember. People could tell him about how she had looked after him when he was a little boy, how she played childish games with him, cleaned his grazed knees when he fell over and told him to blow out candles on his birthday cake, but it would never seem real to him. The things people told him about his past would only ever be stories.

Pauline at least had her memories. It was true her family had effectively disowned her when they found out she was a perceiver, but at least she could remember the love. And, maybe, in years to come when perceivers were accepted out in the general population, she could know that love again.

The table had gone quiet.

Alex was the one to break the silence.

"I have to agree with Pauline," he said. "Telling Norm has the potential to get us into more trouble. I don't see any downside to *not* telling Norm."

"That makes it two against one, Michael," said Pauline.

Sarah looked like she wanted to say something, but had the good sense not to cast her vote.

"Okay then," said Michael, realising he wasn't going to win the argument. "We say nothing."

"Agreed," said Alex.

Pauline nodded. "Yes."

"That means no levitating beer mats," Michael insisted. "Not even to impress a girl."

"Oh, he can do other things to impress me," said Sarah with a grin.

The others perceived Alex's arousal before he could hide it from them. "Possibly," he said.

"Alex, you're so funny," said Sarah.

"Am I?"

Michael finished his drink. "Anyone want another one?" he asked, holding up his empty glass.

They all did, meaning the evening was going to turn out to be more expensive than he had planned.

But it gave him a moment to step away from the others. As the barman filled the orders, Michael looked back at Pauline and thought about what Alex had said to him not so long ago. Maybe it was time to tell her about his past so she understood about his family. He just had to find the right moment.

TEN

MICHAEL tapped the 'enter' key on Patterson's keyboard and the picture on the screen changed from one white middle-aged man with a large nose to another middle-aged man with a large nose. Both of them had done something or other to get their mugshots into the police database, but neither of them looked like the image of the man Michael had pulled from Rebecki's memory. Not as if he was sure that he would recognise him if he saw him. The police pictures were well lit, detailed and clear. Rebecki's memory had been brief, shady and retrieved involuntarily.

Around him, other detectives got on with their own cases, their heads hunched over their computer screens. Or they leant back in their chairs talking on the phone. A few of them were talking with each other, discussing their cases or last night's TV. It created a hubbub in the room that was starting to give Michael a headache. Every now and then, a snippet of conversation would drift over to him and his mind would latch onto it as far more interesting than looking at photographs of ugly criminals. Then he remembered what Patterson had told him, 'the quicker you look through the mugshots, the sooner it will be over' and he went back to his assigned task.

A change in the timbre of the hubbub caused Michael to turn around and see that the officers were reacting to the arrival of DCI Mulgrew. She stood in the doorway, a collection of papers clutched in one hand, as she looked around the room. "Where's Patterson?" she said.

One of the other detectives called over. "He was here a minute ago."

"He went out to get me—" Michael didn't finish his sentence before Patterson was at the door, weaving his way past Mulgrew with two coffees in cardboard cups from the takeaway place outside the station. He handed one to Michael and peeled the lid off the second to take a sip. Only then did he realise that Mulgrew was at his shoulder.

"Did you get my report on Rebecki?" he asked her.

"Yes," she said.

"We think if we can identify the people who supplied him with the drugs, we'll have more of a handle on what's going on."

But Michael perceived that Mulgrew wasn't interested. "Inspector," he said. "I think DCI Mulgrew has come to tell us something."

Patterson put his coffee down. "Oh?"

"I want you to stop the drugs investigation," she said.

"What?" said Patterson.

"I just got the pathologist's report back on Farron." She held up the collection of papers in her hand. "There were no drugs in his system. No cocaine, no heroin, no ordinary street drugs … I've ordered a more detailed toxicology report, but it seems like the drugs angle is a red herring."

"That doesn't make any sense," said Patterson. "Both Farron and Conte were taking the drugs, it can't be a coincidence."

"Not according to the pathologist's report." She dumped the papers on Patterson's desk.

"Then how do you account for them both going off the rails?" said Patterson.

"They were both in stressful jobs, people lose it sometimes," said Mulgrew. "Or there's the espionage angle. You did good work on his financials, Inspector, you should follow that lead. It doesn't make sense for someone to pay Farron to take drugs, but paying him to spy on his company, that has a lot more credibility. As for shooting dead a third of the board of Power Grid UK, that sounds more like a terrorist act, wouldn't you say? Perhaps the people who paid him got as much information as they could before getting him to do one last job."

"But, Elizabeth—"

"It's what you wanted isn't it, Anthony? To go back to investigating terrorists? The drugs angle is a dead end, I need someone to follow up on the gun Farron used. Where did he get it? What about the phone calls his wife said he took in the last weeks before the shooting? We checked his mobile phone records and there's nothing there, so maybe he had a second phone. Find that phone, Inspector."

DCI Mulgrew headed for the door.

Michael called after her. "But Rebecki was being paid by someone else to deliver the drugs to Farron and Conte. Don't you think that's interesting?"

Mulgrew stopped at the doorway, turning back and leaning on the doorframe, keeping her body half out of the office. "Of course it's interesting, but that's why we have a drugs squad. Write up what you know and pass it over to them."

She continued her path through the door and was gone.

Patterson sat down on the edge of his desk in defeat. His bottom touched the side of the cup of coffee, knocking it straight over.

Michael jumped up as steaming brown liquid flooded all over the desk, soaking into the pathologist's report, seeping under the keyboard and mouse until it spilled over the edge of the desk and dripped onto the floor.

Patterson turned round and looked at the mess he had made. "Perfect."

ELEVEN

THERE was an unnatural chill in the air of the gym, as Michael stepped inside. The air conditioning had sucked out every drop of sweat and body odour from the atmosphere so that it made the room smell sterile and unwelcoming. Music with a fast beat played out of speakers high in the ceiling, thumping in time to the feet of two women on the treadmills by the window, who ran as they chatted to each other between snatched breaths. The other equipment sat unused. But then, it was not long after dinner and most people stationed on the base were digesting. Michael, in fact, could still feel the weight of the jacket potato he had eaten and had no desire to disturb it by doing something like running on a treadmill. He had come to find Peter.

Peter, wearing a combination of sweaty vest top and baggy track-suit bottoms was at the far end of the room where the weights were kept. He had a large dumbbell in each hand and was alternately lifting them, puffing out his cheeks with the effort as each bicep bulged. Michael caught a glimpse of himself in the mirror as he walked towards Peter, skinny in comparison and somewhat overdressed in his perceiver greys.

Michael leant against the rack of free weights, arranged in ascending order from lightest at the top to heaviest at the bottom, and waited for Peter to notice.

Peter kept lifting the dumbbells as Michael felt his perception flit around the edge of his filters. "What do you want?" said Peter, lowering the weights to the length of his arms and walking over to place them back on the rack.

"To talk to you," said Michael.

"I can perceive that. Talk to me about what?"

"You can draw, can't you?" asked Michael.

"You know I can." Peter perused the rack of weights and picked up a couple of dumbbells a bit smaller than the ones he had put back.

"You can draw stuff from things you see in people's heads?"

Peter held the smaller dumbbells parallel with his hips and raised them out sideways until they were level with his shoulders, then brought them back down to the starting position and repeated the move. "I do it all the time in my job."

"Could you do it to me?" said Michael.

"Maybe," said Peter between lateral raises. "But if you're asking me to draw some imagined fantasy landscape for your girlfriend's birthday card, I charge a fee."

"No," said Michael. "I saw the images of a face when I perceived a man, but I can't describe it. I thought, if you could draw it, I wouldn't need to."

Peter gave up with his lateral raises and returned the weights to the rack. "Okay," he said. "But don't get your hopes up, memories of memories can be difficult."

"But we can try it?"

"We can try," confirmed Peter. "I'll have a shower and you can meet me back at my room in half an hour."

PETER'S room was identical to Michael's except it felt completely different. It had the same furniture in more or less the same arrangement, but Peter's personality was embedded in it. Most striking was the wall upon which he had stuck a load of his drawings, in pencil or black ink and occasionally in colour. Many overlapped to form a collage depicting everything from landscapes to people and inanimate objects.

Some of the people Michael recognised as other perceivers from Galen House. The one that caught his eye the most was a pencil sketch of Norm the Norm, his exaggerated face screwed up in the middle of shouting at someone. Michael chuckled. "These are really good."

"Thanks," said Peter, tossing his gym clothes into a wash bag in the corner. "I thought Norm the Norm was going to make me take that one of him down, but I think he sort of likes it."

Michael got closer to the section of decorated wall which lay between the television and the table. They were even more impressive when he could see the individual drawn lines which made up the overall picture. Of all the pictures, there were some images which were repeated, notably one of a child of about ten. The boy was pictured playing with a football, eating dinner and simply looking directly out of the drawing. Michael didn't know much about Peter's background, but he remembered he had at least a mother and one sibling at home. "Is this your brother?" he asked.

Peter deliberately ignored his question, preventing whatever emotion it produced from being perceived and sat on the bed. "So, what is it Alex, Pauline and you are up to these days?"

"Up to?" said Michael. He wasn't entirely sure why, but he felt the need to strengthen his blocks a little. Not enough, he hoped, for Peter to notice.

"Going off camping together, meeting in your room, that sort of thing."

"Oh." Michael waved away any suggestion of conspiracy. "We're friends, that's all. We can't all be Mr Popular."

"Is that what I am?" said Peter.

Peter was loud and entertaining. If ever there was a large group congregating in the communal area, it was usually Peter at the centre of it. "I think you are," said Michael.

"Then you must be Mr Secretive."

Michael supposed he was. But then, he had a lot to be secret about. "How do we do this drawing thing?"

Peter reached over to a cabinet by his bedside and opened the top drawer. After a little rummaging, he brought out a plain A4 pad and a collection of pencils. "When I do this at my job, I spend a long time carefully picking through someone's mind to find the right memory. Hopefully that won't be necessary with you." He looked over to the cabinet where a clock's digital numbers showed it to be a little after half past eight. "Because I was planning on getting an early night."

Michael approached the bed. "Do you want me to project—?"

"Don't project the memory," said Peter. "Just let me see it. That way I can find the little details that you might not be aware exist."

"Okay." Michael sat on the bed.

"Think of the memory."

"Okay."

Peter looked at his face, and into his eyes. Michael felt his perception enter his mind.

"You're still blocking me," said Peter. "You can keep up the filters that stop other thoughts and feelings getting in, but you have to let down the barriers preventing things from getting out."

Michael took a deep breath. It took an immense amount of trust to allow another perceiver full access to his consciousness.

"Think only of the memory you want me to see," said Peter. "That way I won't accidentally perceive anything else."

Michael thought himself back to standing near the security door in the police station. He remembered looking into Rebecki's mind and seeing the flash of a memory. A half-forgotten face emerged from the dark.

A face that gradually manifested itself onto the pad resting on Peter's lap. First in big broad strokes, and then in tiny details which Michael hadn't even realised he had seen.

TWELVE

THE cafe was a ten minute walk from the police station, close enough to pop in for lunch hour, but far enough away that it wasn't full of police officers. It was mostly full of office workers taking time out from their nine-to-five, although there were also a couple of tables crammed with large men in grubby clothes who had been digging up the road just round the corner. Every single one of them made noise, from the chattering to each other, the clinking of cutlery and the rattling of teacups, to the sounds of cooking and the coffee machine behind the counter. Enough noise for other people not to overhear Michael and Pauline's conversation.

Pauline had chosen a cheese and ham toastie while Michael had gone for a sausage roll and chips. When they arrived at their table, he regretted his decision — her lunch smelled better.

Pauline bit into her toastie and melted cheese oozed out by the side of her mouth. It must have been hot because she immediately sucked in air and waved her hand frantically in front of her face to generate a cooling breeze.

Michael laughed. He decided to wait before delving into his own hot food. Instead, he pulled a piece of folded paper from his pocket which he unfurled and pushed across the table towards her.

She put down her toastie, wiped her hands on a paper napkin and pulled it closer. "Is this Peter's sketch?"

"Yeah," said Michael.

"It's good, isn't it?"

Staring up from the table at them was a man with a dark fringe swept across his face. Peter had done well to accurately reproduce the image, perhaps too well as, just like Rebecki's memory, it was shadowy and indistinct.

"How do we find out who it is?" asked Michael.

"Didn't you think of that before you asked Peter to draw it?" said Pauline.

"I thought if I saw the image on paper, it would help me compare it to the mugshots in the police database. But, to be honest, it hasn't made it any clearer than it was in my head."

"You could ask some of the officers in the drugs squad if they recognise him. You're handing the drugs case over to them anyway, aren't you?"

"That's what your boss wants my boss to do," said Michael.

"Mulgrew thinks the drugs squad are better suited to follow that lead and Patterson is better suited to look into where Farron got the gun from."

"So you're on her side?" said Michael.

"I'm presenting her argument, it's not the same thing."

Within the dozens of perceptions of people in the cafe, Michael suddenly felt someone familiar.

He wasn't sure if Pauline perceived it too, or if she had just seen who had walked in the door, because she hunched herself lower over the table and took another bite from her toastie. "Keep your head down," she said.

Michael turned to see Patterson had stepped into the cafe. He looked cold without a coat and red faced from having walked from the police station. He was carrying a cardboard file in his hand. Michael sat up in his seat and gave him a wave.

Pauline kicked him under the table. "Michael! What did you do that for?"

He had no time to answer because Patterson had walked the few steps to their table, becoming disappointed when he saw Michael had company. "Oh, hello, Pauline," he said.

"Inspector," she acknowledged as she continued to eat her toastie.

"In your text, you didn't say you were with someone," said Patterson to Michael.

"You asked me where I'd gone and I said to the cafe for lunch," said Michael.

"I wouldn't want to play gooseberry," said Patterson, stepping away. "I'll see you back at the office."

Michael could perceive Patterson wanted to tell him something. "No, it's okay, we were talking shop anyway." He threw a thought over to Pauline, *Tell him it's okay.*

"It's okay," she called to Patterson. "You might as well stay now you're here. Why don't you buy yourself a sandwich or something. The ham and cheese toastie is nice."

Patterson relented and five minutes later was sitting next to Michael with a cup of coffee in a white cup and saucer.

"You can talk in front of me," said Pauline. "Just because I work with DCI Mulgrew, doesn't mean I can't keep a secret if you want me to. Michael's been showing me the sketch of the person who supplied the drugs to Rebecki."

Michael passed the piece of paper across to Patterson, explaining how it had been drawn.

"Do you know who it is?" asked Patterson.

"Not yet," said Michael. "So, what is it you wanted to talk about?"

Patterson looked uncertainly across the table at Pauline, then pulled out the file he had brought with him, laying it open on the table. Michael recognised the pages inside as the same ones Patterson had been poring over the other morning.

"Isn't that the private detective's report?" said Michael. "I thought you went through that already."

"Something about it has been bothering me," said Patterson. "I took a fresh look at it this morning and saw what had been staring me in the face."

Pauline leant forward, trying to read the report upside down across the table. Michael looked over Patterson's shoulder. All he saw were a list of times and places detailing Farron's movements across several days, some entries with a lot of comments, others with very few.

Patterson reached into his inside jacket pocket and pulled out a pen. He clicked the button on the top to extend the writing tip and held it poised above the file. "Look at this: the 28th of October, Farron leaves the office at 6.32pm," he read. "He stops off at Sainsbury's at 6.48, buys four bags of shopping and gets home at 10.02pm." He circled each recorded time with a swirl of blue ink.

"I don't see it," said Michael.

"Look at the times," said Patterson.

"I get it," said Pauline. "There's more than three hours between him stopping off at the supermarket and getting home."

"Right!" said Patterson. Then he gave her a quizzical look across the table. "You're not perceiving me, are you?"

"No!" she said. "Cross my heart." Her finger traced an imaginary cross on her blouse.

"Doesn't necessarily mean anything," said Michael. "It might be a long way to his house from the supermarket or he might have got stuck in traffic."

"Except, I would expect a private investigator as meticulous as the one who was following Farron to have made a note of something like a traffic jam. He didn't, and yet on the 28th of October, a journey that normally took Farron about an hour, takes three times as long. It's not the only discrepancy in the report, either."

The table fell silent, as silent as it could be with the clang and chatter of the busy cafe around them.

"You think he was meeting someone," said Pauline.

Patterson looked up from his papers. "Now you *are* perceiving me," he said.

Pauline smiled. "I am a little. Michael is right, your thoughts are very loud."

"So yes," said Patterson. "I think he was meeting someone. Someone that someone else doesn't want us to know about."

"The obvious question would be 'who?'" said Michael.

"My bet is on Etchin," said Patterson. "He was all ready to have the report couriered straight over to me as soon as he got back to his office the time we first saw him, and yet it took him several days. I think he read the report, saw something he didn't like and decided to doctor it before passing it to the police."

"I have another obvious question for you," said Michael. "Why?"

"I'd hazard a guess it has something to do with the reason he had Farron followed in the first place," said Patterson.

"He really was spying on the company?" said Michael.

Patterson shrugged. "I don't know yet, but I think it suits Etchin to paint Farron as a drug addict who went a bit crazy and shot his colleagues, rather than admit that he had a mole in his organisation."

THIRTEEN

PAULINE was a welcome sight, all smiles and light in her face, despite her usual black clothing. She must have recently been outside of the police station because her long hair looked like it had been ruffled by the wind. Not that it mattered to Michael, he decided he liked the wild look. He opened his perception to feel her positivity and noticed something else — that her mood also lifted when she saw he was still at his desk.

Not as if he actually had a desk. It was Patterson's desk, really. As a 'consultant' to the Metropolitan Police, he got the feeling that someone in charge didn't expect him to be hanging around long enough to need one of his own.

"I wondered if you were ready to go home?" said Pauline.

Michael stood from the chair where he had been sitting for too long. "I am *so* ready," he said. He stretched out his arms and his legs and felt the blood flow into them. *Is this what it feels like to be old?* he thought.

Pauline giggled.

I didn't mean you to perceive that.

"Where's Inspector Patterson?" she said.

"Gone to hand in his report to the drugs people. He spent all day writing about it and moaning about it."

"So you didn't get any further in the investigation, then?"

"We found out where the gun came from," said Michael.

"Where?"

"Manchester, we think. There were a bunch of guns smuggled out of Bosnia after the war which ended up in Manchester. The officer up there said it could have changed hands several times before it ended up in London. Which means it's an illegal street gun. If Farron was getting drugs off the streets, then getting a gun off the streets isn't such a leap."

"Doesn't answer why he did it," said Pauline.

"I think it's like you said happened to Conte with the cricket bat and the fire. He just flipped." *I was in his head after Farron shot those people, Pauline, it didn't feel like he had a plan to kill anyone. It didn't feel like he had a plan at all.* "Patterson has this crazy theory that…"

Michael felt a familiar presence at the edge of his perception and looked up to see Patterson come in. The grumpy man that Michael had had to endure all day was gone, there was even a little bit of excitement spilling out from him. "Patterson has this crazy theory that what?" he asked.

"You think Farron might have been paid to kill senior managers at Power Grid UK."

"What's so crazy about that?" said Patterson.

"For a start, six of them survived," said Michael.

"Didn't the witnesses say he fired indiscriminately?" said Pauline. "It wasn't like he was targeting anyone."

Patterson turned to Michael. "Did you bring her here to gang up on me?"

Michael laughed.

"Anyway, don't bother about that now," said Patterson. "I've just been over to narcotics to hand over that bloody report, and while I was there I showed your sketch to my friend. He said it looks a lot like Robert Fazoni, a small-time criminal the probation office believes is living in a flat above a restaurant on East Finchley High Road."

PATTERSON nuzzled into a parking space on the East Finchley High Road, one that he was fortunate to get on a busy evening. He turned off the engine and sat for a moment in the shade of the night underneath a broken street light. A few metres down, and across the road, was Al's Kebabs & More, a Turkish restaurant-cum-takeaway squeezed between a general store and a nail bar. Above it lived Robert Fazoni, the young man with the dark fringe.

"I just thought," said Pauline from the back seat, "if he's not home, we've driven a long way for nothing."

Patterson turned round to face her through the gap between the two front seats. "Would you have preferred it that I called ahead to give him time to get his story straight?"

"I was just saying," said Pauline.

Michael perceived, and Pauline must have too, that Patterson felt cajoled into having them both tag along. He had learnt to work with Michael, to even respect him, but two young perceivers made him feel like *a stressed father having to take the kids out at the weekend*, as his thoughts had so eloquently put it.

"Here's the rules," said Patterson. "I do the talking, you two do the perceiving. Are we clear?"

But Pauline wasn't really listening, she was looking out the window across the street. She leant forward to take a closer look. "Isn't that the guy you called in for questioning?"

Michael followed her gaze and saw the unmistakable brown bomber jacket of Arnold Rebecki. Part of his face was obscured by a scarf wrapped high around his neck, but it was definitely him.

"What's he doing here?" said Patterson.

"Want me to find out?" said Pauline, scooting across the seat and putting her hand on the door handle.

"We're not here for him," said Patterson.

"Don't you think it's weird he's here?" said Pauline. "I can perceive him for you if you like."

Michael was still watching Rebecki though the window. "He's going into the kebab place," he said as Rebecki disappeared through the door of Al's Kebabs & More.

Patterson's thoughts tumbled with indecision as he both wanted to know what Rebecki was doing there and not to send Pauline out to follow him.

"You two can't go in," she said. "He knows you from the interrogation. But he doesn't know me. It's a public place, I'll be fine."

"Okay," said Patterson, but he wasn't happy about it. "Perceiving only, no confronting."

"Sure thing," she said as she got out of the car.

Be careful, Michael thought, knowing she would hear him.

Of course.

Text me.

Will do.

Pauline darted across the road through the slow-moving rush hour traffic and disappeared through the door of Al's Kebabs & More.

Michael pulled his phone from his pocket.

"What are you doing with that?" asked Patterson.

"Keeping in touch with Pauline."

"Can't you two telepath each other or something?"

"Not at this distance."

They waited in the car for something to happen. People walked by. Cars drove by. Michael's phone remained silent.

A woman went into the nail bar. A man came out of the general store with a bunch of stuff in a blue plastic bag. Patterson shuffled impatiently in the driver's seat.

Michael's phone bleeped. It was a text from Pauline. 'He's not here,' it read.

Patterson leant across to read it. "What does that mean?"

Michael was concentrating on texting her back when Patterson tapped him on the shoulder. When Michael looked up he saw that Pauline had left the restaurant and was dashing back across the street towards them carrying a white parcel.

The smell of cooked greasy meat and spices filled the car as Pauline got in. "Mission failed," she said.

"What happened?" said Michael.

"He wasn't there," she said.

"But we saw him go in."

"I tried perceiving the man selling the kebabs — which wasn't easy because he thinks in Turkish — and as far as I can work out, there's a back door in the restaurant with access to stairs which lead to the flat above. Best guess is Rebecki went up there to see whatshisname."

"Robert Fazoni," said Patterson.

"Yeah, him."

"There he is again," said Michael as he saw the man in the brown bomber jacket come out of the restaurant.

"I'm going to follow him," said Pauline.

"No," said Patterson.

She leant forward and passed her package over to Michael. "Save me some if it's nice. If it isn't, you can eat it all."

No sooner had he taken her kebab parcel than she was out of the car and crossing the road.

"Why did I agree to bring your girlfriend?" said Patterson.

"Because she'd tell Mulgrew you'd gone to interview the drugs guy when she told you to pass it on to the drugs squad."

"Hmm," said Patterson.

"And she's not my girlfriend. She's just a friend."

"Right."

REBECKI got on a bus and Pauline got on after him.

'He's furious,' said Pauline's first text.

'About what?' Michael texted back.

'Not sure. Mind full of swear words.'

Michael chuckled.

Patterson pulled out from his parking space and tried to follow the bus without looking like he was following the bus. It zipped along in the bus lane where cars were not allowed while Patterson was stuck behind traffic going nowhere, his blood pressure silently building inside of him.

Pauline texted again. 'He's angry he's being made to do another drop. He told them, no more after the cops pulled him in.'

"He's making a drop?" said Patterson. "If he's delivering more of the drugs, then who to? Farron and Conte are dead."

Michael texted Pauline the question.

'Can't perceive. Hold on.'

The bus pulled in at a bus stop. Two people got on. A few people got off. Patterson relaxed a little as the traffic nudged forward and he caught up with the bus again.

'Woman sitting behind him got off,' Pauline texted. 'Going to sit closer. Going to perceive deeper.'

The bus forged ahead in the bus lane, sailing past green traffic lights up ahead, which turned amber as the car in front of Patterson was approaching. It obeyed the law and stopped as the lights turned red, leaving Patterson frustrated behind it. "Who is this idiot? Doesn't he know you can get away with driving through the lights on yellow? Everyone in London goes through the lights on yellow!"

Michael ignored his rantings and watched the black screen of his silent phone.

The bus continued its journey further up the road and disappeared from view.

"Police can use the bus lane if I put on my flashing lights," said Patterson.

"Won't that draw attention?" said Michael.

Patterson gripped the steering wheel tighter and stayed in the line of slow-moving cars.

Michael pulled up the internet on his phone and searched for the bus route. "The bus should continue on this road for a while yet."

Patterson's yo-yo blood pressure calmed as a combination of the bus waiting at a few bus stops and his aggressive driving brought them to within visual range again.

Michael's phone bleeped, lighting up with Pauline's text. 'He's meeting a woman at Brent Cross,' it said. 'He's too angry to care who it is.'

Michael checked the bus route again to see how far it was before they got to Brent Cross.

Another text came through. 'He got suspicious when I got close. I had to pretend I was asking for directions. He thinks I'm going to Golder's Green.'

The bus route revealed Golder's Green to be after Brent Cross. "If she follows him when he gets off," said Michael, "he'll know she was lying."

"Tell her to stay on the bus," said Patterson. "She can find somewhere safe to wait for us like a coffee shop or something. We'll deal with Rebecki."

The bus eventually left the busy main road and journeyed through a series of residential streets which had been built long before the massive Brent Cross Shopping Centre had come to dominate the area. Patterson continued to follow behind the bus, keeping enough distance to suggest to any casual observer that he wasn't following it. Up ahead, a railway bridge signalled they were close to a train station. The bus slowed as it approached, the yellow light at its bottom left corner indicating it was pulling in.

Patterson slowed too, bringing the car to a stop at the kerb. He turned off his headlights and his car hid in the night. Only the purr of the running engine, and the two people inside, distinguished it from a parked car.

The bus waited under the bridge as Rebecki got off, the glow from the street light illuminating the brown of his jacket as he stepped onto the pavement. As the bus drove off, carrying Pauline with it, Rebecki was momentarily obscured from view. When it had gone, all that could be seen was a bus shelter sticking out from the wall and a barren expanse of pavement stretching into the dark.

"Where is he?" said Patterson.

Michael strained his younger eyes to look. Behind the clear perspex of the bus shelter was a shadow which, if the shelter was empty, shouldn't be there. "I think he's sitting in the bus shelter."

"Then that's the drop-off point," said Patterson. "Is there anyone with him? I can't see."

Michael opened his perception, blocking out the loud thoughts of Patterson by his side, spreading his antenna wide as interference piled in from the houses in the street. It was hard to pick out Rebecki's mental signature and he wouldn't have been able to if he hadn't perceived him before. Even then, all he could do was detect his presence. He couldn't make out his thoughts or tell if any other of the perceptions belonged to a second person in the bus shelter or were just the general background noise of other people.

"I'm too far away," said Michael. "We need to get closer."

"I don't want to spook him," said Patterson. "We need to know who he's meeting."

"I think I can get close enough to find out." Michael reached for the door handle.

"He'll see you," said Patterson.

Michael pulled up the hood of his top. "You were the one asking the questions in the interrogation, he barely noticed me." With his hood up, all of his head and part of his face were covered.

Patterson sighed. "Walk straight past, don't look directly at him, and be careful."

"Sure thing," said Michael, echoing Pauline's phrase from earlier.

He got out of the car and shut the door with a click rather than a slam. He skipped across the road and began his slow walk towards the railway bridge.

Being on the other side of the road put Michael at a better angle and, even as he kept his face half hidden by his hoodie, he saw that there were two shadows sitting on the bench in the bus shelter. One was the familiar shape of Rebecki, the other was a woman much smaller, thinner and largely hidden under a full-length black coat.

He ambled towards the bridge while targeting his perception. The woman's nerves twittered around her mind like birds around a bird feeder on a frosty day. *Come on, come on, come on*, her thoughts were saying, almost as a mantra to hide whatever else she might be thinking.

Michael padded forward, his trainers hardly making a sound on the damp ground. He saw her white hand reach out from her black coat and take a brown-wrapped parcel from Rebecki. Her relief was partial, calming her twittering birds, but she wasn't safe yet. She stood up to go. Michael turned to look, ready to perceive more, but he must have turned too fast.

The movement caught Rebecki's eye and he stared straight across the street, right at Michael. Michael perceived his sudden recognition. Rebecki was, as Patterson had said, 'spooked'.

Looking around in all directions, Rebecki noticed Patterson's car with the silhouette of someone sitting inside. He couldn't possibly have recognised Patterson at that distance, but Rebecki had a criminal's instinct. *Cops.*

Rebecki jumped up and ran off in the other direction like a man half his age.

The woman was so startled she dropped the package. *The drugs!* screamed her mind as she grabbed the package back and thrust it under her coat. She looked at Michael and he perceived a moment of confusion before she chased after Rebecki like an adult who hadn't run since her last school sports day.

Michael glanced back at Patterson. He was out of the car and running towards the bridge, but Michael couldn't wait. If he was going to find out who the woman was, he needed to go after her. And this time, when he was close, he wouldn't hesitate to push her surface thoughts out of the way and burrow until he found out what the hell was going on.

He broke into a run, his trainers making fast progress on the pavement as the woman ran ahead of him, tottering on shoes that weren't meant for running as she reached into her coat pocket.

Michael heard the jingle of keys and the clicks of car locks unlocking as she pointed her hand at a hatchback parked up ahead. It responded with the flash of yellow indicator lights.

He was closing on her, but not quickly enough to stop her from getting inside.

Michael reached the bumper as the engine started with the roar of injected petrol. *Come on, come on, come on!* her thoughts were saying. Michael ran round to the front of the car and slammed both his hands on the bonnet with the bang of hollow metal. He stared straight at her through the windscreen, getting into her mind at the same time as his body blocked her car's escape.

Her thoughts were so full of panic he only perceived what she was going to do a split second before he heard the gears crunch into reverse. The car sped backwards, swerving out of control and mounting the pavement. Michael stood his ground out in the road, concentrating only on her mind, intending to pull at least a name from the mess of her thoughts.

The gears crunched again and that's when Michael perceived she was going to drive the hell out of there.

The car shot forward. Michael stayed steadfast in the road so she couldn't get past. But she didn't care and she drove right at him.

At the last moment, he jumped out of the way, almost stumbling over his own feet as the car sped off, its engine roaring as it pumped out the grey smoke of an overworked engine.

He turned and watched it go, only thinking about reading the number plate when the car was too far away to see.

Patterson finally came up behind him, puffing unfit breaths and staggering to a stop. "Did you find out who she is?" he panted.

Michael had only managed to find a first name. "She's called Theresa, I think. Or Tina."

He perceived Patterson's disappointment. "Did you get the number plate?"

"No," said Michael. But there was something else about the car he had recognised. Something that he was only just remembering he had seen before. "There was a sticker on her car windscreen. It had a picture of a black circle with a lightning bolt in the middle."

"The Power Grid UK logo?" said Patterson.

"Yeah. I think it was a parking permit."

FOURTEEN

THE smoky-grey glass doors at the front entrance parted with the quiet whir of electronic motors, allowing Patterson and Michael to walk in. The reception area at Power Grid UK had been cleaned up since they were last there. Cleaned up to the point that dirt was not merely absent, it had been banished.

Everything Michael remembered from the aftermath of the boardroom massacre was gone. The building was still there, in terms of walls, windows, ceilings and doors, but everything inside of it had been ripped up and thrown away, to be superseded by something new. The purple colour scheme which had once welcomed visitors was gone and replaced with bold blue walls, a pristine maroon carpet and bright red sofas which branched out at a right angle from the corner beside the entrance. Even the reception desk, an impressive semi-circular affair made of light-colour wood looked almost yellow in the bright spotlights that shone down upon it.

Patterson self-consciously wiped the dirt from the car park off his shoes by rubbing them thoroughly on the mat provided. The receptionist, meanwhile, looked up from behind her yellow desk and smiled at him with thin lips which she had painted with vibrant red lipstick. "Can I help you?"

For once, he had his identification ready as he approached. "Detective Inspector Patterson."

The receptionist's smile faltered as she examined his police badge. "That's real, is it?"

Patterson was taken aback with the question. "Of course it's real," he said. *I forgot to pack my fake one*, he thought.

"I'm told I have to be careful," the receptionist explained. "Journalists will spill any lie if it will get them inside the building. The other receptionist said it wasn't enough that the people she worked with had died, the vultures in the media had to descend as well."

Patterson put his ID back in his pocket. "Other receptionist?" he asked.

"She's off on compassionate. I'm a temp."

"Ah," said Patterson with disappointment.

"I'm still quite capable, I can assure you."

"It's just that we're looking for someone who works here called Theresa," said Patterson. "I was going to ask if you knew her."

"Theresa what?"

"Theresa's all we know, I'm afraid."

"Or possibly Tina," added Michael.

"We believe she works here," said Patterson. "Her car had a Power Grid UK parking pass on the windscreen."

The receptionist pursed her red lips into the opposite of a smile. "I'll ring HR and see if they know if any one of the five hundred employees is a woman who has a first name beginning with 'T'."

"Thank you," said Patterson.

"Why don't you take a seat?" she said, with a tone that implied, *Please go over there and keep out of my way*. If Michael had perceived her, that's probably what he would have heard, but he decided it was immaterial what the temporary receptionist thought and so he spared himself the trouble.

Despite her sarcasm, the woman made her phone call as promised and came back with a positive answer. "It turns out we do have an employee called Theresa, Mr Patterson."

Inspector, he corrected her in his head, but again he bit his lip.

"Would you like to come with me?"

She escorted them to the lift and took them up to the fourth floor.

The lift doors opened onto a corridor almost a carbon copy of the one Michael and Patterson had been in on their previous two visits to the building. This time there was no blood, no police officers with semi-automatic rifles and no police tape. It looked the same as it must have looked the day before Farron shot up the boardroom, but it felt very different. Michael could perceive there were people busy working behind the walls, all of them a little more timid, a little more uneasy and a little less self-confident than they once were.

The receptionist, by contrast, strode out of the lift with supreme confidence, instructing Michael and Patterson to follow her.

They obeyed until she stopped at a plain brown office door, knocked on it and, without waiting for an answer, went inside.

Patterson was close behind and almost walked into her as she stopped abruptly.

The office was a relatively small room with a desk on one side, a worn purple upholstered sofa pushed against the opposite wall and a window that looked out onto the Power Grid UK car park where Patterson had left his car. There was only one person in the room and it wasn't Theresa. It wasn't a woman at all, but a tall man who had turned round to face them as soon as the door opened, stopping the receptionist in her tracks.

It was David Etchin, looking more assured than he had been on that first day after the shooting. Like the reception area, he had given himself a new look: his arm was no longer in a sling and he was wearing a tie, bright red like his receptionist's lipstick.

"Mr Etchin!" said the receptionist. "I'm terribly sorry, I must have got the wrong room."

"No, this is the right room," he said. "You can leave the inspector and his sidekick and go back downstairs."

The receptionist hesitated for a moment before quickly hustling herself out of the room and closing the door behind her.

Michael opened his perception up to Etchin. There was one over-riding emotion coming from him, and that was smugness.

"I was rather expecting this to be the office where a woman called Theresa works," said Patterson.

"And so it is, Inspector. It's just that she's not here at the moment."

"But *you* are."

"Indeed."

Michael had no patience for listening to the older men play verbal tennis with each other. He leant back against the closed door and allowed it to take his weight as he looked directly at Etchin. He stared beyond the features of his face and into his mind. Clouded by his smug exterior was a nervousness at having the police in his building again, and an uncertainty at what he was going to tell them.

There was also a memory, of the woman who had nearly run Michael over by the Brent Cross bus stop, the woman Etchin thought of as Theresa. He remembered a time when she sat on the sofa in her office. She had bloodshot eyes and the lines of many fallen tears streaked down her face.

The memory faded as Etchin dismissed it and focussed on the now. He leant back against the windowsill, wondering how much Patterson knew and how much he could get away with telling him.

"What's your interest in Theresa?" said Etchin.

"Why are you in her office instead of her?" countered Patterson.

"I asked first," said Etchin.

"But I am the policeman," said Patterson.

"What was she upset about?" said Michael, deciding to break out from his position of sidekick.

"What?" said Etchin.

Michael perceived he had caught him off guard, presented him with a piece of information he didn't expect the police to have. "She was crying in this office. You were in here with her. That sort of thing doesn't go unnoticed in a building of five hundred people."

"I don't know what that receptionist told you—" In his head he was thinking of firing her, but not before she had told him who among his staff had been spreading gossip.

Patterson stepped forward, taking up the mantle. "What she may or may not have told us is unimportant. What is important, Mr Etchin, is that you answer the question."

Etchin smiled. Not with happiness, but with irony. "If you must know, she had been asked to spy on my company."

It wasn't the answer Patterson was expecting and he let it show. "Spying?"

"Someone was paying her to pass information about Power Grid UK."

"I know what spying is," said Patterson. "I wanted to clarify why she was crying. Was it because you caught her?"

"Actually, no. She confessed. She needed the money after her divorce, but she got in too deep and the lying was tearing her up inside. Which is why she came to me and asked for my help."

The memory was back again, of Theresa gasping for air between sobs as she confessed on the sofa of her own office while Etchin sat back, conflicted between consoling her and being angry with her.

"And did you help her?" said Patterson.

"Of course," said Etchin. "I'm a businessman, not a monster."

Michael's perception of that statement was unclear. Etchin seemed to be hiding a lie within a truth. He looked harder, but kept coming up against the same memory, of Theresa sobbing on the sofa.

"How did you help her?"

Etchin pushed himself away from the window and walked across to the same sofa that formed part of his memory. The movement gave him time to think, thoughts that Michael was able to eavesdrop on. *How much does he know?* Etchin wondered. *How much should I tell him?* He sat down.

"Why don't you take a seat, Inspector?" said Etchin. Another delaying tactic. "There's Theresa's office chair over there—" he pointed over to the far wall behind the desk "—or you can sit next to me." He patted the sofa cushion alongside him, hoping it would unnerve the police officer.

Patterson seemed to take this as a challenge to appear even more professional and he took out his phone and stylo. "I'll stand, thank you, Mr Etchin." He noted down something on his phone. "You were going to tell me how you helped Theresa, a woman you say was spying on your company."

"I think I mentioned to you before that Power Grid UK is invested heavily in renewable energy." He crossed his legs, trying to appear nonchalant as, all the while, Michael was monitoring his nervousness. "That's bad news for countries which supply us with oil and gas. We — that is, the UK — import a large amount of fossil fuels to run our ageing power stations. If renewables are a success — wind power, wave power, solar energy, that sort of thing — then those countries stand to lose a lot of revenue; both from us and from other Western nations. Unless they steal the technology and turn around to sell that to us instead."

"That's who Theresa was spying for?" said Patterson.

"She was spying for a rival organisation, even she didn't know which one," said Etchin.

"So you sacked her."

"No, Inspector! What would be the advantage in that? I got her to feed misinformation back to the people she was spying for. That way, I undermine their attempts to rip me off while at the same time they think they have a spy in my ranks and don't go around trying to recruit other people in my staff."

Patterson noted it all down in his phone. "Was Farron also a spy?"

"What makes you think that?" said Etchin. He uncrossed his legs again as his nerves wavered.

"It wasn't me who thought it, it was you. You were the one who hired a private detective to investigate him."

"Yes, and as you know because I sent you his report, the only thing he found out about Farron was his life was rather mundane."

"So it appeared on first reading," said Patterson. "On second reading, I discovered several gaps in his movements. What can you tell me about that?"

"Gaps?" Etchin rubbed his chin as if thinking. "I don't think I recall any gaps." But in his mind, a memory revealed him sitting at his own desk in much larger office, editing a digital version of the detective's document. Michael pushed harder to see the text he remembered deleting.

"Perhaps gaps is the wrong word," said Patterson. "It might be more accurate to say that there were a few entries which seemed to have been altered as if to cover up somewhere that Farron went or something that he did. According to the report, for example, he spent an inexplicably long time in the supermarket on several occasions."

"Did he? Perhaps he liked shopping."

"No one likes supermarket shopping that much," said Patterson.

"He could have been hanging around to delay the point before he went home to his screaming baby. There were a couple of times when my kids were little that I stayed late at work to get some peace and quiet."

Michael pushed in on Etchin's memory, but the more he concentrated on the text on the screen, the more the words blurred into nothing. They weren't real, they were only a memory and Michael could only perceive them if Etchin was remembering reading them.

The memory vaporised as Etchin sat forward on the sofa, trying to reclaim the upper hand in the conversation. "Nigel Farron was just a man who got too stressed to handle life, it was Theresa who was the spy. I hired the private investigator to follow the wrong person."

"Isn't it interesting, then, that we discovered Farron was taking some sort of drug and, when we followed the dealer who supplied him, we ended up bumping into Theresa."

"You did?" said Etchin. He tried to sound surprised, but in his head he remembered how Theresa had opened her shoulder bag and showed him the syringes and vials of liquid she kept in there. "I knew she was screwed up, but I didn't know she was taking drugs. Poor woman."

But Etchin's worries were not about her, they were about his own international espionage efforts. If the police unmasked Theresa, then his route to spread disinformation among his rivals would be cut off.

Just like a gas pipeline to Europe should the Europeans eventually embrace renewable energy.

FIFTEEN

THERESA Barclay lived in an impressive detached house in Surrey, not far from Farron's widow. The journey was a reasonable commute from Power Grid UK and appeared to be the sort of place where people on larger salaries liked to buy larger houses. If Theresa had been short of money after the divorce Etchin had mentioned, it didn't show in her home, which was tucked behind a dense hedge and up a gravel drive.

Michael and Patterson crunched their way to the front door past a dark blue hatchback. In the windscreen was the lightning symbol of Power Grid UK, with the word 'parking' above it and 'pass' underneath. It was almost certainly the same car which had nearly run Michael over.

A dog inside the house barked loudly. Michael hung back and let Patterson ring the doorbell. If the dog was going to attack anyone, he would prefer it not to be him.

No one came to the door. Patterson rang the bell again. The dog barked its head off.

"Can you perceive that dog?" said Patterson. "Is it going to bite me?"

"I don't do dogs," said Michael.

"What good are you?" said Patterson, not unkindly. He leant closer to the door. "Mrs Barclay? It's the police!"

"If she's divorced, she might not like the 'Mrs' thing," said Michael.

"Theresa, I know you're in there! It's Inspector Patterson, I'm investigating the shooting at your office."

"She's coming," Michael perceived.

The door opened a crack and her two eyes appeared. Eyes that stared with the same fear Michael had seen behind the wheel of her car. At her knees, an Alsatian dog bared its deadly teeth as it barked, pulling at the collar around its neck as she held it back. "Identification," she said.

"Oh," said Patterson. He fumbled in his pockets and found his police badge on the third attempt.

It was enough to satisfy her. "Let me put Max in the garden."

She closed the door on them and the dog's barks receded. Patterson looked at Michael. Michael returned his uncertain look.

It was only a moment later that the door was opened to reveal Theresa Barclay in her hallway without the snarling Alsatian. "Come in," she said and led them to the back of the house where a sprawling open plan lounge/kitchen took up the width of the building, with vast patio doors that looked out onto an impressive stretch of lawn. It was edged by borders of straw-coloured flower stems which had died with the passing of summer, and enough trees at the back to make a small copse. Trotting across the grass, without a hint of aggression, was her dog, apparently oblivious to the strangers inside.

"Excuse the mess," said Theresa, even though there was no mess to excuse.

There was not a speck of dirt on the rug laid on the spotless wooden floor. The two cream leather sofas on either side of a clean oak table could have been brand new and there were no ornaments or personal items cluttering up the room. The only things out on display were a computer tablet and a coffee cup resting on a side table by one of the sofas. Theresa tidied both away.

When she came back, Michael perceived her mind. Unlike her house, it was a mess. Emotions ran round it like excited children in a playground, screaming anxiety, doubt, fear and nervousness — all at once. Her thoughts were jumbled and came and went like switching from one television channel to another. *Should I offer them a cup of tea? What are they going to ask me? Does Etchin know? Should I tell Etchin? Is my washing finished? Should I offer them a cup of coffee? Did they wipe their feet when they came in? …*

"Would you like a drink? Can I get you a drink?" she asked.

"We're fine," said Patterson.

"Good." She was filled with relief, a relief much greater than was normal for someone spared a simple task. She sat down on the sofa nearest the kitchen, her nerves twittering.

Patterson took this as an unspoken invitation and sat opposite her. Michael did the same.

"What do you want?" she said.

"Just to ask a few questions," said Patterson. He took out his phone and stylo.

Panic erupted in her head. "Questions? I don't know any questions!" *Or is it answers that I don't know?* She stood up and clutched her hands to the side of her head. Images came into her mind — images that Michael tried to follow as they spun around in blurred flashes. He saw himself in a memory, glaring at her as he stood in front of her car. As soon as he recognised himself, it was gone and replaced with Etchin's smiling face. A memory of being at the vet with her dog when he was much younger, of struggling to keep it on an examination table as the vet tried to administer an injection. Another of Rebecki handing her money and drugs and a horrible feeling of dread. "Where's Max?" she suddenly cried.

Patterson, clearly unnerved by her behaviour, looked out through the glass doors at the Alsatian digging up one of her flower beds. "Your dog?" he said. "He's in the garden."

"He's all I've got left," she said. *I'm not going to let him take Max, I'm not, I'm not!* Michael got the impression that the dog was the one thing she and her ex-husband had fought over in the divorce. It was about the only clear thought in her head.

She ran out of the room. Not towards the garden to get her dog as Michael had expected, but back out into the hallway.

"Where's she going?" Patterson asked him.

Michael didn't know, her mind was too scrambled.

The sound of her running up the stairs told Patterson what he needed to know. He got off the sofa and run after her. Michael was only a little bit behind.

Three doors on the landing were open, allowing peeks into three bedrooms. Only one door was closed and that had to be the bathroom.

Patterson knocked loudly on the door. "Mrs Barclay? Are you all right in there?"

Michael stood beside him. "Theresa," he said quietly.

"Theresa? Are you all right?" Patterson knocked on the door again. There was no answer. He turned to Michael. "Is she okay?"

Michael hadn't thought she was okay from the moment he got a peek into her mind. He pushed his perception through the door. He found the same craziness he had experienced downstairs, a mess of emotions dominated by fear. "On the whole, I would say no."

Patterson tried the door handle. The door remained closed. "Theresa, if you don't open this door, I'll be forced to break it down. I'm worried about you." He put his ear to the door, but was soon shaking his head to indicate he heard nothing. "Theresa, I'm serious about breaking down the door. I'm going to count to three and then I'm going to kick it down. One. Two. Stand back, I don't want to hurt you. Three."

Patterson took a step back from the door and lifted his foot so it was level with the handle. He kicked forward and the impact made a hollow bang, but the door remained closed. His shoe print on the wood's pristine white paint was the only mark he'd left. He tried again. And again. On the third time, the hollow bang of his foot was followed by the sound of splintering wood. The lock broke free and the door swung inwards, slamming against the side of the bath. Patterson fell forward, regaining his balance only as he stepped into the bathroom.

Sitting on the bathmat on the floor was Theresa, her bare forearm resting on the closed toilet seat. Her sleeve was rolled up and a handkerchief was tied around her upper arm. In one hand she held a spent syringe. The syringe's sterile packaging was discarded on the floor, alongside an empty glass vial. A small droplet of blood had formed on the vein in her arm.

"Jesus," said Patterson under his breath.

Theresa smiled. "Can't see into my mind now, can you *perceiver*?"

She looked directly at Michael as if challenging him to use his power on her.

Something suddenly prevented his perception from getting through.

Minutes before, her mind was loud with emotions and tumbling thoughts. All that had been replaced by a sudden and impenetrable silence.

"She's ... *blocking* me," he said.

"What?" Patterson spun round. "Are you saying she's a perceiver?"

"She wasn't when we walked in," said Michael. "But I think she is now."

SIXTEEN

MICHAEL threw off his shirt and chucked it in the corner of the room. He was hot and sweaty from the day and the formal clothes he had to wear for work felt stiff and uncomfortable. He pulled a set of clean grey trousers and T-shirt from the wardrobe and threw them onto his bed. He got as far as unbuckling the belt on his trousers when the door to his room opened.

He saw Pauline standing there in shorts and a vest top, her long black hair tied back in a ponytail and the sheen of sweat on her body. She was breathing somewhat heavily from exercise and he could perceive her adrenaline, which seemed to be fuelling an anxiety. "Is it true?" she said.

"Is what true?" said Michael.

"The drugs."

She said it loud enough for her voice to carry down the corridor. Michael gave her a warning look. He took her hand, pulled her inside and closed the door. "What have you heard?"

"Mulgrew texted me while I was running," she said. "I didn't see it until I went to record my time on my phone. She said those drugs we found are a serum that turns norms into perceivers. I tried to call her back, but it just goes to voicemail. Is it true, Michael?"

"I think so," he said. He turned from her and fished around on his bed for the TV remote control. He pressed a button and pictures of a foreign war appeared on the television while a reporter spoke over the top. He changed the channel and some inane quiz show appeared. *That'll do*, he thought to himself and chucked the remote back where he found it. "If we're going to talk about it, I don't want other people to hear."

Michael sat on the bed and faced the telly. The pictures of people's faces as they tried to work out the answers to the questions amused him. He'd often thought about going on one of those programmes himself, perceiving the answer from the quiz show host and winning a million pounds. Except, apparently, that was fraud and could get him sent to jail. Still, sometimes he thought it would be worth it.

Pauline kicked off her trainers and came over to the bed. She sat opposite him, with her back to the telly, and folded her legs up underneath. "Are you going to tell me, or what?"

He told her about Theresa Barclay. "I suppose if I had concentrated, I could have got through her blocks," he said. "I was there for ten minutes while me and Patterson waited for the ambulance and they were normal perceiver blocks like we use every day. She had them on full blast, though."

"Then Nigel Farron, Benjamin Conte and Theresa Barclay were all taking this stuff?"

"I'm beginning to think that's what made them mad," said Michael. "I only caught a hint of Farron and Conte's madness, but I saw into

Theresa's mind before she injected herself — it was a mess. Scrambled thoughts, jumbled emotions, totally paranoid."

"If you perceived all three of them, it must mean the stuff wears off," said Pauline. "That's why they keep needing more of it."

"The more they take it, the more it effects their minds."

"So why did they do it?" said Pauline.

"To be perceivers," said Michael. "At least for a little while."

She shivered. Partly at the thought and partly because her body had cooled from her run.

Michael got off the bed.

"Where are you going?" she asked.

"Nowhere," he said. At least, nowhere outside of the room. He went to the bottom drawer where he kept a blanket to throw over the duvet when it was extra cold in winter. He brought it back to the bed and wrapped it around her shoulders.

Pauline let him. And she let him perceive that she liked it.

"But look at you," she said, referring to his naked chest. "You must be cold too." She reached her arm across his shoulders and draped part of the blanket around his back. She shuffled her bottom nearer to him and rested her head on his chest. Michael was suddenly warmer, and it wasn't because of the blanket.

"So, Etchin was right," said Michael, hiding the reaction of his body by talking about work. "Farron was a spy, using the serum to turn him into a perceiver so he could look into the minds of his colleagues and gather even more information for the people who he was working for."

"Which would explain why he was both being paid and supplied with drugs," said Pauline. The vibrations of her voice as she spoke rumbled on his chest. "Presumably, that's what was happening with Conte as well. He must have been spying on that company he was working for — what was it called? — Ethical Energy something or other."

"Then Etchin said Theresa confessed to him that she was also a spy. I perceived he was telling the truth about that, but at the same time it sounds a strange thing to do."

"You said she was bonkers, maybe she wasn't thinking straight," said Pauline.

"She must have seen what had happened to Farron and Conte and didn't want the same thing to happen to her. She showed Etchin the drugs — it was in his memory — but he denied it."

"When he had admitted to everything else? Why did he do that?"

"I've been trying to work it out," said Michael. "Norm brains are so confusing sometimes."

"Perhaps we need to work out who they were spying for, then it will start to make sense."

"That's what Patterson said."

She thought about it for a moment. "That's what they want us to do eventually, isn't it? Perceivers, I mean. They want us to spy on people. All this stuff with the police and what Alex is doing in court, it's just training for something bigger."

"I don't know what they're doing. I haven't seen Agent Cooper or any of the others here in a long time. It's like they've put Norm the Norm in charge and forgotten about us."

"I just think they're keeping the people in charge away from us so we don't eavesdrop on their minds and find out their plan," said Pauline.

"I didn't know you were a conspiracy theorist." Michael chuckled, not realising it would make his body move. Pauline lifted her head until it stopped and she was able to rest back on his chest again. The top of her ponytail, where it was tied with a band, pressed into him. He pushed at it gently with his fingers to shift its position. She reached behind and batted his fingers away, opting to pull the band free from her hair entirely. With her fingers, she teased out the strands, slightly damp from her run, and let them fall free, landing softly over his nakedness where a few chest hairs had started to grow.

He dropped all his mental barriers, allowing his feelings to flow from him. Gradually, her mental barriers fell too and he perceived how the warmth from his body made her feel safe and comfortable. That only served to heighten his emotions until Michael took a breath and forced himself to calm down.

"I'm not entirely sure they're in control of us anymore," said Michael. "Alex told me he smuggled that girlfriend of his in here the other night."

"He got away with that?" she said.

"She stayed in his room all night, as far as I know."

"Having a girl in a boy's room," said Pauline. "That's disgusting."

"Shouldn't be allowed," said Michael.

"Absolutely not."

Pauline relaxed again. Her aroused feelings dimmed and her thoughts became subdued. He let her doze.

The lights went out, signalling that their army keepers considered it time for them all to go to bed. Michael was about to shake her awake, but she looked so serene in the glow of the night lights coming through the curtains at the window that he decided not to disturb her. He lay back gently on his pillow and rested her head beside his. The bed was small, meant for one person, but if they cuddled up, there was enough room for both.

Michael started to wonder how he was going to smuggle her out in the morning without anyone seeing, but before he had finished the thought, he too was asleep.

SEVENTEEN

THE meeting room was too big for only four people. It was dominated by a long table, laid out with ten chairs, six of which were empty. Grey clouds which could be seen through the large window added to the feeling of emptiness, cutting down the daylight and causing the indoor lights to turn on automatically. Even the air conditioning seemed to be working overtime, set to cool a room full of warm bodies which weren't actually there.

Mulgrew sat at the head of the table with her laptop in front of her. She had pulled her hair back from her face and scrunched it up on the back of her head out of the way. It made her head look smaller than usual, at the same time as she appeared more business-like. "I know it feels a bit weird in here," she said, looking to Patterson, Michael and Pauline sitting up one end of the table with her. "But I wanted to keep this just between us. Our investigation took an unusual turn yesterday and, to be honest, I'm not entirely sure what to do about it." She turned to Patterson. "Inspector, can you bring us up to speed?"

Patterson looked like he had had little sleep, something that a shower, shave and set of fresh clothes couldn't disguise. "As you know, Theresa Barclay was taken to hospital by ambulance. The doctors couldn't find anything wrong with her, apart from her being a little confused, but I persuaded them to keep her in overnight for observation. She'll be discharged this morning—" he tapped his phone to bring up the time "—has probably already been discharged. I've sent a couple of officers down there to arrest her on suspicion of obstructing an officer. That'll give us twenty-four hours to question her."

"That job will fall to myself and Pauline," said Mulgrew. "I don't expect she'll react well to you boys after you freaked her out yesterday."

"We didn't freak her out," protested Michael. "She did the freaking out all on her own."

"Either way, the end result was the same," said Mulgrew.

"The drugs will have to have worn off if you want me to perceiver her," said Pauline. "Michael said she had her blocks up really strong."

"It's been eighteen hours since she injected herself," said Mulgrew. "I'm hoping that'll be enough."

"Have we heard back from the lab yet?" said Pauline.

"The report came through last night," said Mulgrew. She tapped a few keys on her keyboard and appeared to be looking at a document. Not that any of the others could see from where they were sitting. "If this was a Hollywood movie, I'd show you on one of those amazing projections that hovers in the middle of the room. But, as this is the Metropolitan Police…"

"What does the report say?" said Patterson.

"Essentially, it's a list of chemicals, most of which I've never heard of," said Mulgrew. "The lab tech told me the chemical analysis doesn't match any known substance in the database. It's not cocaine or heroin or any street drug, which we knew already. But he told me — off the record — that some of the chemical signatures were similar to LSD and other mind-altering drugs."

"Sort of makes sense," said Patterson.

"Except he wouldn't be prepared to say that in court," said Mulgrew. "Not as if this case is anywhere near getting to court. Because the drug's new, it's not illegal. We only have Etchin's word for it that anyone was spying on anybody. Farron committed murder, but he's dead. About the only crime we know Conte committed was arson, but he's dead. We're only charging Barclay out of desperation, and that won't stick."

"The drugs are the key," said Patterson. "It's the only thing that links all three of them."

Mulgrew nodded. Then she looked at Pauline and Michael. "I want you to tell me honestly, do you know anything about these drugs?"

Pauline looked across the table at him. *What does she mean?* said her thoughts.

I'm not sure, Michael thought back.

Not getting an answer, Mulgrew asked again. "I realise there are things about the perceiver programme that us 'norms' are not allowed to know, but I promise if you tell me anything, it will stay in this room. I need to know, do these drugs have anything to do with you or the people you work for?"

"No," said Pauline.

"Not that they've told us," said Michael. He looked back to Pauline, *Do you think they could be doing this behind our back? Making some sort of perceiver serum so they don't need us anymore?*

I wouldn't put it past them, came Pauline's thoughts. *But why would they be spying on energy companies?*

If that's really what they're doing, thought Michael.

The pair of them became aware that, outside of their minds, it had all gone quiet and the adults were watching them.

"Okay, then," said Mulgrew. "So we work on the assumption that this is some sort of criminal activity until we know otherwise. We also keep the details about this 'perceiver serum' to ourselves. I've spoken to narcotics and they've agreed to sit on Inspector Patterson's report for now. In the meantime, I don't want MI5 or whoever coming in here and taking over unless it gets to a point where we need their help. Agreed?"

They all agreed.

"So," said Mulgrew. "We continue treating this like a normal police investigation. We track down the people who supplied the drugs to our middle man, Rebecki."

"We'll go back to East Finchley, see if I can finally have a word with Robert Fazoni," said Patterson.

"Good," said Mulgrew. "I have a mad woman to interview."

EIGHTEEN

ROBERT Fazoni came to the door of his flat carrying a bundle of dirty washing. His face looked like the image Michael had seen in Rebecki's mind and in Peter's sketch, except much clearer. He had swept his fringe back from his forehead, revealing a young face starting to form the lines of experience. His police record — which was long and full of petty offences — said he was twenty-two years old and had grown up in the shadow of a more successful-in-crime brother whose downfall came when he was jailed the previous year for running prostitutes.

Fazoni loosened his grip on his bundle of washing, allowing a sock and a bra to fall to the floor, as he saw Patterson and Michael standing in the corridor.

"Who are you?" he asked.

"Police, Mr Fazoni," said Patterson, showing his ID which he had already pulled from his pocket having encountered the eponymous Al of Al's Kebabs & More downstairs.

"How did you get up here?"

"Your boss very kindly let us up."

Fazoni worked for Al in the kitchen of the restaurant-cum-take-away. Al had told them, he'd given Fazoni a job because he felt sorry for him after what happened to his brother. He'd let him stay in the flat above the premises for similar reasons, and because it brought in a little rent. It was a rent that was difficult to get on the open market because the flat didn't have its own front door and, therefore, did not adhere to modern building regulations. Access was either through the restaurant at the front or the kitchen at the back.

"Can we come in?" said Patterson, pushing the door open wide and not giving Fazoni a chance to refuse.

Fazoni stumbled backwards. Michael perceived he was genuinely worried. Not the sort of worried he had perceived from Al downstairs — that he was going to get into trouble for violating building regulations — but genuine being arrested and taken away in handcuffs sort of worried.

"I need to go downstairs and get my washing on," said Fazoni. "I have to do it now before Al puts all his tablecloths in to wash."

Lamest excuse ever, thought Patterson. "Perhaps you can do it after the tablecloths."

Fazoni dropped his dirty clothes — and the clothes belonging to whoever it was who owned the bra — and stood like a man defeated. Michael perceived an overriding sense of guilt coming from him, like he had always lived his life on the wrong side of the tracks and he wasn't sure which misdemeanour the police had come to interrogate him about.

Michael closed the door as Patterson walked further into the flat. It was small with everything crammed into a space about half the size of the lounge/diner at Theresa's house. At one end there was a sparsely fitted out kitchenette with a sink, kettle and microwave. At the other there was an unmade double bed with ruffled up duvet. In between, a narrow strip of worn carpet had just enough room for a TV, two-seater sofa and a small table with food stains on it. At least the flat was relatively bright, with light coming in from a sash window at the front, albeit a single glazed one which let in constant noise from the traffic on East Finchley High Road.

"Do you know a man called Rebecki?" said Patterson.

Fazoni made a point of shrugging his shoulders and looking nonplussed. "Rebecca? No, I don't think so. Who's she?"

His mind knew exactly who Arnold Rebecki was. The man who was in his flat the day before shouting at him for telling him he had to make one more drug delivery.

"Arnold Rebecki," said Patterson. "He was here yesterday."

"Lots of people come here," said Fazoni. "They buy kebabs."

"Rebecki didn't come here for dinner, he came for drugs. Do you know anything about the drugs, Mr Fazoni?"

Words left Fazoni's mouth, but they were meaningless lies. The truth was in his head, playing like a television documentary, explaining how the whole system worked.

He'd be in the kitchen, unpacking the clean plates from the dishwasher when the man with the day's food delivery would arrive. Among the packs of meat, containers of salad and packets of flatbread, would be the parcels that contained the vials of liquid that Fazoni didn't have a name for. Using the excuse that he needed to go to the toilet, he would nip upstairs and secrete the vials in his room. There would also be packets of cash. Some for him and some for Rebecki. He often thought about siphoning off a little extra for himself, but he was too afraid of what might happen should anyone find out, and so he did as he was supposed to. Rebecki was given the drugs and one pile of cash, Fazoni kept the other.

"Where did you get the drugs?" Patterson asked.

"I don't know anything about any drugs!"

Michael decided it was time for him to ask a question. "We know the drugs were delivered to you, where did they come from?"

The sting of realisation that the police knew more than he anticipated ran through him. "If anything was delivered to me, then I wouldn't know where it came from, would I? Why don't you ask the postman?" He was telling the truth this time, he really didn't know.

"So you're telling us," said Michael, "that you are just a middle man. The drugs come to you and you, in turn, passed them onto Rebecki?"

"I'm not telling you anything!" said Fazoni in panic.

"How does Rebecki know where to deliver them?" said Michael.

Fazoni turned to Patterson. "I don't get involved with drugs, Inspector. I've known people who got into dealing drugs, they went to the slammer or they got shot. Those drugs gangs are nasty. Al gave me a job and a place to stay, why would I risk all that to end up like my brother?" It was supposed to be a rhetorical question to the policeman, but in his head he was asking himself why he had been so stupid.

All three of them swivelled at the click of the door handle.

Michael heard the woman's voice before he saw her. "Rob, I couldn't get any semi-skimmed at the shop, they only had—"

She stopped with just one foot inside the door. It was a girl, at least five years younger than Fazoni, anorexically thin with dyed blonde hair cut into a bob. The plastic bottle of full fat milk slipped in her hand as Michael felt her sudden and terrified recognition: *Michael.*

"Sarah?"

There were no blocks shrouding her, leaving her mind wide open. Michael delved, finding a fear that she'd been discovered.

She turned and ran, pulling her mind from Michael's reach.

He darted after her, zipping past Patterson and jumping over Fazoni's mound of dirty washing.

Onto the landing where he saw Sarah's bobbing blonde head as she reached the bottom of the stairs.

He followed, his feet almost tripping over themselves in the rush to get to the ground floor as his mind felt her presence get further away.

In the bottom hallway, two doors offered two choices: back through the restaurant the way he had come in, or another which was helpfully labelled 'kitchen'. The noise of smashing plates and the sense of Sarah's fleeing mind caused him to take the kitchen door.

He crunched onto shards of broken crockery all over the floor as he went inside. He could only guess they had been knocked over by Sarah as she fled. At the far end of the kitchen, beyond the two lines of stainless steel worktops, a door to the outside swung shut. Michael picked his way over the broken plates and out of the door.

He stepped out into heavy rain that spat in his face and soaked into his hair. Looking around the cracked concrete yard lined with plastic restaurant wheelie bins, he couldn't see any sign of Sarah. He couldn't perceive her either which meant, unless she was better at using her blocks than he thought she was, she had kept running.

Outside the yard was a narrow alleyway. To his right was a solid wall: a dead end. So he took the left turn which led onto the High Road. He ran out onto the street and was confronted with the rush of other people's minds. Up and down the road, a landscape of multi-coloured umbrellas and people hurrying to get out of the rain obscured his view. Refusing to accept that he had lost her, he ran up the street and hoped he had picked the right direction.

The bleeping of a pedestrian crossing ahead of him caught his attention. An elderly woman walked ponderously across it, lowering her head against the rain so it fell on her hat and not on her face. Behind her, a younger figure ran past. Michael saw it was Sarah, her thin body unable to disguise itself against the black and white of the road markings.

Michael ran. The lights on the crossing were flashing to warn pedestrians to stop, and to tell motorists they could drive on. Michael ignored them. He raced over the crossing, car horns angrily blaring, as he watched Sarah on the other side of the street, running back the way they had come. He reached out his mind to read her thoughts, but she was still too far away, still too hidden by other people.

She stopped up ahead. Michael couldn't see why, he didn't care why, he just knew it gave him a chance to reach her.

Her head disappeared. Into the body of a black London taxi at the side of the road.

Michael opened his perception as wide as he could, sucking in all the meaningless rubbish from the minds of people going about ordinary lives, hoping to find part of Sarah within the cacophony, or even pull a destination from the taxi driver's mind.

The cab drove off from the kerb and took their minds further away. Michael tried to catch up to them, but his legs were no match for a diesel engine. The taxi's distinctive black bubble entered the bus lane and sped away, going faster than the other traffic on the road.

Michael stopped, defeated and confused, as the rain dripped off his sodden hair and ran a cold, wet stream down the back of his neck.

NINETEEN

MICHAEL threw open Alex's door without knocking. Pauline followed him in and closed the door behind her.

Alex looked up from his bed where he had been sitting propped against his pillow playing a game on his phone.

"Bit early for dinner, isn't it?" he said, but even as the words came out of his mouth, he must have perceived the two of them weren't there to take him to eat. The phone slipped from his fingers.

"What do you know about Sarah?" said Michael. He was angry and he didn't care if Alex perceived it. The more he thought about Sarah, the more enraged he got, and he had no intention of sparing Alex's feelings by keeping it locked up inside him.

"What is this?" He got up off the bed and stood to face them.

Pauline walked past Michael to be closer to Alex. "There's something we need to tell you about Sarah."

"Did something happen? Did Norm the Norm find out she slept here the other night?" Alex's perception reached out to Michael's mind for answers. Michael blocked him.

"Show him, Michael," said Pauline.

"Show me what?"

"Michael saw Sarah at work today," she said. "Not in a way you would like."

"Michael?" Alex turned to him. His perception knocked on the door of Michael's mind. "If something's happened to Sarah, you have to let me in."

"Show him the memory," Pauline urged. "It's the best way for him to find out."

"Okay," said Michael. "You better sit back down again."

Uncertainly, Alex backed away until his legs touched the mattress of his bed. He sat on the edge. Michael sat beside him. "It's been a long time since I've done this," said Alex, perhaps more afraid of what he might see than of the technique he was about to use. "I can't remember how to …"

Michael dropped his blocks. "Look into my mind." He felt Alex enter, harshly at first, too eager to find the answers. "Perceive my surface thoughts." Alex pulled back a little and hung there: waiting. "Experience the memory."

Michael remembered Fazoni's flat, the pile of washing that included a woman's bra, Sarah arriving unannounced with a pint of milk and her fear when she saw Michael. He replayed the chase out into the street, trying to recall every moment until she disappeared into the traffic.

There was no more to tell. Michael felt Alex withdraw and he gradually restored his blocks, but not before Michael had experienced how it made Alex feel. He was bewildered, still trying to understand what it meant. "She had a relationship with this man?" he said.

"I don't know, Alex," said Michael.

"The bra—"

"Could have belonged to someone else."

"You don't believe that."

"No."

"So Sarah was lying to me?" said Alex.

Pauline was suddenly at his side. She crouched beside the bed and took his hand in hers. "Do you think she was lying to you, Alex?"

He shook his head. "It's impossible. I mean, it has to be. I would have perceived a lie, wouldn't I?"

"Would you?" said Pauline. "Even through those full-on blocks she used."

"She said she was shy. She hadn't been with a strong perceiver before, she didn't like people looking into her mind. I respected that." But he didn't believe her excuses anymore and they could both perceive it. "Have I been an idiot?"

"No!" said Pauline. "Of course not."

"Maybe a little bit," said Michael.

"So you need to tell us everything," said Pauline.

"It could turn out that she's only with that other guy because she was a drugs smuggler, right?" said Alex. "He might not be her lover."

"You say that like it's a good thing," said Michael.

"Better that she lied about drugs than she lied about what she felt for me." Alex's embarrassment filled the room. He tried to hide it, but his strength to filter out his emotions was weakened by the shock.

"Just tell us about Sarah," said Pauline.

"Everything you know about her," said Michael.

Alex took a deep breath. "Okay."

SARAH Smith had grown up in the foster care system after her mother died in a car crash when she was two. It was her mother's fault, she had been drinking and swerved into the path of an oncoming car which she only managed to miss by driving into a lamppost. There was no father on the scene and so Sarah spent most of her life house-hopping from children's home to foster family until she reached sixteen and was found accommodation in a shared house with three other girls of a similar background.

All of them were studying in further education of some kind. Sarah was the only perceiver.

Alex had been to the house on several occasions. Sarah had her own bedroom and it was a place where they could be together, safe in the knowledge that none of the other people who lived there could perceive what they were up to with the door closed. It was the one place where Michael, Pauline and Alex might be able to find Sarah and get some answers out of her.

Ordinarily, Michael would have told Alex he was in no emotional state to come with them, but as he was their ticket into the house, they had no choice but to bring him.

The front door was opened by a young woman that Alex's mind knew as Libby. She had to be a couple of years older than Sarah, with wavy blonde hair which didn't look like it had come out of a bottle. She wore a brown T-shirt with a dusting of white powder on one sleeve. "Hi, Alex!" she said. "Sarah didn't tell me you were meeting her here. But it doesn't matter, come in."

"Thanks," said Alex.

As all three of them stepped inside, Michael tried to perceive exactly what Libby meant by meeting Alex, but he didn't need to because she told them everything as they wandered through the narrow house, past the living room and to the kitchen in the back. "Sarah said you were going away for a bit — how romantic! I wish my boyfriend would whisk me away like that. Going as a foursome, are you?"

"Er, yeah," said Alex, turning around to look at Michael and Pauline behind him. They returned his nonplussed gaze.

"It's cheapest that way," Libby rambled on. "Sarah asked me to pack a few things for her, but I couldn't fit all her stuff in the case.

So I left it upstairs on her bed, I figured she could sort it out when she came to pick it up."

"She's coming to pick up her case, then?" said Alex.

"Isn't that why you're meeting here?" said Libby.

"Yes," said Alex, thinking on his feet. "I just thought she might be here already. Did she tell you what time she'd be picking up her case?"

"Later is all she said to me."

They entered the kitchen, a room so narrow it might have been called a hallway if it were in a stately home. Down one wall was a small collection of cupboards and appliances with a single worktop. Down the other wall was nothing but a passageway large enough for one person to stand and another to squeeze by, assuming they weren't a very big person.

"I hope you don't mind making yourself tea, I'm in the middle of cooking a stew." Libby stood beside the one and only worktop where a lump of raw meat sat on a wooden chopping board next to a pile of flour. Libby picked up a chopping knife and began hacking at the meat, cutting it into cubes and coating them in the flour.

Michael looked across at Alex. *Make the tea*, he instructed with his thoughts.

You seriously want a cup of tea? Alex thought back.

It'll look normal. Put the kettle on.

Alex picked up the kettle from the side of the sink and stuck it under the tap.

Libby kept talking over the sound of water filling the kettle. "I'm cooking enough for tonight and to put in the freezer. Stew's really cheap if you bulk it out with vegetables. I'm probably going to be fed up with stew by the end of the winter, though."

Alex plugged the kettle into the wall and flicked the switch. *What if Sarah doesn't show?* thought Alex.

Let's not think about that until we've had at least two cups of tea, thought Michael.

And a bowl of stew, thought Pauline.

The kettle boiled. Libby gave Alex instructions on where to find mugs and teabags in the cupboards and he made four drinks, which his thoughts made quite clear he had no intention of drinking.

A bang rattled through the house. Libby's thoughts recognised the noise as the front door being slammed shut. "Sarah? Is that you?" she called.

All three perceivers focussed on who had come into the house. Michael immediately knew the unblocked mental signature belonged to Sarah. Even through the door, she must have perceived too because her blocks went up almost instantly.

Alex bolted like a greyhound, pushed past the others and was the first out of the kitchen and into the hallway. Michael and Pauline were quickly behind.

Sarah was at the front door, fumbling with the latch, as she looked back at the three perceivers coming her way.

The latch turned, the door opened and she virtually fell outside.

Alex, Michael and Pauline ran through the open front door and out into the cold.

Sarah scurried down the road like a frightened rabbit, her single figure clear under the residential street lights. Alex pursued her, his longer legs and sensible footwear no match for her spindly body on equally spindly heels.

He reached for her, catching her arm and pulling her back so hard that she swung round to face him.

"Let me go. Let me go!" She struggled as he dragged her back to the house.

Michael and Pauline watched as he passed them with Sarah helpless to get free in his grip.

"Take it easy," said Pauline.

"If she has nothing to hide, why did she run?" said Alex.

The front door was still open, banging against the latch as it was buffeted by the strengthening wind. Alex pushed it open and pulled Sarah inside.

Michael and Pauline followed, to see that Libby had come out of the kitchen, still holding her chopping knife with a sliver of raw meat hanging from the blade.

"Sarah, are you okay?" asked Libby, looking halfway up the stairs to where Alex had dragged her.

Tell her it's okay, Alex broadcast his thoughts loud enough for all perceivers in the house to hear.

"It's fine," Sarah called back, almost convincingly. "Me and Alex are just going to talk it through in my room."

"If you're sure," said Libby. Nevertheless, she watched the two of them continue their journey upstairs.

Michael took the precaution of perceiving Libby before he followed. He felt her doubt that Sarah really was okay, but he also perceived that she didn't think it was her place to interfere. She went back into the kitchen and her thoughts turned to making up a pint of beef stock.

When he reached her room, Alex let go of Sarah with a violent shove that caused her to fall back onto the bed where a suitcase and a collection of her possessions were laid out. A stack of clean knickers and a hairdryer fell to the floor.

Sarah pushed her dishevelled hair back from her face and looked with scared eyes back at Alex. Her blocks were raised, but they were faltering, and the same fear Michael had perceived back at Fazoni's place was leaking out. This time, it was stronger. She was obviously more scared of Alex than she had been of him.

"Are you sleeping with him?" demanded Alex.

"Who?" said Sarah, feigning innocence.

"Robert Fazoni," said Alex. "Michael saw your underwear in his room."

Sarah stared back at him. She looked across to Michael and Pauline, as if for help. But with her blocks up, it was hard to tell.

"Is he your real boyfriend and I'm just someone you keep around for laughs?"

"Alex, take it easy," said Pauline.

Alex did the opposite. He stepped closer, allowing everyone in the room to perceive that he wanted to shake the whole truth out of her. But instead of attacking her with his physical strength, he focussed his perception onto her, piercing through her blocks like a diamond drill. Sarah put her hands to her temples and scrabbled away from him. More stuff fell off the bed and onto the floor.

Alex held his ground until he let out an anguished cry and stepped back.

He said nothing, but Michael could see the answer that he pulled from her mind was not the one he wanted.

Pauline had perceived something else. *She's worried about her make-up bag*, she thought.

Sarah, who had been looking at the canvas zip-up bag that had fallen off the bed, turned her attention away, but not quick enough to prevent Michael from seeing.

Pauline crouched down and picked it up.

"There's a compact mirror in it," said Sarah, lying desperately. "If it breaks, it's seven years bad luck."

Even if Pauline hadn't already been tempted to look inside, Sarah's lie made it inevitable.

"Don't!"

But Pauline was already unzipping the bag.

Michael perceived her astonishment. "What is it?"

Pauline turned to her side where there was a chest of drawers scattered with bits of Sarah's actual make-up. Pauline brushed all of it to the floor with her forearm. She turned the make-up bag upside down and a tumble of glass vials containing a clear liquid, two syringes in sealed packaging and a wad of sterile alcohol wipes fell onto the surface.

Sarah's shame leaked through her increasingly fragile blocks.

Michael looked at Pauline's discovery and things started to fall into place.

"What is it?" said Alex. "Is she on drugs?"

"Mulgrew called it a perceiver serum," explained Pauline.

"What does that mean?" said Alex.

"It means," said Michael. "That she's not a real perceiver. She was taking drugs to turn her into one. Isn't that right, Sarah?"

She looked aghast at all three of them. "I don't know what you mean," she said, now sitting so far back on the bed that she was trapped between the wall behind her and the perceivers in front.

"You understand that we can tell when you're lying, don't you?" said Pauline.

"So," said Michael. "Why don't you tell us the truth?"

"Robert had the stuff in his flat," said Sarah. "I thought I'd try it out, be the first to get high on the new drug."

"You're lying," said Pauline.

Michael walked over to the vials, picked up one and held it up to the light emanating from the single bulb hanging from the ceiling. It glistened with clear liquid the same as the others found in Farron's house, Conte's office and Theresa's bathroom. "As I understand it," he told Sarah. "This stuff wears off after a while. I can perceive it wearing off inside you even now. Not like on the bridge, not like in the pub. What did you do? Inject yourself just before you met up with Alex? Disappear into the toilet or the bushes to give yourself a top-up when you needed it?"

He perceived that his guess was not too far from the truth.

"Which means, if I wait here, eventually you won't be able to block me anymore. You will cease to be a perceiver and you will return to being a 'norm'. Boring Sarah Smith, the norm."

Sarah was getting more nervous. Afraid of the perceivers in her room, but perhaps more afraid of what would happen if she told them what they wanted to know. "Alex?" she called out.

He was sulking by the door, not knowing quite what to think, except that he didn't care about what happened to her. He made sure they all perceived it.

"The other option is I can pull it from your mind," said Michael. "Like Alex found out about your boyfriend. Except, I'm more experienced than Alex, and stronger than him too. So, no matter how hard you try, I will get the information I want. So, Sarah, drop your blocks and make it easy for both of us."

"I can't," she said, her voice almost a whisper. "The people the drugs came from, they're bad people."

"What people?" said Michael.

She shook her head. Her whole body was shaking.

He probed deep into her mind. He didn't start out gentle or find the easy path through, he plunged straight in, crashing through her blocks and attached himself directly to her thoughts.

She gasped.

"Michael, be careful." Pauline's voice was at his side, but he barely heard the words.

The first thing he pulled out was the memory of Fazoni showing her how to inject herself. She remembered his loving touch on her bare arm as she hesitated with the tip of the needle wavering above her vein.

"They wanted me to spy on you!" she blurted out.

Michael kept inside her mind, but he stopped his probing. He merely held onto her thoughts as she spoke.

"They wanted to know about the government perceiver programme, but they needed a perceiver to do it. Maybe they couldn't find a real one, maybe they thought it was easier to make one, I don't know. But they wanted me to find out what was going on inside that base where you live."

Alex pushed himself away from the door where he'd been listening, his resolution not to care about her now shattered. "You got me to smuggle you in so you could *spy* on us?"

Pauline stepped in his way. "Let Michael work."

Alex ignored her. "I thought you wanted to lie naked next to me, I thought you *liked* lying naked next to me."

"In that moment before you fall to sleep, you release your blocks and your filters and I can see into your mind, to places where you don't let me when I'm awake."

"Bitch!"

Alex turned his gaze to the last remaining vial and the drug paraphernalia on Sarah's chest of drawers. He lifted them into the air with his mental power. Like the beer mat he had levitated in the pub, they hovered for a moment in the suspension of his thoughts.

They shot straight towards her like debris from an explosion. She ducked as syringes, alcohol wipes and the vial flew over her head. They crashed against the wall, so violently that the vial smashed to pieces. Glass tinkled to the floor and the splash of serum formed into drips that ran down the wall.

The shock caused Michael's grip on her mind to waver for a moment. But he didn't let her go, he seized onto her thoughts, holding them even tighter. "Is that what all that stuff was about at the bridge?" he asked.

"Yes, I had to see if the telekinesis thing was real. If I brought back that sort of information, I knew they would be pleased with me."

"Who?" said Michael. "Who would be pleased with you?" He pushed in.

"No!" she screamed.

Noises came from downstairs. He ignored them. "Who?"

"Someone's coming," said Pauline. She was at the window, pulling aside the curtain and looking into the street below. "Police cars."

Sarah's mind felt relief, but Michael kept pushing. "Who?" He probed deep, looking for a name in the half-shaded images of faces that she tried to keep hidden at the same time as she tried — and failed — to rebuild her shattered blocks.

Even though her mind was captive, her hands were free, and they went to her jeans where she undid the top button and lowered the zip. Even in the grip of his penetrating perception, she was able to focus on pulling them down below her bottom, exposing a thong. She wriggled them down further.

Michael's perception was so deep inside he only realised at the last minute what she was doing.

He pulled out quickly.

She cried out at the pain of withdrawal.

He staggered backwards into Pauline.

The door to Sarah's bedroom opened and two uniformed police officers came in.

"Oh, thank God!" cried Sarah, almost falling off the bed as she staggered towards them with her jeans around her knees. She put her arms around the waist of a startled female police officer. "They were doing such horrible things!" she said and burst into tears.

Michael stared with horror at her naked backside, her two pert bum cheeks exposed as her jeans remained halfway down her legs.

He exchanged hurried thoughts with Pauline and Alex. Nothing they could invent on the spur of the moment would make what they had been doing to Sarah in her bedroom seem innocent to two ordinary norm police officers.

TWENTY

MICHAEL had not been on the other side of a police interrogation table before and he didn't like it. The officers who had brought him in for questioning — PC Maclean, a man approaching fifty, and PC Shain, a woman almost half his age — sat across the table from him not believing a single word he said. To them, he was a gang rapist and possibly a lot of other things besides, and the only reason they were taking a statement was because it was a legal requirement.

"I want to see Inspector Patterson or DCI Mulgrew," Michael said for the umpteenth time.

"You need to answer our questions," said Maclean.

Michael shook his head. He had answered their questions. He had answered them at least twice. Apart from admitting he was a perceiver, he had told them the truth. They didn't believe him. "I didn't touch that girl."

"Her housemate witnessed you dragging her out of the street and into her bedroom," said Shain.

"That wasn't me, that was Alex."

"You're saying that it wasn't you, it was your friend?" She wrote it down.

"No!" said Michael. "It wasn't anyone! Alex and Sarah are boyfriend and girlfriend. Used to be. They had a row. She's making this all up."

"Why would she do that?" said Maclean.

"Because she wants me stuck in here," said Michael. "I guess she got what she wanted."

"From what we understand, you were the one who got what he wanted, Mr Sanderson," said Shain.

"Not true," said Michael.

"We're carrying out tests, Mr Sanderson," said Maclean. "We'll know if you're lying."

"Good," said Michael. "I consent to a DNA test." He opened his mouth wide, like people do when the police take a swab from the side of their cheek. "In fact, I demand a DNA test. You can test my blood if you like too." He rolled up his shirt sleeve and slammed his naked forearm on the table. "Take a whole arm's worth if you must."

"That won't be necessary, Mr Sanderson," said Shain.

Michael leant back on his chair and decided to stop talking. Talking was useless.

He remembered Rebecki when he was sat in the suspect's chair. He stood up. "I know my rights and I know I'm free to go if I'm not under arrest."

Maclean looked at Shain and in that moment Michael perceived that he had been foolish to call their bluff.

"Michael Sanderson," said Maclean. "I am arresting you on suspicion of sexual assault. You do not have to say anything, but it may harm your defence if you do not mention, when questioned, something which you later rely on in court. Anything you do say maybe given in evidence."

"Sit down, Mr Sanderson."

Michael sat on the hard wooden chair. They could legally keep him there for twenty-four hours and then they could — probably would — charge him. Then things would only get worse.

The door to the interrogation room opened.

Michael perceived the welcome presence of DCI Mulgrew. She walked in — furious at him — but at least she was there.

"For the benefit of the recording," Shain began, "DCI Mulgrew has entered—"

"Terminate the recording," said Mulgrew. "Have you charged him?"

"No," said Shain.

"Then don't. Leave the room."

"Ma'am?" said Maclean.

"You heard me."

Shain formally ended the recording and she and her colleague left.

Mulgrew watched them go. "What the hell were you doing?"

"I didn't touch her, I swear," said Michael. "The girl was a suspect, you can ask Patterson."

"I did," said Mulgrew. "I rang him and woke him up, seeing as it's goodness knows how long past any sensible bedtime. You won't be surprised to learn that he wasn't happy."

"But he told you about Sarah?"

"Yeah, he told me. That doesn't give you the right to go off questioning her on your own. You work *with* the police, you are *not* the police. Do I make myself clear?"

"It was a perceiver thing—"

She waved away his excuses. "I don't want to hear it. The fact is, the young woman made a serious allegation against you. I don't believe it's true, but I believe it's the police's duty to take all allegations of this nature seriously. Therefore, you'll be released on police bail pending further inquiries."

"Seriously?" said Michael, even though he perceived she was absolutely serious.

"Until then, I'm going to have to suspend you from the police investigation. Pauline too."

"You can't! Someone has created a serum that creates perceivers and they're using it to spy on people. You *need* me and Pauline."

"I need a good night's sleep after a long day, but it appears I'm not going to get that either."

Michael perceived she wasn't going to change her mind.

He closed his eyes and decided for that moment — for that tiny moment in the blank, bland, depressing interrogation room — that he didn't care. He wanted to go home.

TWENTY-ONE

THE wail of an alarm screamed into Michael's head. It pulled him from the comfort of sleep into the harsh reality of his room. The light had been turned on remotely and its brightness hurt his eyes. Squinting at his phone to see the time, he confirmed it was early.

He could perceive others in the accommodation wing being woken too, their disorientation and confusion, distant but very much there.

He pulled on yesterday's trousers, grabbed his T-shirt and went into the corridor. Someone equally as half dressed as him ran past. He was too sleepy to see who it was. A door further up the corridor closed and he saw a girl called Jan look around her. She saw Michael. "What's going on?"

"Don't know," said Michael.

"Is it a drill?"

"I don't know."

She ran down the corridor, sliding in socks as she carried her shoes past him. Michael followed, his own bare feet slapping on the hard floor.

The communal area was full of perceivers milling about, their voices whispering questions as their minds asked, *What's going on?* Michael saw Jan sat on the floor and putting on her shoes. He put his T-shirt on.

Pauline found him. Somehow she had found time in all the rush to get fully dressed. Even her hair was up in a ponytail, although it looked hastily brushed. "Do you …"

He shook his head. She didn't need to finish her sentence.

A booming, commanding voice echoed through the room. "FALL IN!" The unmistakable bellow of Sergeant Norman Macaulay. He marched from the entrance, a striding figure in khaki dress uniform that separated him from his young charges in grey.

They fell into four rows of eight. But as they snapped their shoes or naked ankle bones to attention and straightened their arms rigid at their sides, it was obvious three people were missing. *Who's not here? Where are they? Who is it?*

Norm the Norm stood in front of them, his body tall, his chest out, the pride in his uniform on display for all to see. He looked into the eyes of the teenagers in front of him. Michael stared back from the second row.

"Oh God!" a girl's voice gasped from the front. She broke the formation, stepping sideways as her hand clasped at her mouth.

Her self-control over her barriers and filters disappeared and let out the horrific news: *Peter is dead.*

Peter is dead? Peter is dead? The thoughts ran through their heads like the rumble of a train along tracks. She must have perceived it from Norm. In that instant, they all focussed their perception on him and they all perceived it.

The discipline of the four lines wavered.

"ATTEN-TION!" Norm screamed.

Shell-shocked teenagers tried to stiffen their poses as their minds were falling apart.

Norm walked the length of the formation, looking at each and every one of them. He turned and walked back down the line, speaking words that they already knew. "I regret to inform you that Peter Falcon was involved in a tragic accident last night. He was taken to hospital, but I'm afraid the doctors could do nothing for him. He died in the early hours of this morning."

Silence followed. One that was filled with the collective shock of perceivers, some of them sharing the emotions of their minds with others, some shutting themselves down in private grief.

The creak of the entrance door opened and Kev came in, the one perceiver out of all of them who could be described as Peter's best friend. The civilian clothes he wore were soiled with mud and his hair was a mess. His mind, suddenly bombarded with a deluge of perception requests, remained shut tight.

Kev, what happened? Kev, are you all right? What happened to Peter? Were you there?

He shuffled further inside.

"Form your place in the regiment," said Norm.

Kev made no move to obey. "Are you serious? I just left my best friend's body at the hospital."

"I lost friends when I went to war," said Norm. "I always attended roll call the next day. The fight goes on or the battle is lost."

"But I'm *fifteen*!" cried Kev, blinking away the tears forming in his eyes. "Peter was *fifteen*. He'll never be sixteen."

Kev collapsed to the ground and sat on the floor.

Norm, sensing that he was losing his authority — and knowing that everyone in the room could perceive it — said nothing more.

Peter said his powers could be stronger if he faced death, said Kev's thoughts, broadcasting out to them all. *He said the fear would cause it to emerge inside of him, like his perception emerged when he became a teenager.* "I can show you the memory," he said, looking up at them all. "But only once, and then I want to forget it."

Michael perceived Kev lower his blocks. The others did too, because he felt their anticipation around him as well as their anxiety.

With Kev's barriers down, his emotions were laid bare. Even though he tried to hold them back — to deny them even to himself — the grief, the distress and the exhaustion was poised ready to explode.

Kev remembered a flat rooftop. It was night and he was high up. The lights from myriad buildings in the distance created a starscape out ahead of him. It had stopped raining, but it remained wet underfoot and the wind was strong. Peter was there, and another perceiver called Lucy.

The memory skipped to a little later, like a clumsy edit in a movie. Peter was lying in the wet with half his body stretched out over the edge of the roof. He waved his hands free in the air while the balance of his body, lying on the building from the waist down, kept him safe.

Kev and Lucy held his ankles as he wriggled himself further over the edge.

Lucy was giggling, Kev was smiling as Peter asked, "Have you got me?"

Kev remembered the weight of Peter's body as it passed tipping point, holding tight onto his ankle as Peter dangled over the side. Peter's cries of excitement changed to ones of fear as he must have realised how far he had to fall if they let go.

"Bring me up!" he called.

But Lucy called back. "Make something move with your mind."

"I can't!"

He panicked. His body started to thrash. Kev struggled to hold onto Peter's ankle. He looked across to Lucy. "Let's pull him back," he remembered saying.

"Just a bit longer."

Long enough for her hand to slip.

Kev suddenly held Peter's entire body-builder's weight in his hands. It pulled him forward, almost dragging him off the roof. Lucy was screaming. Peter desperately called for help. Kev grabbed tight onto Peter's shoe.

He replayed the horrific slow-motion memory of the shoe sliding from Peter's foot.

Kev fell backwards — suddenly no longer holding onto Peter's weight. Holding only his empty shoe.

Peter's petrified screams faded into the distance as his body plummeted past the many windows of the high-rise building, until his voice stopped with deathly abruptness.

Kev pulled himself from the memory, like he had pulled his perception from Peter's mind before he experienced the horror of his best friend's death. But the echo of his screams and the sound of his body as it landed like a slab of meat on the concrete below stayed with him.

If the silence that greeted the discovery of what happened to Peter was total, then the silence that followed the experience of perceiving it happen was in the negative. No one thought, no one breathed, no heart dared to beat.

Kev broke down into sobs. His body, his mind, his life totally destroyed.

"Corps dismissed," said Norm, without shouting it, without ordering it.

The four lines of perceivers disintegrated.

They splintered into factions. Some went over to console Kev, others went back into their rooms to experience grief in their own way.

TWENTY-TWO

MICHAEL got back into his room to find Pauline and Alex already there. He hesitated in the doorway then closed the door so they were alone.

"What are you doing here?" he asked, even though he knew.

"Peter killed himself because of us," said Pauline. She appeared agitated, standing there by his bed, twirling the end of her ponytail round and round her finger and thumb. Not that Michael had any intention of letting either of their emotions through his perception barriers. He had just experienced enough emotion to last him a lifetime.

"That's not true," said Michael.

"Isn't it?" said Alex. He was leaning back against the windowsill, his arms folded resolutely. "Didn't you perceive Kev's thoughts? Peter tried to do what I did, except he died doing it."

"What do you expect me to do about it?" said Michael. He went to his unmade bed and sat on the corner. The springs sank under his weight.

"We have to do something," said Pauline.

Michael shared her desire to take action, but what was there to do? They had all perceived Kev, there was no doubt that Peter was gone. They had powers beyond the norm, but even they could not bring someone back from the dead. "How did Peter know about near death experiences provoking telekinetic power?" he said, looking up at them both.

Pauline shrugged. "I don't know."

"Not from me," said Alex.

"Are you sure?" said Michael. "You weren't showing off levitating beer mats and Coke cans, were you?"

"No! We agreed we would say nothing. I said nothing."

"Nothing to nobody? You didn't let it slip from your mind over breakfast or allowed someone to perceive your inner thoughts without realising."

"Hey!" said Alex, leaving the window and closing in on Michael. "I wasn't the one who let Peter into my head to sketch my memories."

Michael stood up again. "You think I would be as foolish as to reveal something like that?"

"It's what you're accusing me of doing."

Pauline stepped in between them. "Put your testosterone away, both of you! Our friend just died."

"You're right," said Michael. "Sorry, Pauline."

"It wasn't me, that's all I'm saying," said Alex.

"It doesn't matter who it was," said Pauline. "It could have slipped out of any of our minds at any time. The fact is, Peter knew about it and he tried it. I know we said we wouldn't tell anybody, but that was before. I think we should tell someone now."

"No, Pauline," said Michael.

"What do you mean, 'no'? You were the one who last time said we should."

"I'm just saying, I don't want to be blamed for what happened to Peter."

"Even if we deserve the blame?" she said.

"We weren't the ones encouraging him to climb up on that roof, we weren't the ones who dangled him over the edge and I'm certainly not going to take the blame for not realising shoes can slip off someone's feet. I know you feel guilty, I feel guilty too. I could drop all my perception barriers and you could share in my guilt if you want, but it won't help Peter."

"So," said Alex. "What shall we do?"

"Wait awhile for everyone to calm down. That includes the three of us." He walked up to Alex, unthreateningly. "Excuse me, Alex."

Alex stepped aside, revealing where Michael had left his shoes and socks from the night before. Michael retrieved them and went back to the bed to put them on.

"Where are you going?" said Alex.

"Out," said Michael. "To clear my head before Norm the Norm issues a directive to lock us up in here."

"I'll come with you," said Pauline.

"Not this time," said Michael. "I want some time on my own."

No one spoke as he tied his shoelaces. Michael got up, grabbed his jacket, and went to the door. He thought about telling them to lock up when they went back to their own rooms, but he decided they could figure out that bit for themselves, and left without a word.

MICHAEL had been sitting on the doorstep so long that his buttocks had forgotten they existed. He knew they were there, of course, but the cold had long soaked through his trousers and taken the heat from his bottom, leaving it numb. At least the rain had decided to hold off for a change. There was even a bit of blue sky up above, despite it being cold in the wind.

A car turned into the concrete drive in front of him, a red Ford Mondeo grimy from the road. Michael stood, his buttocks complaining as warm blood ran back into them.

The driver's door opened and Doctor Rachel Page stepped out. It had been nearly two years since he had seen her and her brown hair had grown long again. He perceived how she was unused to being around other people like her and her mind freely allowed her surprise at seeing him there to spill out.

"Michael!" she said.

"Sorry for dropping round like this," he said. "But I need to talk."

"What about?" She looked at him curiously, perhaps trying to perceive him. "I forgot how people like you can block me."

"Sorry, habit," said Michael. "But I don't want you to perceive it all at once, it's complicated."

"Okay," said Page. She went to the back door of the car, opened it and leant in. At first, he thought she was going to bring out a bag of shopping, but then he listened to what his perception was telling him. There was another presence in the car, an immature presence of someone excited by the newness of life.

Page lifted a little girl down from the car and lowered her so she stood on the driveway. Michael wasn't very good with ages of young children, but he guessed she must be two or three. She turned to rush to the front door, but saw Michael standing there and stopped. Her wide brown eyes grew wider as she stared at him.

"Emma, this is my friend Michael."

Michael smiled down at her, feeling about as competent at dealing with little girls as he had dealing with Theresa's barking Alsatian dog. "Hello Emma," he said.

She side-stepped and grabbed hold of Page's coat.

"I didn't know you had children," said Michael. He thought back to their last meeting: she hadn't mentioned it and he hadn't perceived it.

"She's my step-daughter. She moved in when Graham moved in."

"Oh," said Michael, backing away from the front door. "I didn't realise you had family, I don't want to disturb anyone."

"My perception skills maybe a bit rusty, but even I can work out you've been sitting on that doorstep so long you're cold through to the bone. Come inside and I'll make you a warm drink." She selected the house key from her keyring, took Emma by the hand, and led all three of them inside.

EMMA sat in front of the television watching an episode of Shaun the Sheep, or 'Shaun Sheeps' as she called it, allowing Michael and Page to sit up the far end of the living room and talk undisturbed.

Page had made Michael a mug of hot chocolate which, even though it was a children's drink, tasted amazingly good after the hours he'd spent travelling to her house.

She lived in a lovely house. Not as grand as Theresa Barclay's, but it had nice things in it, and the sense that it was occupied by people, not laid out for an estate agent to bring round prospective buyers. There were Emma's toys everywhere, stacked in multi-coloured plastic piles or left in odd places like in the magazine rack. The house didn't have carpets, Page explained, because of Emma's asthma, and she had had expensive oak wood floors laid throughout the downstairs. The two sofas where they sat were black leather, greyed a little through years of usage. After spending a fortune on the floor, she had had no money left for furniture and so Graham had insisted the sofas came from his old house to replace the dust-trap fabric ones that Page used to have.

"Tell me about Graham," said Michael.

"He's a norm," said Page. "Because I know that's the first thing you were going to ask. He works at a bank — everyone says that sounds boring, but he leaves his boring stuff at work so he can bring the interesting bits back home to me. We both don't like mayonnaise on our sandwiches." She laughed. "It's a stupid thing to have in common, maybe, but we got talking at the sandwich shop one lunchtime and that's how we met. Graham lost his wife through cancer, tragically, so I guess he was lonely. Which was okay, because I was lonely too."

Michael sipped his hot chocolate. "Sounds like you've told that story a lot."

"Yeah," she acknowledged with a smile. "Apart from the norm bit, I don't usually mention that. I thought the only man for me would be a perceiver, but there aren't many natural borns around my age. So Graham's all right. He's good, actually. Sometimes you don't need to perceive people all the time."

On the television, an animated sheep was inexplicably stealing cakes from the farmer's kitchen. Emma was mesmerised.

"I perceive you didn't sit on my doorstep for an hour to hear about my love life," said Page.

"No." Michael finished his hot chocolate. He looked around for somewhere to put his mug. There wasn't actually a table, so he put it on the wooden floor at the side of the sofa and hoped it wouldn't leave a ring. "I don't know where to start."

"The beginning is good."

There was a squishy green frog on the sofa next to him that squeaked when someone pressed its tummy. He knew it did that because he had sat on it when he first got there and it frightened the life out of him. Page had said it was one of Emma's toys that she must have been playing with and left lying around. Michael looked at the frog. He wrapped his mind around it and held it in his thoughts. He willed the frog to lift into the air. Its green body rose from the sofa cushion, the wide painted-on grin of its mouth making it look like the frog was enjoying himself.

Page watched in disbelief.

Michael squeezed the frog with his mind and it squeaked. Page's body visibly jumped at the noise. He brought the frog back down to sit on its cushion.

"How…" Page breathed. "How did you do that?"

He told her about the times he thought he was going to die and how the power emerged to save him.

"Because you're stronger than most others?" Page speculated. "Because you're the son of two perceivers?"

"No. I thought that could possibly be it, but no. We tried it with my friend Alex." He told her about the bridge and the train.

Page sat dumbstruck for a moment, trying to process all the information. "Me and your father did tests in the early days, but we never discovered anything like that. We thought we stretched our perceiver abilities as far as we could."

"Perhaps our minds are evolving."

"Perhaps," she said. "I'd like to run some tests. I don't know what sort of tests yet, but this is amazing!" She stopped talking for a moment and perceived him. "This isn't what you've come to tell me, is it?"

He told her about Peter. His emotions were still raw and he knew she must have perceived some of them, but he couldn't help but let them out.

"What do I do, Doctor Page?"

"Call me Rachel. How many times do I have to ask?"

"That's not an answer."

She sighed. "I'm sorry about your friend, Michael. Sounds like he was being foolish, but that's not reason enough to die. I also don't think the knowledge of what happened is a burden you should have to carry. I'm pleased you told me and, with your permission, I'll tell Agent Cooper."

"Tell Agent Cooper?" Michael remembered Pauline's warning in the pub, that Cooper would tie every young perceiver to a set of train tracks and make them believe a steam locomotive was going to run them over.

"I won't if you don't want me to, but isn't that why you came to see me? It'll be better coming from me. I still have a little sway with Bill Cooper, I'll make sure nothing happens to you."

"You don't think we should keep it quiet?"

"There'll be an investigation into your friend's death. The two people who were with him survived, so it's only a matter of time before the truth comes out. It's best if Bill hears it from me first."

"If you think so, Doctor Page." As he said those words, he felt a genuine relief. One that he hadn't expected.

"Rachel," she prompted.

"Rachel."

The lively end music from *Shaun the Sheep* blasted from the television.

"More Shaun Sheeps! More Shaun Sheeps!" said Emma.

"All right, Emsy. I'll give you more Shaun Sheeps." She looked back at Michael. "One more episode and she'll be hungry. Why don't you stay for dinner? You can meet Graham."

"Does Graham know about me?"

"He doesn't have to know about you to meet you."

"I mean, know that you're my biological mother. That sort of means you have an eighteen-year-old son. Biologically speaking."

He perceived that the thought shook her confidence. "In actual fact, he may not be back from work for another hour or two. Perhaps it would be better another time."

"Yeah," said Michael.

"I can give you a lift to the station or wherever you're going. I'll have to put Emma in the back of the car, but it won't take long."

He looked over at the little girl who had picked up the television remote control and was pressing buttons like she must have seen her step-mother do. "It's fine," said Michael. "I'm sure she'd much rather stay and watch her sheep programme. I can walk. I'd like to walk, it'll give me time to think."

Michael took the opportunity to use the toilet before he left and they talked a little more as Page walked him to the front door.

"It's been good to see you, Michael."

"Yeah," he said, somewhat awkwardly. "I'm glad you've got, you know, a sort of a family of your own."

"Me too," she said.

She gave him a hug before he stepped out on the doorstep and he perceived that uneasy love she felt for him. A love that she had never been able to properly express because he had grown up with his father and the woman who gave birth to him. Not as if he could remember any of it.

It was something they both understood and something they perceived in each other, which meant there was nothing more to say.

He waved goodbye to her and walked from her driveway, past her car, to the street. She stood on the doorstep and waved back, watching him go until he was too far away for either of them to perceive.

TWENTY-THREE

THIRTY-ONE pairs of boots stamped mud from outside into Galen House, sounding hollow as they marched into the building.

"Perceivers Regiment!" Norm the Norm shouted. "FALL IN!"

A grid of four lines of eight perceivers formed in front of the sergeant. Only one gap remained unfilled in the third row: the place where Peter should have stood.

Michael felt himself breathing heavily as he listened to the solid beating of his heart. They had been marching for two hours? Three hours? Round and round the inside of the perimeter fence like rats in a maze unable to get out.

Norm stood before them, a little sweat on his face, but otherwise unfazed by the exercise. His doctors told him it would do his heart good to exercise, Michael perceived, although Norm had little truck with their suggestion that he not overdo it. "After lunch, you will return to your rooms. There, you will wait for details of your assignments. These will be delivered in due course. In the meantime, you will not leave your rooms, except to go to the toilet. You will not fraternise with others and you will not contact anyone outside of the base. Do you understand?"

"Yes, sir!" they answered in unison.

"Dismissed." Norm turned from them and walked away, over to where the stairs led up to his office.

The formation disassembled in ones and twos and they went to get lunch, which was soup and a bread roll. There was a choice of sorts, tomato soup or chicken soup, brown roll or white roll.

Michael chose tomato with a white roll and sat at a table where Pauline and Alex subsequently joined him. They said nothing for many minutes, they were hungry and the soup was surprisingly nice. There was a subdued atmosphere around them. Since what had happened to Peter, nobody felt like talking much.

"What do you think he means by 'assignments'?" said Pauline.

"Somebody saw an army officer going up to Norm's office," said Alex. "They perceived that they were planning to send us all on training exercises. Survival training and endurance training on Salisbury Plain and that sort of thing."

"I heard that too," said Michael, dipping his roll into the soup and watching the white bread turn red as it soaked up the liquid. "But no one seems to know who it was who perceived it, so it's still a rumour."

"I tried to perceive Norm the Norm," said Pauline. "But he kept on thinking about his last doctor's appointment, round and round in a loop."

"Classic norm blocking technique," said Michael. "I meant 'norm' as in non-perceiver, not 'Norm' as in Norm the Norm."

Pauline smiled. "That's almost funny."

On another day they might have laughed. But not that day.

Alex kicked Michael's foot under the table. "Who's that?"

Michael turned to see a man in a civilian suit coming through the entrance behind him: *Agent Cooper*. Michael tried to perceive him, but he was too far away.

"What's he doing here?" said Pauline.

Michael didn't reply.

"You know, don't you?" said Alex.

Michael finished his soup. "I'm going back to my room to think about what I'm going to do," he said. "If they're going to make us play solider, I don't want to stick around."

"You think we have a choice?" said Pauline.

"That's what I'm going to think about."

As he walked back to his room, his phone bleeped. It was a text from Pauline. 'Are you all right?' it said.

'I will be,' he replied. 'I just need time.' He put his phone back in his pocket and kept walking.

IN the quiet of his room, sitting up on the softness of his bed, the words that Peter had said to him not much more than a week ago were loud in Michael's memory:

What is it Alex, Pauline and you are up to …?

It had seemed an innocent question. The three of them were always hanging around together and didn't talk much to the others, so it made sense for him to be curious. He just couldn't shake off the suspicion that it was something more than that.

If Peter had somehow seen Alex practising with the Coke can, or perceived something from one of them in an unguarded moment, then it was conceivable he might have searched for more information. Michael couldn't dismiss the possibility that he went searching in his head. When he'd let Peter in to see Rebecki's memory, he had been careful to isolate it and Peter had promised not to probe further. But could he have seen something when he was sketching? Something that even Michael's perception hadn't detected?

He closed his eyes and buried his head in the pillow. The thought that he was somehow responsible for Peter's death did not go away.

A knock on the door roused him from his self-pity and he sat up to see Agent Cooper walk into his room without waiting for an invitation. The man had a few more streaks of grey in his hair since they had last met and his belly was a little larger, but essentially he looked the same.

"Hello, Michael. This is a bit like old times, isn't it?"

"I think last time you came into my room, it was called a jail cell."

Cooper bristled at the memory. "I suppose it was."

He closed the door behind him.

"Did you speak to Doctor Page?" said Michael.

"Yes," said Cooper. "I'm sorry about what happened to your friend."

Michael perceived that he genuinely was.

"Rachel tells me you and Alex Buckley have developed a new power."

"Yeah."

"Show me."

Michael looked around the room. The easiest thing to use was his phone. He felt its smooth edges and modest weight with his mind and willed it into the air.

Cooper watched with amazement as the phone floated towards him, and hovered right in front of his face. He plucked it from the air and turned it around in his hand, examining it for potential hidden wires or trickery. "Incredible," he said.

"It took a bit of practice, but I find it easy now," said Michael.

"Can it do more?" Cooper was getting excited now. "Can it stop bullets? Throw grenades? Divert falling bombs?"

"I don't know."

"I will get Doctor Page to devise some tests."

He searched Cooper's mind for what tests he was planning to do, but the man didn't know. This was new information to him and he was still processing.

"It's funny," said Cooper, walking up to Michael's bed and perching on the edge. "You wait all year for a phone call about Michael Sanderson, then two come along at once."

Cooper was thinking about buses for some reason, adding to Michael's confusion. "Sir?"

"Your friend Inspector Patterson rang me. I was surprised because he's not supposed to have my number, he's not even supposed to know about me. I get reports sent to me about your work with the police, of course, but they come through to my senior officers via his senior officers."

"I didn't give it to him," said Michael. "He's a detective, finding out stuff is his job."

"That's very similar to what he told me," said Cooper. "He also told me that you are suspended, and he told me why."

Michael felt embarrassed. Almost ashamed.

Cooper reached out with his hand — so suddenly that Michael didn't perceive he was going to do it — grabbed his wrist and pulled him closer to get his full attention. "Tell me honestly, did you touch that girl?"

"No!"

"Are you sure?"

"Me and Alex perceived her, but we didn't … do what she said. You can get someone to perceive me if you don't believe me. Someone who doesn't like me, if you want. You could use Richard."

"That won't be necessary." Cooper let go of Michael's wrist. "She withdrew her allegation."

Michael took a moment to perceive that it was true. "What happened?"

"Apparently, there was no physical evidence to support her claims and she confessed that she had made it up to get back at her boyfriend."

"Then we won't be charged?"

"No," said Cooper.

Michael closed his eyes in a moment of relief. When he opened them, he saw that Cooper was holding up a piece of paper. "What's that?"

"It's a pass to allow you to leave the base."

Michael looked at the unassuming folded white slip that represented freedom. At least, a freedom of sorts for someone enrolled in the Perceiver Corps. Except, he knew that when a gift came from Cooper, it didn't come without strings attached. "What's going on?"

"Patterson told me about the perceiver serum."

So that was the real reason for Cooper to be in his room. As exciting to him as the telekinesis was, it was the serum he more interested in. "We don't know much about it," said Michael. "We agreed we wouldn't say anything until we knew more."

"I don't think your policeman friend wanted to tell me either, but he needed leverage to get you back on the case. I got the impression that, without access to a perceiver, he is stuck with the usual police methods and he's getting a little frustrated."

"You're going to let me go back to work?" He reached for the pass, but Cooper pulled it back so it remained just out of his reach and Michael had to sit back with nothing in his hand.

"I need to find out more about the serum," said Cooper. "I need to know who's making it and why. I could send another team in to investigate, of course, but I don't want to risk alerting the people behind the serum. Better to let the police handle it, especially as I have an 'in' with the police investigation who can read minds."

"Yes, sir," said Michael, keeping an eye on the tantalising piece of paper, still being held out of his reach.

"Do whatever you need to do, and that includes bypassing police procedures and protocols if you have to. The job of the police is to make a case that will stand up in court. I don't care about that, I need to know who is behind this."

He handed Michael the pass. Michael unfolded it and read the words inside — relieved to see it proscribed no restrictions on his freedom — then he folded it back up again and put it in his pocket.

TWENTY-FOUR

PATTERSON'S car had developed a stale and musky 'lived-in' smell from the hours he had sat in it without getting it cleaned. Michael opened the passenger window a crack to let in some air, but the cold and damp of the autumn day did little to chase away the lingering smell of week-old greasy chips and takeaway coffee which seemed to have embedded themselves into the upholstery.

"Thanks for getting me out," said Michael, as they sat parked in a resident's parking bay, looking out for traffic wardens and the subject of Patterson's investigation.

"You make it sound like a prison," said Patterson.

"Sometimes that's exactly what it's like," said Michael.

"Then why do you stay there?"

The inspector was curious to know more, Michael could perceive he was, but it wasn't a conversation he wanted to have. "You were going to tell me about Anton Ivanov."

Ivanov was the man Patterson believed was behind the perceiver serum operation. When Patterson had shown him a picture of the heavy-set Russian, Michael recognised it immediately as the same man whose image had been in Sarah's head. But that's all he knew.

"When you discovered Fazoni was getting the serum delivered to Al's Kebabs & More, I questioned the drivers who work for the delivery firms and, even without a perceiver, it was clear they knew nothing," said Patterson. "They worked different shifts, anyway, week to week, so there would be no guarantee it would be the same driver each time. So I started looking at the supply chain, going back to the manufacturers, delivery depots and stop offs. It took hours. The only thing that popped was a stop off on the delivery route to a nightclub owned by Anton Ivanov."

Michael looked out the car window at the nightclub with a neon sign behind its black closed doors, unlit in the daytime, revealing it to be called The Living Dream.

"It stuck out because the only thing they deliver there is cocktail cherries," continued Patterson. "It's an expensive way for a business to get hold of cocktail cherries. When I saw Ivanov was the owner, I knew it had to be the place where someone is slipping the serum into the kebab shop order."

The double doors to The Living Dream remained closed and innocuous, sandwiched between a hair salon and a dentist's surgery.

"If Ivanov is a known criminal, why isn't he in prison?" said Michael.

"Ivanov is a clever sod," said Patterson. "Always coming up in police investigations, but never leaving behind enough evidence to be charged. He was arrested once, but let go after questioning. We think he brought his particularly nasty form of organised crime over from Russia about ten years ago, first on mainland Europe and now in Britain. Annoyingly, he knows the law backwards. He won't talk to us unless he's arrested, and he knows we haven't got enough evidence to arrest him, let alone get a warrant to search his place."

"Which is why you want me to perceive him."

"I've come up against a brick wall with normal police methods."

Michael stared at the club doors until he could see the brush strokes in the paint, but they didn't move. No one came out and no one went in.

"Are you sure he's in there?" said Michael.

"As sure as I can be. He has an office on the upper floor where he works from."

"We could be sitting here all day!"

Patterson laughed. "Welcome to the exciting world of police work."

A man came out of the dentist's looking pale and shell-shocked. A woman went into the hairdressers with her hair hidden under a woollen hat. The double black doors of the club remained closed.

Michael was getting that nagging feeling of needing to pee soon. His tummy rumbled. He was also getting hungry and it was ages until lunchtime. He wasn't sure how much longer he could sit there without having to deal with both bodily urges.

"How do you do it?" said Michael. "Sit here all day, I mean?"

"When I was a young copper, I used to sit here and work out how much money I was earning for every minute I sat on my bum doing nothing. It's complicated because you have to work out how many working days there are in the year, minus holidays and weekends…"

Michael tuned him out as something bright and blonde caught his eye across the street. The bobbed hairstyle, sitting atop a matchstick body in a long grey coat was instantly recognisable. "Sarah," he said to himself.

Reaching out his perception to touch her mind, he caught a snatch of her presence, even at that distance, telling him for sure it was her, walking with tottering steps past the dentist's. He got out of the car to perceive more, squeezing himself out of the tiny gap between the door and the body of the car as he tried not to get run over by passing traffic.

Sarah reached the club as Michael's hand slipped from the handle of the car door and it slammed shut behind him. In the built-up environment of the street, the noise echoed off the nearby buildings, causing Sarah to turn.

He perceived her instant recognition like hearing a person's voice say his name across a crowded room.

Michael felt conspicuous. He wanted to climb back into the car and hide away, but it was too late.

One of the black doors opened and she disappeared into the darkness inside. As it closed, Michael's perception of her was cut off.

Behind him, he heard the whir of an electric motor as Patterson wound down the passenger window and leant across the passenger seat. "What are you doing?"

Michael got back in the car. "It was Sarah."

"We're not here for her," said Patterson. "After what happened, you need to stay well away from her."

But Michael was thinking, if Sarah was at the club, it proved they were in the right place.

It was a hopeful glimmer in what continued to be another couple of hours of nothing.

Eventually Michael had to obey his body and go find somewhere to take a leak. There was a stretch of parkland beside the road, but it was too public with daytime joggers and dog walkers to find a secluded spot behind a tree, so he was relieved when Patterson agreed that he could make a quick trip to the coffee shop down the street.

Two takeaway cups in return for the use of the facilities was a fair exchange, he thought, and he rushed back to the car in case Sod's Law was in operation.

Sod's Law — or Surveillance Law, as Patterson called it — said that the moment you leave your assigned spot, especially to obey bodily considerations, your subject goes on the move. They weren't so lucky with Ivanov. Nothing happened at the club. They sat and drank coffee until darkness descended on the afternoon and they ran out of things to talk about.

Until the neon light flickered The Living Dream into life.

Moments later, the black doors opened and a large white man, both fat and muscular, strode out onto the street with the self-confidence of someone unaware that the police were watching him. His face, clean shaven with a bulbous nose and receding unnaturally dyed-black hairline, looked similar to the photo from police records, but had a stronger resonance to the image from Sarah's memory.

"We're on," said Patterson.

Michael got out of the car with the timidity of someone who didn't want to be spotted. Closing the door behind him with a careful click this time, he walked along the road parallel to Ivanov, keeping pace a few steps behind. At a gap between the traffic, he skipped across the road, trying to appear just like anyone else who was walking along the street. All the time, he scoured with his perception, rejecting the minds of innocent people walking around him.

Focussing on Ivanov was hard. Harder than it should be. He knew it was possible to perceive a moving target, especially one at a constant distance from him, but even after eliminating the thoughts of others around him, he was unable to get a firm grip on Ivanov.

Michael took the decision to move closer and quickened his pace. Not easy, as the Russian was taller than him, with longer legs, and appeared to be in a hurry.

He turned, disappearing into nowhere. Michael panicked. Without a hold on his presence, he was relying totally on his eyes which saw Ivanov apparently vanish between two shops. As he got closer, he saw it was an alleyway. One of those claustrophobic spaces dating back to old London when no one cared about getting anything much bigger than a person around the back of a building.

Ivanov's large frame was silhouetted in the passageway by a security light at the other end. Michael knew that following him up there could risk exposing him, but letting the man go without perceiving him would have been a waste of a day. He waited a few moments to make it less obvious and followed, entering the alley just as Ivanov reached the far end and his silhouette turned into a receding shadow.

Michael's shoes, which he wore as part of his smarter work wear, echoed uncomfortably loudly over cobbles as he dashed towards the security light, leaving behind the confusing mass of minds of other pedestrians behind him. Still he perceived nothing from Ivanov, and was beginning to fear the man had gone. Perhaps into the back entrance of one of the shops, or even driven off in a car secretly parked there.

He stepped out of the alley into a medieval courtyard. It was like stepping back in time as he was suddenly faced with wobbly walls made of old uneven red brick, interspersed with the black beams on which the buildings were constructed. Only the single security light, shining from high above, kept the courtyard firmly in the present.

"Are you following me?" The gruff Russian accent filled the space.

Startled, Michael turned to see Ivanov's impressively tall and bulky frame looming over him like a medieval ogre.

Michael realised what he should have realised back in the street: Ivanov's mind was closed to him. Closed like it belonged to a perceiver.

But Ivanov's barrier was fragile. As Michael perceived him, fragments of the man's sense of his own superiority leaked through. It was like looking into a room through the crack of an almost-closed door. He caught a glimpse of Ivanov's confidence, but only for a moment before he was perceiving nothing again.

"I'm sorry, I must have taken a wrong turn," said Michael, hiding his nervousness behind his own blocks in case Ivanov was monitoring his mind.

"Tell your boss," said Ivanov, scrunching both his hands into a fist, "that he will get nothing from me. Not from my mouth, not from my nightclub and not from my mind."

Unable able to read Ivanov's intentions, Michael thought he was going to hit him. Michael cowered back against the wall, but Ivanov turned on his heel and walked back down the alley with his mind still enclosed in a perceiver's block.

Michael listened to his footsteps recede before he let out the breath he was holding.

Left alone in the glare of the security light, he realised his day of surveillance had been for nothing. He had learnt nothing from Ivanov, but Ivanov had learnt something from him. He now knew who Michael was.

TWENTY-FIVE

MICHAEL stood by a tree in the park across the road from Ivanov's club, walking around on a tiny patch of worn grass, wishing he had put a jumper on under his coat. He glanced across the road where the sign for The Living Dream was lit up in pinky-blue neon. The black doors underneath remained closed, but as the night got later and colder, customers would arrive and the doors would finally open.

Pauline and Alex stood with him in the shadow of the tree cast by the street lights. They were better dressed for the night weather, but equally restless.

"I don't know if I want to see Sarah again," said Alex, kicking at a weed which had bravely grown where the grass from the park met the earth under the tree.

"But that's why we're here," said Michael. "She's our way into Ivanov's inner circle and to finding out more about the perceiver serum."

"That might be why you're here," said Alex. "I'm here because it got me a pass to get off the base." The toe of his boot finally uprooted the weed he was toying with. He pressed his heel down and ground it back into the dirt, leaving it crushed and dying.

"Can't we go undercover in the nightclub?" said Pauline, plunging her hands deep into the pockets of her long black coat, looking like she was starting to feel the cold now. "It'll be open soon."

"Neither of you are eighteen yet, so that's going to be difficult," said Michael. "Not as if we're likely to find out anything in the public areas and I don't know how we would break into Ivanov's office, especially as he knows what I look like."

"We could still perceive people," said Pauline.

"Ivanov made it clear he wasn't going to let that happen," said Michael.

"Are you sure he had taken the serum?" said Alex. "If he was blocking you, he could be a real perceiver, like we all thought Sarah was when we first met her. I know he's old, but he could be a natural born."

"Except Sarah had practised her blocks," said Michael. "Do you remember? She said she had learnt the technique from perceiver forums. Ivanov was not practised. His blocks were patchy and sloppy. Sarah must have told him I was watching him and he injected himself with the serum to make a point."

"What makes you think Sarah will help us?" said Pauline.

"She won't," said Alex. He left his position by the tree and jumped down onto the path, turning round to look Michael directly in the eye. "He wants us to use mind control, isn't that right, Michael?"

Michael nodded. "It's the easiest way."

"Assuming she's off the serum now and you can get into her mind," said Pauline. "Even if you can make her go into Ivanov's office, once she's in, you have no control. She can carry out the tasks you programmed into her, but if anything goes wrong, or if she's caught, she'll have no free will to get herself out of the situation."

"Does that matter?" said Alex.

"If you want her to come out of there with any information she gets for us, then yes," said Pauline. "Putting aside any reservations I might have about making people do things against their will."

"You're forgetting that she lied to us," said Alex. "And she spied on us. Don't waste your sympathy on her."

Throughout the conversation, Michael kept watch on the ever-closed doors of the club.

A slight movement caught his eye, a change in the reflections in the gloss black of the paint that make him look across the road. "Shh," he ordered.

The three of them fell silent against the background of passing traffic. The left hand door opened slowly, just enough for a thin person to emerge. Michael hoped to see the tell-tale blonde of Sarah's hair, but the head of the person was black. He couldn't see who it was because the person had their face turned away, so he perceived them. He was surprised to sense a familiar presence: it was Sarah. She had pushed her hair up inside a black woolly hat and pulled it down over her ears.

We're on, said Michael's thoughts.

Unspoken replies from the others acknowledged him.

Are you sure you're okay with this, Pauline? Michael thought.

It's what Agent Cooper wants us to do, isn't it? was her reply, suggesting she wasn't sure but had no choice.

She turned to take her pre-arranged route, a right turn towards the main park entrance.

Michael glanced back at Sarah: she had turned left out of the club and was walking down the street.

Alex ran out ahead to the second park gate and exited onto the street where he slowed to walking pace on the opposite side of the road to Sarah.

Michael didn't run, but kept pace with Sarah: she on the opposite side of the road to the park, he on the path just inside the park railings. He soon reached the second gate and, like Alex, walked out onto the main street.

He turned behind to check Pauline was walking behind all of them. Her role was to keep an eye on everything and step in when necessary.

Sarah, across the road and slightly ahead of Michael, didn't appear to notice. He checked with his perception to be sure and confirmed that she was involved in her own thoughts, apparently unaware of anyone following her. He couldn't perceive her deeply as she moved, but it was enough to confirm her mind was like that of a norm, not of a person under the influence of the serum.

At a break in the traffic, Michael hopped across the road. He was only a couple of metres from Sarah now and walking directly behind her.

Less than two minutes to catch the bus, her thoughts said as her small footsteps hurried along the pavement. She was thinking of Fazoni and the short bus ride that would take her to him. The memory of her boyfriend represented comfort and security.

Up ahead was the bus stop: a perspex shelter with a blue-sprayed graffiti tag over the front of it. Sarah slowed. Michael slowed. He perceived Pauline slacken her pace behind him as Alex, across the road, kept going.

Alex, this is it. Michael wasn't sure if his thoughts would reach his friend, but Alex must have heard because he stopped and turned to pretend to be looking in the window of a shop.

Sarah pulled into the bus shelter, glancing back to see if the bus was coming.

What she saw was Michael. She gasped as recognition fired across her brain. She turned to escape, but a large woman carrying at least four bulging bags of shopping was standing behind her, waiting for the bus.

With Michael directly in front of her and the bus shelter and the shops on either side, she was penned in.

He perceived her desperation in a brief moment before she stepped backwards into the large woman and pushed her out of the way. The woman was knocked sideways with her shopping and a collection of loose apples spilled from the top of her bag, bouncing off down the pavement as Sarah ran.

Michael dashed after her. Out of the corner of his eye he saw Alex break into a run and, behind him, he perceived Pauline getting closer.

Alex weaved through traffic to the sound of angry taxi horns to cut off Sarah's escape. Seeing what he was doing, Sarah bolted like a scared rabbit into the road. The skidding of rubber tyres screamed at her. A car braked hard. It only just missed striking her with its bumper before she made it across.

Bollocks! said Alex's thoughts as he realised he had made the wrong move. All three of them were now on the wrong side of the road. Sarah, still running, was heading back the way she had come. Michael doubled back too, stretching his perception as much as he could towards her. Sarah knew that part of the road well, he perceived, and aimed to lose them in the park.

She's going into the park! Michael broadcast, and sensed Alex had perceived him, although he had lost track of Pauline.

Michael kept running, keeping an eye on the traffic, looking for a window of opportunity to cross the road without being run over. To his frustration, he saw Sarah disappear through the smaller second park entrance and disappear into the trees. His perception of her dwindled to almost nothing. Alex was halfway across the road after her, but she had a sizeable head start over him.

The cars, taxis and one view-obscuring London red double decker bus slowed to a stop and Michael took his chance to cross. Weaving in and out of vehicles, he reached the opposite path as Alex disappeared through the gate.

Michael followed into a world of shadows. He stopped and opened his perception, but he couldn't sense Sarah. As he reached out further, background minds from people in the street behind him chattered. If Sarah's mind was among them, he couldn't find it.

Alex? Pauline?

But they were too far away to hear his thoughts.

Knowing he was close to the end of the park, he took a chance and headed towards the main entrance, hoping that's where Sarah would have run. After a few steps, he broke into a jog, keeping his mind open for her presence and cursing himself for letting her get away.

He saw green foliage in the dark around him and realised she could be anywhere. She was too far away for him to perceive her — unless she had injected herself with serum and was blocking him. Then she could be hiding behind a bush close by, laughing at him, and he wouldn't know it.

He kept jogging and searching with his mind.

A single thought from Pauline — distant and unexpected — reached him: *She's here!*

Where are you? He reached out to find her presence. It was on the edge of his perception, but it was enough to hold on to.

He ran towards it — tripping and almost falling over a fallen branch from one of the trees.

As he did so, he thought he could sense Sarah. Sarah's presence was less solid: oscillating at the edge of his reach, like hearing only some of the words of a sentence carried on the breeze.

A nearby bush rustled. Pauline — almost camouflaged in the night by her black coat — was suddenly with him. "She tried to get out the main entrance, but I was waiting," said Pauline, breathing heavy from running. "I went after her, but ..."

"You lost her?" said Michael.

"Sort of. She's close by."

Michael nodded. *Alex?* he called out with his thoughts

Yeah?

Find us.

Michael searched with his perception again and this time, he sensed all the words of the sentence that made up Sarah's unique signature. She was not blocking him, she had not taken the serum, her mind was that of a norm.

Find her in your mind, he told Pauline and Alex. *If we all close in on her, she can't get away.*

After a few tentative steps forward, Michael's fix on Sarah's mind became stronger. He perceived Pauline could sense her too. He gave a signal and the two of them fanned out to cover more ground.

A twig snapped in front of him. Michael paused. To his left, foliage twitched and the blur of a grey coat emerged from hiding.

Sarah ran full-pelt into the open, her mind hoping she could outrun the others.

But suddenly Alex was there: blocking her way. She turned and ran from the three of them, panic clouding her mind as they corralled her in one direction.

Straight into the impenetrable iron railings at the edge of the park. Sarah grabbed the rails, as if checking they were real, then turned her back on them to face Michael, Pauline and Alex.

"Let me go, please."

"There's nothing to worry about," said Michael. "We just want to talk."

"I don't know anything!" Sarah protested.

Ready? Michael's thoughts asked the others.

Be gentle, cautioned Pauline.

Be there to guide me, thought Michael. He enclosed his mind around the edge of Sarah's thoughts, feeling a fear he didn't understand. He needed to get deeper to program her to spy on Ivanov, but her emotions were so strong, it hurt to push past them.

"Don't violate me again!" she said. "Alex, make them let me go."

Alex's emotions — a reawakened anger — spilled over into Michael's consciousness, disturbing his concentration. "You lied to the police about us," said Alex. "I spent half the night in a cell because of you."

"You violated me!" she screamed.

"You may have lied to the police about it, don't think you can lie to me," he said.

Alex, not now. But Michael's thought bounced of his friend's anger like water off oil.

"You violated my mind," said Sarah. She turned to Michael and evoked the memory of being in her room while he probed her thoughts.

He was feeling it from her perspective for the first time. Her rage and pain exploded at him so violently that it threw him out of her mind.

"You didn't rape my body, but you raped my mind!"

She collapsed helpless to the ground and clasped her hands to her head.

Michael took a step back and looked at her pathetic figure on the ground. He remembered what he had done to her in the bedroom. He had been looking for facts, spying on her secret thoughts like they had been taught by Cooper and the people who worked for him. It was his job to probe into other people's minds and he never questioned it. But now...

He re-evaluated the horror of the police officer who had walked in on them. The officer had misinterpreted what had been going on — Sarah had wanted her to — but Michael suddenly realised he was guilty of stripping Sarah naked in a way that was perhaps even worse than taking off her clothes.

"Michael?" It was Pauline's voice. He opened his eyes — only realising at that moment that they had been closed — and saw her worried face looking at him.

His skin was cold, but inside he was hot. He perceived from her that he looked pale.

Sarah hugged her knees to her chest as she sat on the damp ground of the park, shaking like a terrified child. "You trespassed on me," she said. "You forced yourself inside me to a place where no one should be allowed to go. Where I keep the real me."

A single tear rolled down Sarah's cheek.

"She's bluffing," said Alex. "It's a trick, like back at the house."

"Perceiver her, Alex," said Michael. *She's not faking.*

The four of them remained in stalemate, forming a circle of three perceivers and one perceiver victim. Thoughts buzzed unseen between them as they battled with what to do next.

"I think I'm going mad," Sarah whispered, so quietly her words were barely audible. "The others went mad, didn't they? That's what they told me. Not before the injections, of course, only after. After I'd stopped. After they'd finished with me because I wasn't useful to them anymore. I keep seeing … There are things in my head … I forget, and then I remember." She looked up. "Alex, you've got to help me."

"Me?" Alex looked to Michael and Pauline. "But she betrayed us. Cooper has given us a mission, we have to follow it."

"I can get you information about the serum, if that's what you want," said Sarah.

"You can't trust her," said Alex.

"Let's at least hear what she has to say," said Michael.

"Ivanov has an office above the club, I can get you in there," said Sarah. "I don't know what you'll find, but he has computers and stuff in there. Robbie recruited me to spy on you, he gave me the serum, but once I was in and I was gathering information, it was Ivanov I reported to. Until you found out about me — then he cut me off and I became just another norm."

"If you're not taking the serum anymore, why were you at his club?" said Pauline.

"Because Ivanov won't let me go," said Sarah. "He said, if I did what he said, he would give me enough money to set up on my own.

I was going to open a hair salon in Manchester, a long way away from London, but he said because I got caught, I broke the deal."

"You could have cut your losses and left," said Pauline.

"You don't *leave* Ivanov," said Sarah. "It's all right for you with your cosy accommodation provided by the military and your nice little salary and guaranteed job for life. It's not so easy on the outside. If I run away, Ivanov will find me. He says I still have a debt to pay. He says he wants to see if I go mad like the other people on the serum who killed themselves — you have to help me."

"Okay," said Michael.

"Michael!" said Alex.

"It's like Pauline said, if we use mind control then we have no flexibility if things go wrong. She'll blindly do what I program her to do no matter what happens to her. This way, we have a better chance of succeeding."

"You can't trust her," said Alex.

Perceive her, Michael told them as he turned to Sarah. "Sarah, can we trust you to help us?"

"If your Agent Cooper can get me out, set me up with a new name, with a hairdressing business up north, then yes."

Nothing about the mind that Michael perceived suggested she was lying. That, as far as he was concerned, was enough for them to take her up on her offer.

TWENTY-SIX

MICHAEL sat cross-legged on his bed in underpants and a T-shirt. He had stripped down to the basic set of clothes after coming back from the park and his plan had been to sleep in them. But all he had done was lie down in them: thinking.

Morning had arrived and he didn't want to face it. The dim light of day filtered through the window behind him, but he didn't want to open the curtains to let it in. He just sat, with the headboard at his back so he faced the door. From that position, he could see the whole room. All of his possessions were in that room, a meagre reflection of a life that belonged to other people. Whether it be Norm the Norm or Agent Cooper, he was their pawn, doing the job that they told him to do, living where they told him to and they even imprisoned him in the base — a sad excuse for a home — if he did not do what they wanted. No matter how strong his mind powers were, he felt powerless.

He stared at the pair of shoes he had taken off just inside the door. They were running shoes, really, with rubber quiet-approach soles which were more comfortable to wear than the shiny, squeaky, formal shoes that Norm would expect him to wear for inspection. He used to think of them as informal, civilian wear, but now they were soiled with dirt from the park. A thick line of brown clung to the edge of the sole where it had oozed when Michael had run through soft mud. He grabbed the ugly shoe with his mind and willed it into the air.

The muddy trainer sprang off the ground as if launched from a trampoline, then hovered like a hawk above the other half of its pair. Michael willed the trainer to fly around the room and it obeyed: circling around and around above his head. While it spun, his mind turned to the pair of jeans crumpled on the floor. They rose up to the ceiling and circled with the trainer, loose legs flapping as if in the wind. The rubbish bin took to the air, rising up to join the spinning clothes. With a flick of his mind, Michael tipped the bin upside down and all the bits and pieces inside of it — an old drinks can, a used tissue, a broken pen and a chocolate wrapper — spilled into the whirlwind and defied gravity as they twirled above his head like clothes in a giant tumble dryer. Faster and faster as his anger fed their energy and they became one circular blur of colour.

The door opened. He did not allow himself to be distracted. The objects continued on their spinning trajectory.

It was Pauline in her regulation army greys. She looked above her, saw what was happening and quickly closed the door.

"Michael, what are you doing?"

"Practising."

"You weren't at breakfast, I thought you might have over-slept."

"Nope."

Michael, stop it!

He stopped looking at the centrifuge of colour above him and lowered his eyes to look at Pauline. She was the one good thing about the place where he lived, beautiful even in the drab uniform they were told to wear, with her hair untidily pulled back into a ponytail.

He slowed the spinning objects until it was possible to make out the individual pieces once again. She stepped further into the room as he lowered them and was hit in the face by Michael's flying jeans.

She tore them from her face and threw them on the floor. *Michael, enough!*

Michael commanded the objects to stop with his mind. In that moment they froze mid-air, then he allowed gravity to slowly take them and they returned to the ground with the grace of a hot air balloon.

"She really got to you, didn't she?" said Pauline.

"Who?" said Michael.

"You know who."

The question he had been asking himself, one that he had been afraid to articulate, at last came out of his mouth. "Did I rape her mind?"

Pauline stepped over the rubbish bin which had landed between her and Michael's bed and sat on the edge next to him. "Don't think about it."

The anger he thought he had spun out of him with his display of telekinesis was suddenly back. "I was so focussed on getting the information out of her that I didn't think. I went in and I took what I wanted."

"Maybe you went a bit too far, but Alex is right, she was the one who hurt us first."

"Does that make it any better?" he asked, genuinely wanting the answer to be yes, fearing that the answer would be no.

"It excuses what you did. What we all did."

"You don't need to make excuses for me, I need to know the truth."

"The truth is, someone has developed a serum which can turn norms into perceivers. I can only begin to imagine what that will mean for the world. Who will use it? The military? Terrorists? Presidents? Prime Ministers? And what happens to them when they do? Will they be tempted to use it too much and send themselves mad? Do you want a bunch of mad people running the world?"

"Isn't the world already being run by a bunch of mad people?"

"You know what I mean."

He nodded. He understood what she meant but he wasn't sure if it was more of an excuse than a reason. "If you're saying the end justifies the means, then I don't know if it does anymore. I've spent too long in this building and spent too many hours in training to know if I'm doing the right thing or just indoctrinated into thinking I'm doing the right thing."

Pauline reached over and took his hand. A feeling of calm seemed to flow out of her body and into his. He held her fingers tight, grasping the comfort that it gave him. "You're a nice person," she said.

"I don't know about that," said Michael.

"Well, I like you."

He smiled. "I like you too."

"Do you like me enough to come to breakfast with me?" she asked. "I've eaten already, but I can drink tea with you."

As lovely as breakfast with Pauline sounded, he didn't want to go. "I can't face a hall full of perceivers."

"Barely half-full. Some of them have gone off on Norm's re-indoctrination training exercise. Most of the others have eaten and gone already."

"No," said Michael, thinking that somehow an empty hall would be worse, with its vast echoing space. "I need to have a shower and report to Cooper. I have to persuade him to honour our half of the deal with Sarah."

"He will," she said. "If the information's as important to him as we think it is."

"That's what I told myself."

"You still need to eat something. I'll go to the hall for you and bring you something back, even if it's only a banana."

She stood up to go, but Michael kept hold of her hand and she stayed standing by the bed.

"What?" she said.

"Thank you," he said.

"You're welcome."

He allowed her hand to slip from his fingers and he watched her go from his room, taking her calming presence with her. He wished he had the courage to say something more to her, to let her know his true feelings. But, then, she was a perceiver. Maybe she knew already.

SARAH was waiting for Michael by a cobbled alleyway that led off the road which ran around the back of Ivanov's nightclub. A cigarette smouldered in her hand, the tube of ash steadily growing at the end as it burned. She held it like she was holding it for a friend, away from her body, shifting her position every now and again so that the plume of smoke didn't blow in her direction.

Michael nonchalantly adjusted the straps of the half-empty rucksack on his back and looked around at the quiet street. It was narrow, with traffic only allowed to travel one way, and was lined with a row of terraced houses on one side of the road which butted up to the pavement, and the back of the shops and restaurants from the high street on the other. He made sure no one was watching him and approached Sarah.

"You smoking that?" he asked.

She looked at the cigarette clasped inexpertly between her two fingers. "Smokers hang out on street corners all the time," she said. "I told Ivanov I needed a new drug if he wasn't going to give me the serum. It's an excuse to get out of the building."

"What about getting *into* the building?" said Michael.

"Did you speak to your boss?"

Michael nodded. "He'll get you away from here and set you up with a new name and enough money to start a hairdressing business, if that's what you want."

"He better. I'm risking everything."

Sarah looked past Michael to something behind him. As he turned, he saw it was a delivery van, dirty white from the grime of the road with a blue logo on the side. Its left indicator flashed yellow to show it was turning. Sarah stepped back from the corner of the alleyway and Michael joined her as the van squeezed its way onto the cobbles.

Sarah dropped her cigarette to the floor and ground it under her heel. "This is how we get in," she said.

She led him down the alleyway which opened up into a courtyard, similar to the one where Ivanov had threatened him. Among the less than salubrious plastic rubbish bins was parked a silver Mercedes Coupé, so clean that it was almost as shiny as a mirror. The van pulled in beside it and two men got out of the front. One of them was a tall, skinny, pale man who had a mobile phone clamped to his ear.

"Yeah, yeah," he was saying. "Right, yeah. I know, right? Yeah, yeah, cheers mate." He hung up, put the phone into his pocket and went to the back of the van to join his colleague, a shorter and more muscular man whose face was almost entirely hidden by a trimmed beard.

As Sarah approached, she smiled at the thin one and he returned a cheeky grin. "Just in time," she said.

"Yeah," he said.

None of it made any sense to Michael, so he perceived the limited vocabulary man. It seemed he and his colleague were making a drinks delivery to the club and the phone call was to ask someone inside to release the fire door so they could gain access. Sarah's comment meant she had arrived just in time to get let back into the building without having to ask for permission herself.

It was then that Michael saw the double doors in the side of the building with no handle or lock on the outside. Just two pieces of wood painted dark green, looking as if someone had cut a hole in the brickwork and stuck them in.

The left door — with a sign, FIRE DOOR, DO NOT BLOCK — was opened a crack and the shorter man was already heading towards it carrying a box he had pulled out of the back of the van. The box was labelled with the logo for Carlsberg lager and looked heavy, even for a delivery man who presumably spent most of his day carrying heavy boxes of alcohol in and out of buildings. He kicked at the door, it swung open and he disappeared inside.

"Do you want a hand?" Sarah asked the thin one.

"Yeah," he said, using what appeared to be his favourite word. He stood at the back of the van, staring in at his Aladdin's cave of boxed booze. "Why don't you take this one?"

He handed her a box with a Schweppes Tonic Water logo on the side. Sarah braced herself for a heavy box, but when it landed in her arms she was able to carry it easily. As she walked off through the fire doors, the man planted a heavier box of lager into Michael's arms and he struggled to follow her quickly in before he dropped it.

Getting into the nightclub was as easy as that. He walked straight into the heart of the building, between two sets of tables that circled the dance floor. It was a dark and empty space in the daytime which made the squeak of Sarah's shoes on the wooden floor sound almost mournful. As he followed her towards a door at the far side of the room, he glanced back at the inside of the fire door which had a similar warning sign about blocking the exit, and an extra one warning that the door was 'alarmed'. He smiled at the concept of the door having an emotion, but it explained why Sarah had got the delivery man to ask for the doors to be opened for them from the inside: she had needed someone to turn off the alarm without arousing suspicion.

They deposited the boxes in a store room behind the bar where the deputy manager was waiting. Michael felt a flutter of nerves as they came face to face, but the man just thought he was one of the delivery guys and asked him to put the lager with the rest. After that, the real delivery men went back to the van to get more boxes while Sarah led Michael into the back of the building.

Away from the swish modern decor of the public areas, the age of the building was more obvious. The ceilings were low and the walls thick and painted white on uneven plasterwork. There was a draught coming from somewhere he couldn't see and, even when getting near to an old-style cast iron radiator pumping out heat in the hall, the place was cold.

Without a word, Sarah led Michael up a narrow winding staircase to the top floor with a cramped landing and three doors. One door was labelled 'Toilet', the second was labelled 'Storage' and the third, 'Office'. Sarah stepped towards the office.

Her mind revealed that she expected it to be locked, but she tried the handle anyway. The door did not open.

"You can perceive if anyone's coming, right?" she whispered.

"Sure," said Michael. He opened his perception as wide as possible until he could just about sense the deputy manager and the delivery men downstairs, then dialled it back again so he felt just Sarah and himself.

He felt her confidence give way to nervousness as she pulled a bunch of keys from her pocket, clasping them in her hand so that they didn't jangle. Her thoughts revealed that she didn't know for sure if they were the right set of keys. So, as she tried the first one in the lock and it didn't work, her nervousness grew. She rattled the second key to get it in the door, but it was not until the third try that the key turned and they were in.

It was a large room for an office and looked like it might once have been a bedroom. There was even a wardrobe at the back of the room with a full-length mirror set into one of the doors, bouncing back light from the expansive bay window which faced onto the high street below. A fireplace added to the feeling that the building was a converted house, although the actual fire had been replaced by a plug-in electric heater. Above it was a mantelpiece which had bowed over the years and become a handy place to dump junk mail.

The rest of the room was more like an office and had two desks, a computer, chair, filing cabinets and several piles of stacked boxes that once held beer and now appeared to be stuffed with papers.

Sarah pushed the door closed with the click of the latch behind them. "Do whatever you've got to do and be quick."

"How long have I got?"

"Piece of string," she said, which meant she had no idea.

Michael pulled the memory stick Cooper had given him from his pocket and wiggled the mouse on the desk, bringing Ivanov's computer to life. He was confronted with a window asking for a password. Michael ignored it and plugged the USB stick into the base of the computer. He hit CTL+ALT+DEL and chose re-start. The computer did as it was asked and, as it rebooted, it ran the software installed on the stick and started pulling all the data from the machine. Michael didn't know how it worked exactly, he just knew he had to wait until it was finished.

"Where does he keep the serum?" Michael asked.

Sarah shrugged.

"Right, start looking," he said.

"The deal was I get you in here. I didn't say anything about searching the place."

"The quicker we find what I'm looking for, the quicker we can leave."

Sarah frowned. "What are you looking for?"

"Anything and everything to do with the serum."

Sarah looked around at the clutter in the room before looking in the wardrobe. There was nothing in there other than one coat and two jackets hanging above about half a dozen pairs of neatly placed shoes. She moved on to the desk by the window piled with papers.

Michael took the rucksack off his back, put it on the floor in front of him and opened the zip. He delved inside and pulled out a plastic bag containing two small electronic bugs. Their range was short and listening in would require someone with a receiver to be close to the building, but if they didn't get enough information during the break-in, this was their only backup. He placed one under Ivanov's desk and the other in the fireplace.

Sarah pulled a multi-coloured leaflet from the pile of papers she was looking through. "I've found the pizza menu," she said.

"What?" said Michael, standing up from the fireplace and narrowly missing cracking his head on the mantelpiece.

"Didn't you want to order pizza?" She waved the leaflet she had found in his direction.

Michael might have thought she was joking if he hadn't perceived that she was being deadly serious. "We're looking for details about the serum," he reminded her.

"Are we?" Her brain whirled. She remembered. She dropped the pizza leaflet on the table and looked away, embarrassed.

"Sarah, are you all right?"

"Yes, of course! I just thought you might be hungry." But in her mind she feared she wasn't all right.

Michael wished he had time to talk to her about it, but he didn't know how long it would be before Ivanov came back. He walked over to the filing cabinet and pulled open the top drawer. It contained a load of unsorted receipts and invoices relating entirely — as far as he could tell — to the nightclub business. Both the middle and bottom drawers were locked. All the more reason to get into them.

He pulled the top drawer out all the way until it stopped. With a few tugs at several experimental angles, he managed to pull the whole thing off its runners and lower it to the floor. With the top drawer removed, he was able to get to the contents of the second drawer.

He found more papers stuffed into suspended cardboard files. He pulled out a few and looked at them. They were mostly printed papers, almost all of them in Russian.

"This is it," said Sarah.

Michael turned to see she'd abandoned the clutter on top of the desk and was on her hands and knees underneath it where she had found what looked like a small metal cupboard. The door was open and her face was aglow from a light inside. What she had actually found was a small fridge, humming from where its refrigeration unit was plugged into the mains.

Michael came over. Inside were stored five vials of what was almost certainly the perceiver serum, along with two cans of Red Bull energy drink.

"Do you want the serum?" said Sarah.

His instinct was to say yes, but to steal it would make it obvious someone had been in the room, and the police lab already had the vials taken from Farron, Conte and Theresa. He decided to take one, but as he reached inside, a slamming sound from downstairs caused Sarah's body to shudder.

"What is it?" said Michael.

"The front door." She got up and looked out of the window, trying to be quick so she wasn't seen. "I can't tell who it is, but it's too early for the nightclub staff. It must be Ivanov."

"I thought you said he was going to be out for at least an hour."

"Usually he is."

"Are you sure it's him?"

"No! You're the perceiver, can't you tell?"

Michael tried, but the person's mind was out of reach. "It might not be him or he might not come up here," said Michael.

"But it might be and he might do," said Sarah.

He left the fridge and went round to the front of the computer. Meaningless code (at least, meaningless to him) was scrolling up the screen, and lights on the front of the base unit were flashing rapidly as it accessed the hard drive. There was no way to tell how much data had been collected by the stick and how much was left to go.

The presence of someone new touched the edge of his perception. It could be Ivanov, but he hadn't perceived him before and it was difficult to tell. The one thing he could work out was that whoever it was, was getting closer and Sarah was getting increasingly nervous.

"We've still got time," said Michael. "We put back everything the way we found it, then we leave."

"We leave now!" Sarah insisted.

"Thirty seconds and he won't be able to tell we've been in here."

Sarah capitulated, her thoughts revealing that doing what he asked was probably quicker than arguing about it.

She helped him lift the top filing cabinet drawer back into place and that's when he realised he wasn't having to try to sense the mind of the person who had entered the front door. It was closer.

"What?" said Sarah. She must have seen him flinch.

"We're in a hurry." He closed the filing cabinet drawer and looked around. There was still a glow from the open fridge under the desk. He pointed. Sarah got back on her hands and knees and pushed it shut.

He turned to the computer. The meaningless code was still raining down the screen. Hoping that getting out with some data was better than getting caught with all of the data, he pressed the power button on the base unit. Too many long seconds passed before the computer shut off abruptly. He pulled the stick from its slot. Better than yanking it out while data was still being written to it. Or so his minimal experience with computers told him.

Clasping the stick in his hand, he followed Sarah onto the landing, only to hear the sound of a heavy footstep on the stairs below. The perception of Sarah's sudden panic magnified his own.

'Ivanov?' she mouthed silently.

Michael perceived the owner of the footsteps. He was thinking in Russian. She was almost certainly right.

Sarah grabbed Michael's hand and pulled him towards the toilet door. But the sound of the footsteps were continuing to climb and, after only a couple of steps, both she and Michael could see the top of the staircase.

If they could see the stairs, then the person climbing the stairs could see the people on the landing. She turned and pulled Michael back into the office they had just left.

Closing the door behind her, Sarah went straight to the wardrobe. She piled all the shoes up one end and they stepped inside together.

Sarah pulled the door closed as best she could and held her breath.

It might not be Ivanov, Michael thought, wondering if she could hear him. *He might be coming up to use the toilet.*

She didn't react, she didn't breathe. She almost certainly didn't hear his thoughts.

Michael perceived the man on the stairs. Aside from the Russian words in his mind that Michael didn't understand, there was no sense that he wanted to go to the toilet. His footsteps bypassed the toilet door, headed straight for the office.

Michael felt Sarah's body tense next to him. He tried, like her, to be perfectly still. But they could not stay that way forever. Soon, they would both have to breathe.

TWENTY-SEVEN

THE heat from their two bodies filled the wardrobe as they tried to breathe silently. The damp from their breath added to the heat, bringing a jungle-like humidity to the wooden box in which they were trapped.

The crack between the two doors of the wardrobe gave them their only window on the rest of the world. Through that thin sliver, Michael saw Ivanov enter his own office and perceived the man's unease as he questioned himself on whether he could have left the door unlocked or whether someone else had been in there while he was out. As he looked round the room, Michael remembered all the things he and Sarah had touched and hoped they had put everything back where they had found it. Judging from the unease in Ivanov's mind, there had to be signs that things had been disturbed, but thankfully the mess in the room meant he couldn't be sure and he dismissed the possibility as he sat down at his computer and wiggled the mouse to wake it. Nothing happened.

"Chert!" he swore at the blank computer screen. He wiggled his mouse more violently and tapped on the keyboard, but still nothing happened. He resorted to pressing the 'on' switch and the computer bleeped as electricity flowed through its circuits again.

Michael inwardly breathed a sigh of relief as Ivanov left the computer to go to the window and so didn't see the warning message on the screen that told him the computer had shut down unexpectedly. He crawled under the table and retrieved a can of Red Bull from the little fridge.

Walking back, he stopped to check his image in the mirror of the wardrobe. Michael held his breath and listened to Sarah's fear. She thought he was going to open the door to put away his jacket and shoes, but all he did was comb his untidy hair back with his fingers before turning away and sitting at his computer.

The warning message had gone from the screen and it was asking for his password. Michael eavesdropped as Ivanov typed it in, but the man was thinking in Russian and the password in his mind remained undecipherable. Ivanov leant back in his chair, opened the ring pull of the can and sipped his drink as the computer loaded. Michael could see about half the screen through the gap between the wardrobe doors, the rest of it was obscured by Ivanov's shoulder.

The bleepy music of someone calling in via Skype rose from the computer. Ivanov took another sip of his Red Bull, letting the caller wait, then answered. "Allo?"

"Allo, Anton," said a voice from the computer. The video picture of a young-ish man with a full beard appeared on the screen.

The men talked in Russian. Michael tried to perceive what they were talking about, but he only had access to one of their minds, and Ivanov's emotions only revealed him to be vaguely interested in their conversation.

All the time he was pressed uncomfortably close to Sarah in the wardrobe. He could feel her body touching his side and smell her sweat mingling with his own. He wasn't sure how much longer they could stand still like that. He considered running for it. With Ivanov sat down at the computer, they could be out of the wardrobe and down the stairs before the Russian was barely out of his seat. But then he would know they had been in his room. Michael decided to wait a little longer in the hope he would finish his Skype call quickly and leave.

Ivanov's Skype call dragged on, all of it in Russian. It was an ordinary conversation, even their body language was relaxed. They could have been talking about their respective shopping lists as far as Michael could tell.

After what felt like half an hour, but was probably only five minutes, the bearded man on the screen was distracted by something to his left. Michael thought he heard another voice off-mike, but he wasn't sure.

"Ask about the girl," the voice shouted in English. Still off-mike, but loud enough for Michael to hear.

"Peredai emy, chto Sarah v poryadke."

Sarah flinched beside him at the mention of her name.

"Ya dumayu on khochet znat' bolshe chem eto," the bearded man replied.

Ivanov replied in Russian. The bearded man responded.

"Is she going mad yet?" the English voice chimed in. The voice of a man and closer this time. "Get out of the way and let me talk to him."

The bearded man was suddenly gone from the screen. Another man put his face in front of the webcam, which struggled to focus. It showed the pinky blur of a white man's face with grey hair on top. As the image sharpened, it revealed the man to be older, probably in his fifties, with black square-rimmed glasses.

Michael gasped with recognition. A tiny intake of air, sounding louder in the echo chamber of the enclosed wardrobe than it would have done in the open. Sarah's shock was so loud in his perception, it stopped him sensing whether Ivanov had heard or not. Michael prayed he hadn't. He stopped breathing and willed his body to stay perfectly still — he would have stopped his heart from beating if he could.

Ivanov had heard. Something. But he seemed confused as to what it was. For a moment, his eyes settled on the gap between the wardrobe doors. But it must have been too dark inside for him to see and he looked away.

Michael breathed again. But only enough to stop him from passing out.

On the computer, the man he had recognised as Doctor Saul Lucas was chastising his Russian associate. "Well, Anton? You are supposed to be reporting on how the serum is affecting her and your latest report is late."

"She is not mad," replied Ivanov in English. "Well, maybe a little crazy, but she has not flipped like the others yet. I think, maybe because she is young…"

"All the more reason to send me your report."

"But she is useless for the spying," Ivanov said in less-than-accurate English. "I not give her serum anymore."

"But I must know the threshold for madness. You need to keep injecting her until she 'flips' as you put it."

Michael could feel Sarah's body shaking against him as the horror of the conversation filled her mind. They had already kept still for longer than their bodies could stand. She lost her balance and her arm touched the side of the wardrobe.

Ivanov definitely heard it that time.

He rose from his chair and spun round. He reached for the wardrobe door and flung it open — revealing the two teenagers huddled inside.

Sarah screamed. So loud and so sudden that Ivanov stepped back in surprise.

Sarah took her chance and jumped out of the wardrobe. She was at the door before Ivanov could grab her.

But Michael wasn't so quick. Strong, Russian hands reached into the wardrobe and grabbed the straps of the rucksack over his shoulders. "You little bastard," he said in English, pulling Michael's face so close to his own that Michael felt his spit land on his cheek.

"What the hell's going on?" called Lucas from the computer, his voice sounding pathetic through the tinny speakers.

Michael willed the computer monitor with Lucas's confused face on it to come closer. The whole thing lifted from the desk and pulled at its power cable. The cable was wrenched from its socket and the display plunged into darkness. Michael continued to use his telekinesis to pull it close, as it tugged at the data cable still secured to the back and brought the desk noisily with it.

Ivanov turned to look as the cable broke free and the monitor swung and hit him in the face.

Ivanov dropped the rucksack and Michael stumbled backwards into the wardrobe door. Regaining his balance, he dashed for the landing, leaving Ivanov stunned with his hand on his cheek and staring with disbelief at the monitor which had attacked him.

Michael ran down the stairs as, above him, Ivanov shouted in Russian.

He ran to the public area of the club, across the empty dance floor and to the fire doors. He pushed on the bar that ran across the middle of the nearest one and, as it opened, he tumbled out into the courtyard. An alarm wailed an electronic scream.

That's where he saw Sarah. In the centre of the courtyard, her arms pinned tightly behind her by the deputy manager of the nightclub.

"Michael!"

Sarah struggled, but the man was too strong for her stick-like body.

"Help me!"

Michael looked around for something to throw at Ivanov's hench-man, but the only things in the courtyard were the Mercedes and the bins. Michael focussed on the green recycling bin and, in his mind, willed it to tip backwards onto its wheels. The deputy manager glanced over, but soon turned back to keep an eye on Michael. There was confusion in his mind, but he knew better than to let go of Sarah.

The bin wheeled itself across the cobbles, wobbling over each uneven stone, spilling the remnants of cardboard boxes and cellophane wrappers from inside. Michael maintained his concentration as he stepped away from the fire door, looking for a chance to attack the man with the bin, just as he had attacked Ivanov with the monitor.

Striking him with the bin would almost certainly cause the man to lessen his grip on Sarah and allow her to break free.

But concentrating on the bin took all his energy and Michael didn't perceive Ivanov coming out of the club behind him.

"Stop your mind power!" Ivanov's voice boomed from the open fire door. He stepped into the courtyard with a semi-automatic pistol in his hand. He pointed the gun at Michael's chest and placed a finger ready on the trigger.

Michael gasped. His mind forgot about the bin and it fell over backwards, scattering rubbish over the cobbles.

"What were you doing in my office?" said Ivanov.

"Looking for whatever you've got on Sarah that makes her afraid of you," Michael lied. He stared at Ivanov's pistol. It was a different model than the one he had used briefly during his army training but he knew it would hold just as much explosive power.

"I don't believe you," said Ivanov. "She spied on you, why would you help her?"

"Because you made her do it."

With a burst of mental energy, he willed the gun to fly out of Ivanov's hand across the yard.

The gun lurched to the left, but Ivanov held it so tight that it took his arm with it. In an effort to keep hold of it he squeezed the trigger and a shot rang out around the walls of the old buildings.

Sarah screamed as the bullet exploded from the barrel, flew past her body and made a hole in the rear wing of the Mercedes.

Ivanov spun back to face Michael, the gun still firmly in his hand and pointing at Michael's head. "Don't try that again. Next time maybe I shoot the girl. Or I shoot you."

Michael didn't doubt it. He stood frozen to the spot in the courtyard, not knowing what to do next.

Ivanov reached into his pocket where he must have had the keys to the car because the doors of the Mercedes unlocked with a flash of indicator lights. "Put the girl in the car," he called to his deputy manager, not taking his eyes off Michael.

The deputy manager opened the back door and bundled Sarah inside.

Part of Michael hoped she would use that moment to make a break for it, but the other part looked into Ivanov's mind and saw that he meant what he said about shooting her.

Ivanov backed towards the car. "Don't try to rescue the girl," he warned, not taking his eyes off Michael and not wavering the aim of his gun. "She's not worth it."

Michael stood, helplessly, as Ivanov got into the driver's seat and started the engine.

He saw Sarah's terrified face through the rear window as the car pulled away and drove down the narrow alleyway.

Michael followed as it pulled out into the road. The last he saw of Sarah was her face looking desperately through the glass as she mouthed the words, 'help me!'

TWENTY-EIGHT

MICHAEL had remembered his coat that morning, but still the wind blew at his body, cutting through the artificial fibres and pushing its chill inside them. The wind carried with it a light drizzle which spat in his face, leaving his skin cold and damp. He wanted to turn his back on it and nuzzle into the wall of the police building for protection, but then he risked missing the arrival of Inspector Anthony Patterson.

It was early and still dark, like it would be for three months at that time of morning before spring arrived. The lights of the arriving police cars shone brightly in his eyes and blinded him for a moment before he got used to the darkness again. A couple of the arriving officers and civilian workers recognised Michael by sight and gave him a cursory, 'good morning'. He smiled and gave them a 'good morning' back and they passed him without concern. Only a few of them, he perceived, were secretly wondered what he was doing there, but they said nothing.

At the point where Michael began to fear that he had misunderstood Patterson's work pattern and he wasn't going to turn up, Patterson's car entered the compound. Michael left his draughty spot and approached the car. Patterson stopped and wound down his window.

"I didn't expect to see you this morning," said Patterson, as drizzle blew into the car and left droplets on his wiry hair.

"I'm not supposed to be in," said Michael. "Can we talk?"

Patterson nodded. "I'll just find somewhere to put the car and we can go up to my desk."

"Not here."

The horn of another arriving car honked to tell Patterson to get out of the way. "I need to park. Will the cafe do?"

"That will do," confirmed Michael.

Patterson found a parking space and the two of them walked the ten minutes to the same cafe where he had talked to Michael and Pauline about the private detective's report.

They were damp when they arrived, but the cafe was warm and full of inviting smells that made the walk in the drizzle almost worth it. Patterson ordered a bacon sandwich and a tea, even though his thoughts revealed he had been planning to eat a healthy banana at his desk. Michael was too wired for food and ordered a coffee.

A man and woman in business suits were just vacating the table they had sat at the last time and they were able to take their place at the back. One of the staff members came over to give the table a quick wipe and take away the couple's empty crockery.

Office hours had begun and the number of people in the cafe had thinned to a handful, but there was still enough ambient chatter to allow them to speak without broadcasting their business to the whole establishment.

Michael pulled a computer memory stick from his pocket and placed it on the table between them.

"What's that?" said Patterson, biting into his bacon sandwich, causing a blob of tomato ketchup to ooze out on the other side and drop onto the plate in front of him.

"The contents of Ivanov's computer," said Michael. "At least some of it."

Patterson looked at him with questioning eyes as he chewed his bacon.

Michael sipped his coffee. It was warming, bitter and made him feel more awake, even before he had swallowed it. "We broke into Ivanov's office," he said, keeping his voice low.

"You what?" Patterson put his sandwich down. The emotion coming from him was more betrayal than anger.

"The people I work for," Michael began. "The people I *really* work for, not the police, wanted me to do it. They don't care about warrants and due process."

"And this is a good thing?"

Michael ignored his question. "I downloaded everything I could onto a memory stick before Ivanov came back. I have to give the original to Agent Cooper, but I took a copy first. I thought you might find it useful."

Patterson picked up the stick from where it lay on the table and turned it around in his greasy fingers. "What's on it?"

"I don't know, I had to stop the download before it was finished and I couldn't read any of the files. I think it'll need a computer expert to piece them back together. It might have some of his contacts or his underground businesses on it, or it might just have his porn collection. It's difficult to say."

"I can't use any of this in court, you know that?"

"But the information could lead you to find out something you could use in court."

"Hmm." Patterson put the stick into the pocket of his jacket, his thoughts revealing his uncertainty about whether to be grateful to Michael or angry at him.

Michael drank more of his coffee, hoping to draw more strength from it than the caffeine could provide. "Ivanov came back sooner than we thought. I managed to get away, but Sarah …"

"Sarah?"

"The girl from Robert Fazoni's flat."

Patterson raised his eyebrows in surprise. "Is this the same girl who said you—?"

"It's complicated," said Michael.

"Evidently."

"Ivanov took her away somewhere and I feel responsible. I was hoping you could find her. Kidnap is a crime, isn't it?"

"Yes, but—"

"She was being driven in a silver Mercedes. I looked it up on the internet, I think it was a C Class Saloon. I didn't see the number plate. I got Pauline to look through my memory, but I don't think I ever looked at it, so all she can see is a blur where the number plate should be. I'm hoping you can find out where the car took her after it left the club. I can tell you what time it drove off and in which direction it went. I mean, there's traffic cameras all over London, isn't there?"

"What about the people you work for? Don't they have resources for that?"

"Cooper doesn't care about Sarah, he only cares about the serum. I promised her protection — please, you have to help."

Patterson sighed. "I'll pass it on to CID, I'll say it was an anonymous tip-off. What possessed you to break into Ivanov's office in the first place?"

"The serum," said Michael. "But it turns out Ivanov is just another middleman. We should have realised. He's a smuggler, a trafficker, a gangster. He might have been bringing the stuff in, dishing it out and collecting the information, but I saw into his head and he's no scientific mastermind. There's no way he created the serum."

"Then who did?"

"Doctor Lucas."

The name caused a spike of recognition to ripple through Patterson's mind, just as seeing his face had done for Michael. "The scientist who ran away to Russia?"

Michael nodded. "As soon as I saw his face on the webcam talking to Ivanov, it all made sense. He was researching perceivers even before he fled the country, if anyone is capable of making a perceiver serum, it's him."

"Then what's the serum doing in Britain?" said Patterson.

"I spent all night thinking about it and I think we were given the answer right at the beginning, right after Farron died. Remember when we first interviewed Etchin, he told us he was worried about industrial espionage?"

"Yeah, that's why he claimed he didn't have a digital copy of the private detective's report on Farron. He said he was worried about being hacked."

"Right. He also said Power Grid UK was heavily into researching renewable energy to replace oil and gas fired power stations. Who do you think stands to lose if Britain stops using fossil fuels and switches entirely to stuff like wind and solar power?"

"The people who supply us with oil and gas."

"Who are?" said Michael.

"The Russians!" Patterson sat back in his chair and shook his head, his mind asking why he had not made the connection before.

"I looked it up," said Michael. "Not all of our supply comes from Russia, obviously, but a lot of it does. If they could sabotage our renewable energy programme, or even steal the technology and sell it back to us, they don't lose, they win."

"Seems a lot of effort to go to," said Patterson.

"Unless Lucas was using it as a way of testing the serum. If the Russians want to develop perceivers to spy on people, then the energy industry is a low risk one to target if it all goes wrong. And it did go wrong, didn't it? It drove the spies mad in the end."

"I still don't understand why they couldn't test it in Russia where it would attract less attention."

"Maybe the early tests were in Russia and this was the first test in the field. Or maybe no one thought it would attract any attention — I mean, Britain is the only place where perceivers are common after so many were born to mothers who took the fake vitamin pills."

"If you're right," said Patterson, "and the serum was developed in Russia and the Russians were running Farron, Conte and Theresa through Ivanov, then it stops being a police matter and becomes one for the intelligence services."

"So, what are you going to do?"

"I'll take a look at the data on the memory stick and see if there's anything useful, but our investigation may have gone as far as it can go."

"But you will look for Sarah?"

"Of course," said Patterson. "If Ivanov really has kidnapped her, then she could be in danger and that's a police matter."

Michael wasn't sure whether to be pleased because he had Patterson's help or unhappy because their investigation together was over. "I have to get back," he said. "I'm due at a briefing with Agent Cooper."

Patterson picked up the paper serviette which had come with his bacon sandwich and wiped his hands. "I can give you a lift back if you like, I'd be interested in seeing this mysterious base you live in."

Michael shook his head. "Now's not a good time, it's pretty crazy back there at the moment. Anyway, I want you to start looking for Sarah."

"Then we should walk back to the police station."

Patterson dropped a few coins for a tip on the table while Michael put his coat back on and they walked out onto the street together. The wind was still strong, but the drizzle had stopped, so the walk was not unpleasant. Halfway there, Michael should have turned off and made his way back to the base, but he didn't. He wasn't sure how much longer Cooper was going to allow him to continue working with the police and, it might seem odd, but he wanted to say goodbye properly.

Saying goodbye was the last thing in Patterson's thoughts. He was too busy going over the information Michael had told him about Doctor Lucas. So, when they arrived at the entrance to the police station, Patterson didn't so much as give him a smile and a wave.

"Text me if you get any news about Sarah," said Michael.

"I can tell you tomorrow when you come in," said Patterson,

"But if there's any news before then, you will text me?"

"Okay."

"Bye then."

"Yep, bye." Patterson entered the police station without another glance back.

TWENTY-NINE

 think Sarah is in Russia.'

Patterson's text came through to Michael's mobile two days after their meeting at the cafe. If it was true, then she was almost certainly out of reach. At least the message didn't say they had found her dead body.

'Are you sure?' Michael texted back.

'It's our best guess,' texted Patterson.

In the flurry of messages that followed, Patterson told him that a witness had seen someone matching Sarah's description getting out of a silver Mercedes at a service station near Chelmsford and being bundled into another car. The witness had assumed the man was her father until the car drove off and he had second thoughts and decided to report it. CCTV at the service station hadn't captured the incident, but had managed to record the car she was in, a blue Vauxhall Astra, driving onto the A12. It also recorded the car number plate which was picked up later that day on cameras based at Harwich ferry port. There, the car boarded a ferry heading for the Netherlands. Europol was able to track its journey to Poland, but after that the trail went cold.

So, there was no firm evidence the car went all the way to Russia. But, with both Ivanov and Lucas having Russian connections, it seemed likely that's where Sarah's captors had taken her.

'What do we do now?' Michael texted Patterson.

'Russia is way out of my jurisdiction,' he replied. 'Let me ask around and I'll see what I can do.'

Michael texted an 'OK' and watched the display on his phone until the screen went dark. All he could do was wait.

IT was another day before Michael was ordered into Cooper's office. The Agent barely ever worked out of Galen House and his office had remained the same blank canvas that it had been when first assigned to him. There was a desk, a chair, a landline telephone plugged into the wall and a window which looked out onto the grounds. The carpet had hardly been walked on and retained that new, sponginess underfoot as Michael approached the near side of the desk.

Cooper leant back in the black, leather executive chair which the army had provided for him and it squeaked with neglect. Cooper's mood was difficult to judge, even for a perceiver, as it was a jumble of excitement, annoyance and concern.

"What is it with you and that bloody Inspector Patterson?" Cooper demanded, looking across his desk at where Michael stood with his hands clasped behind his back — there being no second chair in the office for visitors.

"Sir?"

"I've had him on the phone about that Sarah girl."

"Oh?" Michael felt a flutter of optimism.

"He wants me to send you to Russia to get her back."

"Me?"

Mixed emotions swirled inside him. He felt guilty that he had escaped while Sarah had been caught, but he also remembered when he was last in Russia and the memory chilled him. He could almost feel the cold steel of the handcuff around his wrist and how it dug into his flesh when he tried to pull away from the radiator he'd been chained to.

"Patterson is frustrated he can't close up the case. I can understand that."

"I can't go to Russia," said Michael. "I don't speak the language."

"People who speak Russian I'm not short of," said Cooper. "People with your skills are a rare commodity. One that is sorely wasted hanging around with the Metropolitan Police."

"You're not seriously thinking about it?" said Michael, perceiving that Cooper seriously was.

"There's some things I didn't tell you about Doctor Lucas," said Cooper. "We lost track of him after he experimented on you, as you know."

Michael's body involuntarily shivered. He still didn't know what happened to him during the time Doctor Lucas took his unconscious body out of the room where he'd been kept prisoner.

"An English scientist with a rudimentary grasp of the Russian language is difficult to hide for long. We discovered about a year ago that he is now based at a military facility outside of Moscow."

"You think Sarah was taken there?"

"She was one of his research subjects, it makes sense. Not that we know for sure."

"Do you think we can get her out?" said Michael.

Cooper let out a long sigh. "Honestly? No. Breaking a civilian out of a Russian military facility is a long shot, but it gives us an excuse to go out there and try to find out more about Lucas's perceiver programme."

"You're sure he's the one behind it?"

"From the information you acquired in Ivanov's office, I think it's almost certain."

"Don't you have Russian agents you can send?"

"Not ones who understand perception, who will know what they are looking for, and who can look inside Lucas's head and pull out all he knows."

"I've never done anything like that before."

"Then it's about time that you did. I think both of us know that it's time to stretch your ability."

Cooper's thoughts were so loud, it was like he was inviting Michael to perceive him. Like Patterson was frustrated at the limitations of being a British policeman, Cooper was frustrated that the special teenagers that he had recruited weren't using their talents to the full. Now that they were older, now that his superiors were pressurising him to show results from his expensive perceiver project, Cooper felt it was time to test them.

"I want you to go with Pauline, you two work well together and are up to speed on the police investigation, so it makes sense. Alex too. He knows the girl and also has telekinetic power which has yet to be tested in the field. I've also agreed that Patterson will accompany you."

"Patterson?" said Michael.

"I need an adult to keep an eye on you, he knows more about the perceiver project than his security clearance should have allowed and he practically begged me to be included on the mission."

"I don't think he speaks Russian either."

"You will fly to Moscow where you will meet a local contact. They can fill you in with the details of the mission and deal with any 'speaking Russian' duties."

Michael still didn't feel comfortable. "I appreciate your confidence in us, sir, but are you sure we're the right people to send?"

"We *need* to know more about the perceiver serum," said Cooper. "We need to confirm that Lucas is the one behind it and ascertain if he is working with someone else. We know it's been tested in Britain, but we don't know if it's been deployed elsewhere and how advanced those tests are. I can't think of anyone better to find that out than a perceiver. I want you to come back to Britain with full details of Lucas's work, do you understand?"

"Yes, sir."

"You leave tomorrow. Pack for the cold."

"Yes, sir," said Michael, turning to go and thinking about what he was going to say to the others.

"You're not dismissed yet, Michael."

Michael stopped at the door. "Sir?"

"I shouldn't have to say this, but I'm going to say it anyway. You're not to breathe a word of this to anyone. Leave it to me to brief Pauline and Alex. I need all three of you to keep your mouths shut and your minds closed while you are on the base. Fortunately, half the Corps is on exercise, but even so, secrecy is of the utmost importance. I could be draconian and confiscate your mobile phone, but I trust you to instigate full security protocol."

"Yes, sir."

Michael touched the cold metal of the door handle and turned it. As he walked out into the corridor, he heard Cooper pick up the telephone and order that Pauline and Alex be sent to his office.

He dawdled on purpose as he walked back to his room and passed Alex as he was led out of the accommodation corridor by a norm soldier.

What's going on? Alex asked with his thoughts.

Michael wanted to tell him, but Cooper's warning over secrecy was still in his mind. *Can't say*, thought Michael.

Is it bad? thought Alex.

I hope not.

In his need to share something with his friend, even a few cryptic thoughts, he had caused Alex to become apprehensive. But he only perceived it for a moment before the two of them had walked away in different directions and became out of range.

THIRTY

A Russian agent met them off the plane. She was an unimposing, slight woman, only in her twenties and entirely the opposite of what Michael was expecting. Perhaps that was the idea.

She said her name was Julie, but Michael and the others perceived it was a lie. Her real name was Marta, a fact that she had endeavoured to keep secret in case they were captured and questioned.

She had clearly not worked with perceivers before.

Patterson took off his glove and offered his hand for her to shake. "Pleased to meet you," he said. "I'm Tony Patterson."

She kept her hand hidden in her black leather glove as she accepted his handshake. "We need to go," she said in a heavy Russian accent. "The car is in short-term parking."

Patterson nodded. "Right."

He's so nervous, thought Alex.

He'll be fine, thought Michael.

Filter him out, thought Pauline. *It's what I usually do.*

Michael stopped himself from laughing out loud as Julie led them from the airport building and they stepped out into the icy Russian wind. Julie tucked her long plait of blonde hair up inside a woollen hat which she pulled down over her ears. Michael wished he had paid more attention to Cooper when he had told him to pack for the cold.

The car Julie spoke of was a large four-by-four which she had either hired or borrowed or procured — Michael wasn't sure which — for the mission. He only knew because when people got into 'their' car, he always perceived they had some sort of connection with it. A connection that went deeper than if they had got on a bus or into a taxi. Julie's feelings about the car were detached and she had a certain unfamiliarity with the controls which suggested she had not been driving it for very long.

The light gave way to the dark in the hour and a half drive out of Moscow. Tall, modern buildings gave way to smaller and older concrete blocks and, eventually, to electric lights twinkling out of the night. Patterson tried to engage Julie in small talk as he sat next to her in the passenger seat, but she was reluctant to talk about herself because of the need for security and he soon gave up. Michael, Pauline and Alex exchanged thoughts in the back for a little while before fatigue from the journey caused them to retreat inside their own minds.

Julie took them to an apartment located in a small town near to the military facility where, it was believed, Lucas was based.

A faint smell greeted them as they stepped through the door which Michael could only identify as something between mouldy damp and chicken soup.

As she led them into the kitchen, the food smell grew strong enough to mask the smell of damp and it turned out Julie had prepared a meal for them. On the hob was a pan of chicken and chunky vegetable soup which she re-heated as the others sat around the kitchen table.

The table was the only thing about the room which was solid enough not to look like it would fall to pieces any second. It was made with real wood, possibly oak, with a few knocks and gashes on it which suggested it had been put to good use for many years. The rest of the kitchen, by contrast, was fitted with chipboard cabinets which didn't close properly and a stainless steel sink splattered with water marks which didn't look like it had had a good clean for some while. The table, like the British people who sat round, felt out of place.

Julie handed round bowls of soup for everyone, along with hunks of white bread thickly dotted with blobs of butter which were too cold to spread. The soup was welcomingly warm and filling after their long journey, even though they had eaten on the plane. Michael used the back of his warm soup spoon to spread out the butter a little bit better, then dunked the bread in his bowl. He held it there long enough for some of the butter to melt and create a shiny yellow pool in the middle.

Julie didn't dish out any soup for herself, but sat at the table and watched them eat. Michael tried to perceive her, but although her surface thoughts were easily accessible, they were all in Russian and the woman remained a mystery.

"As much as it would be nice to spend a day acclimatising yourself after your flight, we have business to do," she said when they had nearly finished. "The longer we stay here, the more we are likely to get noticed. So, I'll brief you tonight and we go to work tomorrow."

Julie brought a laptop computer over from where it had been sitting on the worktop and opened it on the table. "Your target, Doctor Lucas, works at a military establishment a short drive from here," she said. "Many of the civilian scientists are housed in the surrounding area, but for some reason, Lucas lives somewhere on site. He's probably considered a security risk. So, to get to him — and his research — you need to go onto the facility. It is a large site situated at the top of a hill and protected by an electric fence and regular patrols. The easiest way in is to go through the main gate dressed as soldiers. I have uniforms for the three of you."

"Three?" questioned Patterson.

"You will be our driver," said Julie. "We need to be dropped off as near to the facility as possible without being seen. You will then wait for us until you get the signal to pick us up. You're also our man on the outside should something go wrong."

"Nothing will go wrong, will it?" said Patterson with a nervous chuckle.

Julie looked at the three perceivers sitting round the table. Michael could not the Russian thoughts he perceived from her, but he had sensed that feeling before. She regarded them as inexperienced children.

He couldn't help but share her anxiety because he knew she was probably right.

"You will also be armed with Russian standard issue pistols." Julie walked over to one of the ageing kitchen cupboards and retrieved three semi-automatics and three magazines of ammunition. "The P-96 is similar to the weapons you have used, yes?"

Michael held the gun in his hand and felt its relative lightness without the magazine inside. He pulled back the slider with ease, feeling how the mechanism would have loaded the first bullet had he slotted in the ammunition. It felt small compared to the Glocks he had used briefly in training, but he knew how to use it if he had to.

"Unfortunately," continued Julie, "dressing up as soldiers won't be enough to get us in, even with fake IDs. But I am told you have a skill which will make them believe that we have the authority to enter the facility."

It took Michael a moment to realise what she was talking about. "Mind control?" he asked the others.

"Mind control," agreed Alex.

Pauline nodded.

Julie opened a file on her computer which brought up a satellite image of a collection of buildings which looked like rectangular blocks with flat roofs. She pointed to one near the middle. "We think Lucas works out of this building."

Michael perceived she wasn't sure. "You *think* he does?"

"According to our latest intelligence, that's where his research lab is, but that intelligence is six months old, so it's what you English call our 'best guess.'"

Great, thought Pauline with sarcasm.

"This needs to be a quick in an out operation," said Julie. "Get whatever you can, plant the computer bugs, then retreat without attracting attention."

"What about Sarah?" said Alex.

"Who?" said Julie.

"The girl," prompted Patterson.

"Oh," said Julie. "We have no intelligence on her. I was led to believe she is low priority."

"Low priority?" said Alex.

Michael had thought Alex didn't care about her anymore, that he was angry about what she had done, but he clearly still had some feelings for her, despite everything.

"She isn't a security risk," said the Russian agent. "If we find her, then my orders are to bring her out if possible, but the main target is Lucas and his research."

We have to find Sarah, thought Alex. *It's why we're here.*

Of course we'll find her, thought Pauline.

If she really is here, thought Michael. *We don't know for sure she actually made it to Russia.*

Julie was unaware of the perceivers' conversation among themselves and was still talking. "… need someone who can speak Russian and so I'll be going into the facility with you. You can then use your power to locate Lucas."

"What do you mean?" said Pauline.

"You can perceive an English mind separate from a Russian mind, can you not? Then once we have entered the research building, you will be able to locate Lucas."

"Perceiving through walls is difficult," said Michael. "We can't just walk in and say he's on the second floor in the middle room or something."

"Then we will split up to search. A large group of unfamiliar faces would be likely to draw attention in any case."

Patterson had said little during the briefing, instead he had sat picking nervously at a piece of dirt which had wedged itself into one of the gashes in the wood of the table. As his nervousness hit its peak, he pushed his empty soup bowl so it covered the gash and looked Julie straight in the eye. "I said I would be here to protect them," said Patterson. "I can't do that if I'm stuck outside waiting in the car."

"We need a driver and we need someone outside. You don't speak Russian and you don't have their power, so it has to be you. We'll keep in touch via radio, but if you came into the facility with us, you would only be in the way."

Patterson looked warily at the guns and ammunition laid on the table. "I'm uncomfortable with this plan."

"These are our orders. If you don't like it, you can talk to London, but I can assure you that they include protecting the perceiver assets as much as possible."

Michael flinched at being described as a 'perceiver asset'. Pauline and Alex did the same.

Julie turned away from Patterson, blanking him completely, as she addressed the 'perceiver assets'. "Now," she said. "Tell me about mind control."

THE apartment was not vast and had only two bedrooms. One had twin beds and was reserved for the 'boys' as Julie called them, while Pauline had the other room to herself. Patterson was given a sofa bed in the living room while Julie went somewhere else for the night. Once the adults were out of the way, Alex confessed to being a snorer and it was agreed he would swap rooms with Pauline.

Michael lay in his single bed, looking up at the bare ceiling and trying to ignore the smell of damp coming from the plasterwork, as he ran the details of the plan over and over in his head. Julie had been frustratingly difficult to perceive, but two things he had picked up on from her continued to bother him: the way she regarded them as inexperienced children and the sense that she agreed with Patterson's unease about the plan.

"Are you awake?" came Pauline's voice from the other bed.

"You can perceive I am," said Michael.

"It's polite to ask, though, isn't it?"

"I suppose."

"Do you think we'll be all right?" said Pauline. "Tomorrow, I mean."

"Of course," he replied. "Three young English people breaking into a Russian military facility — what could go wrong?"

She didn't reply to his sarcasm and, for a moment, his thoughts began to drift towards sleep.

Then his perception told him Pauline's mind was closer. He opened his eyes to see her standing next to his bed, her lithe naked body wrapped in a duvet. Despite his sleepiness, his body reacted to the sight in a way he was embarrassed for her to perceive.

"Are you cold?" she said.

He had never warmed up from the icy blast of Artic air which had rushed over them when they walked out of the plane at Moscow airport. "A little bit."

"Me too."

Without asking, she slipped her body under his covers and mixed her body heat with his. She laid her duvet on top, but Michael found his body was suddenly hot without the need for it.

"Pauline—"

"Don't say anything."

She was letting him perceive her. He felt her vulnerability, her need to be close to someone, a need for comfort.

He dropped his blocks and allowed her to explore his feelings. She relaxed him and excited him all at the same time. Her smell, musky from their long journey, was so sweet he could almost taste it. He loved having her body next to him. It touched him just enough so he felt the smoothness of her skin and the tightness of the muscles beneath. In a foreign country where he couldn't speak the language, on the eve of a dangerous mission, she made him feel safe.

"I sometimes think I should have had the cure," she said.

"Pauline!"

"I do. I had the choice back then. Cooper wanted me to sign up, but I could have turned my back on all this and become a norm."

"It would have changed the person you are," said Michael. "I like the person you are."

"There's a girl my age who writes a blog I've been reading. She opted for the cure. It was bad at first, but now has loads of norm friends, she goes to parties and she's thinking about university. I don't have any of that — I'm never going to have any of that."

"Are you saying you would take the cure now?"

"I might," she said. "My family might accept me again. When I think about spending another Christmas without them …" She allowed her feelings of loss, denial and resentment to fill her mind. There was no need to finish the sentence.

Words formed in Michael's head. Words that he had wanted to say for a long time, but had never had the courage. "I had the cure once," he said.

"No you didn't."

"You can perceive I'm not lying."

She still battled with the contradiction. "But you're a perceiver. Perceivers who have the cure turn into norms."

"I *was* a norm for a little while," said Michael.

Pauline sat up in bed, holding the duvet up to her chest so it just covered her breasts. She stared down at him, the ambient light of the room picking up the brown of her eyes. She perceived him. "You're serious."

"My father wanted to stop me falling into the hands of Agent Cooper," said Michael. "Like you, he thought if I was a norm I could turn my back on all of this. But I was too strong. Halfway through the procedure, I broke out of it. It damaged me."

"It…?" The question only half formed on her lips before it died, unspoken.

"It wiped my memories."

"Memories of what?"

"Of everything. I don't remember ever having a family Christmas, although I guess I did. I don't remember growing up, I don't remember school, I don't even remember my mother. I met her, once, a couple of years back and she was a stranger."

"You can't remember anything?"

"It's all gone," said Michael. "Everything before I was given the cure might as well never have happened."

Pauline shivered. Perhaps from listening to his story, perhaps from sitting up with naked shoulders.

She lowered herself back under the covers and laid her head on Michael's chest. Her hair was soft and the warmness of her cheek was comforting.

"So," she said. "Why aren't you still a norm?"

"I got the procedure reversed," said Michael. "The cure only stops a person from accessing their perception. Restoring access is like unclogging a pipe. But the memories were in a part of my brain that didn't survive."

"I didn't know," said Pauline.

"I don't talk about it."

"Must be awful."

"I don't remember what it was like before, so I don't miss it," he said. "It just means I can't join in with stuff sometimes, like talking about what football team I've supported since I was a boy, or what it was like growing up and discovering I was a perceiver."

"That last one, you're better off not remembering," said Pauline.

"So I hear."

"Michael?" she asked after a moment. "Is it okay if I sleep here tonight?"

His body wanted it. It wanted it so much, even though both of them knew the bed was really too small for them both. "Of course."

"I perceive you're not sure."

"I think Agent Cooper wouldn't approve if he was here. But he's not here, is he?"

"No."

Michael stroked Pauline's hair and felt her sink further into the bed as any remaining tension disappeared from her muscles. His heart was pumping blood strongly through his body, but eventually it understood that the joy of being close to Pauline was all that mattered. As her breathing slowed and he perceived her conscious mind moving into sleep, he too felt the pull of unconsciousness.

They slept for a full eight hours before the sound of Julie coming back into the apartment woke them for their big day.

THIRTY-ONE

THE Russian uniforms they were issued with were not much different than the ones worn by British soldiers back home. Green camouflage for use in military campaigns in forests was, it seemed, more or less the same everywhere. Expect that, over the top of the camouflage fatigues, the Russians were issued with a camouflage coat far more substantial than the average British soldier was offered. Whatever material it was made of, it did the job as it caused Michael to sweat as he sat in the warmth of the car.

Patterson drove them to the pre-arranged secluded area, the Russian equivalent of a country lane through a stretch of woodland, only just about wide enough for two cars to squeeze past each other. The bare branches of trees reached up to the sky on either side and sheltered them from view.

As Julie got out of the passenger seat, Patterson turned around to the three teenagers in the back. Michael perceived, as the other two must have also, that he was doubtful about leaving them there. "I should be coming with you," he said.

"We need someone on the outside," said Michael. Julie had been right about that, even though the familiar presence of Patterson at his side would have been reassuring.

"I didn't expect to come all this way to be a getaway driver."

"A driver we can trust," said Michael.

But still Patterson's doubt remained.

A blast of cold air came into the car as Julie opened the rear door next to him. "We haven't got time for a chit-chat."

Michael gave Patterson an apologetic smile and the three perceivers clambered out of the four-by-four.

Patterson wound down his window and peered out. "I'll be on the radio if you need me," he said.

"You should go," said Julie. She was impatient, a little nervous and — the more Michael perceived her — the more he felt she had developed a dislike of Patterson.

"Of course," Patterson told her. Then he turned his attention to Michael and the others. "Be careful, okay?"

They said that they would.

Patterson pulled his head back inside and the engine roared as he drove up the lane while waving one hand out of the window. Michael watched him go and perceived his doubt as it receded into nothing.

"It's a ten minute march from here," said Julie. "Remember, to anyone who sees us, we must look like Russian soldiers returning to our base."

She led them in the opposite direction to which they had come, and they followed: left, right, left, right.

The air was dry and icy and the bare branches of the trees around them did little to lessen the breeze. Despite the protection afforded by the military coats and gloves they wore, it sucked the heat from their faces until they were numb.

Michael thought of the other perceivers they had left behind who were probably doing much the same thing in the more familiar environment of England, marching to the monotonous beat of their leader. He had once thought himself lucky to escape the exercises that Norm the Norm had ordered the others to take part in, but he was beginning to wonder if he wouldn't have been better off braving the hills of Salisbury Plain with the rest of them. No matter how miserable the exercises were back home, at least they were unlikely to come up against armed Russian soldiers who were liable to shoot them if they found out who they were.

They had marched for little more than five minutes when Julie stopped at the side of the road and huddled into the relative shelter of a bush at the edge of the surrounding woodland. "We should test our communications," she said.

Julie pulled a black box, no bigger than the palm of her hand, from her pocket and flicked a small switch on the top. Also in her pocket was a little listening bug, which she secreted in her ear, and a microphone, which she clipped onto her collar.

The others did the same with their communications equipment. The black box was a radio transmitter and receiver which they could hide in their pocket, allowing the earpiece and microphone to be small enough not be detected by a casual glance. The technology had not yet been invented, however, to make them invisible and they wouldn't be able to risk wearing them all the time.

"This is J," said Julie. "Receiving me, over?"

The split second delay between hearing her speak at the side of the road and those same sounds being relayed through the earpiece produced a disconcerting echo.

"This is M. Confirmed," said Michael.

"This is P. Confirmed," said Pauline.

"This is A. Confirmed," said Alex.

"Tony receiving you, J, M, P and A," came Patterson's voice through the earpiece.

With the test completed, they removed their earpieces and microphones and put them back in their pockets until they needed them.

I wish we could communicate with our minds, thought Pauline.

That's not going to work if we're too far away from each other, thought Michael.

And the norms can't hear us, thought Alex.

Sometimes that can be a good thing, thought Pauline.

The road turned and they found themselves on a stretch of tarmac which led directly to the military facility they had seen in the satellite photograph. It was built like an ordinary road, but its effect was like a driveway, sloping gently upwards to a collection of buildings encased in a ring of high electric fences with barbed wire snaked around the top. The only gap in the enclosure was marked by a booth where two guards were stationed next to a barrier which blocked the entrance to unauthorised vehicles.

The barrier appeared identical to the ones used on military bases in Britain: an electronically controlled metal bar painted red and white with a skirt of railings beneath.

Two guards emerged from their hut, with their rifles slung casually across their torsos.

"Privet!" said Julie in a cheery tone as the first one approached.

Michael could no more speak Russian than he could land on the Moon, but he knew that word meant, 'hello'.

The guard mumbled the same word in reply.

Michael entered his mind.

At the same time, Pauline and Alex dealt with the second guard.

Michael cut through the first soldier's superficial emotions — his need for a cigarette and the cold in his feet — and aimed straight for the centre of his brain.

The guard trembled and a hand reached towards his gun.

Perception is normally a passive power, a sixth sense that 'hears' the thoughts and feelings of others. Even when probing beyond the surface, the person doesn't feel it. But, on this occasion, Michael had no time to be subtle. He went in hard and he went in deep.

Michael seized the man's mind and his hand stopped before it reached his rifle. In his head, his routine of checking newcomers at the gate became locked in suspended animation. Like a video paused by remote control, he could not move forward and he could not move back. He was trapped in the procedure.

It took all of Michael's strength to hold off the guard's free will as he examined the guard's routine. Like a series of shots in a film, the steps formed a pattern which only changed if something out of the ordinary happened — something unordinary like a Russian agent and three British perceivers trying to get into the facility. Michael had to delete the bit of his routine where he checked their credentials so the guard moved straight to the part where he opened the barrier and waved them through.

It sounded drastic, but it wasn't much different to what the human brain does sometimes when it's distracted. Ask anyone who's been thinking of something else while making the coffee and discovered they've poured themselves a cup of hot water with milk and sugar because they'd forgot to add the actual coffee.

Michael had almost completed his task when startled Russian words from the other guard broke into his consciousness. It suggested Pauline and Alex were having problems.

"Hurry up," said Alex. "I can't hold this one for much longer."

Michael struggled to maintain control of the first guard while Julie went to help the others. Michael was aware of a scuffle at the periphery of his vision. Julie had the guard pressed against the booth while Alex was in his mind and Pauline monitored.

"It's done," Pauline said after a few moments. "Release them in: one, two, three."

They both let go of the guards' minds.

It was an anxious few seconds as the perceivers waited for the guards' conscious minds to return to the job in hand.

Michael perceived them: there was a moment of confusion and then they were back to normal without, it appeared, any memory of what had just happened.

The guards' emotions were mundane. They were bored at being stuck for hours on guard duty and irritated to have been dragged out of the relative warmth of their booth to attend to people wanting to be let in.

Michael's guard nodded to Alex's guard who returned to the booth and flicked a switch for the barrier to rise.

Painfully slowly, with the creek of a mechanism that was overdue for an oiling, the barrier lifted to the upright position and the way was clear for them to walk through.

"Spasibo!" said the first guard, and waved them into the facility.

Michael had never perceived so much relief in all his life.

He could tell Julie was impressed, but outwardly she didn't show it. "That wasn't as quiet as you said it would be," she said.

"Quieter than them shooting us," he said.

The road continued up the slope through a grassed area to the cluster of buildings which formed the military facility. Approaching them, they appeared both larger and more substantial than they had from the satellite photograph. The other thing that was different from the satellite image was that, in real life, there were no labels on the buildings and he wasn't sure which was which. He hoped Julie was better than him at interpreting where they were heading.

Two soldiers walked past them, talking to each other in Russian. Michael perceived them and felt their disinterest at the four newcomers heading for the buildings. He put his hand into his coat pocket to feel the side arm strapped to his leg. Its presence was reassuring, but he realised that if the soldiers had turned to challenge them, he would not have had time to remove his glove, pull his pistol from its holster, disengage the safety and fire it at them before they fired at him.

Julia strode on ahead, took a right turn and headed for the concrete building which Lucas worked out of, according to her out-dated intelligence.

It was a far cry from the sort of modern laboratory that might be found in the West. Those modern, steel and glass constructions which towered into the sky would have appeared as futuristic fantasies next to the grey rectangle which sat on the edge of the grass area. The only things which broke up the grey were the windows, each one identical to the next and placed in regimented rows three storeys high.

Its entrance was equally mundane. There was no plush, expansive reception area manned by a smiling receptionist. Instead, there was an ordinary door which opened with a simple turn of a handle. It led into a functional lobby not much bigger than the inside of a lift and furnished with a tiled floor, bare painted walls and a sign printed in Russian.

No guard stopped them. No one questioned them. No one was there at all. It was like walking into an ageing and run-down apartment block. It had a corridor which turned to the left, another which turned to the right and stairs in front which led to higher floors.

Julie kept her words to a whisper. "We'll take the ground floor and work up," she said, referring to herself and Michael. "You two take the top floor and work down."

Pauline and Alex nodded.

"Put on your communications devices," said Julie.

Good luck, Michael thought as Pauline and Alex began walking up the stairs, fiddling with their earpieces as they went.

You too, came Pauline's reassuring thought.

Don't wait to call us if you need us, thought Alex.

Michael watched them disappear up the stairs, leaving him with Julie. She nodded to the corridor on the left and led the way.

It was a stark tunnel lit brightly from above with more painted bare walls and the continuing tiled floor that went on for what was probably the length of the building. On either side were plain white wooden doors that led into unknown rooms, equally spaced just like the regimented windows on the outside. The only thing that differentiated one door from another was a square plaque screwed into the top right hand corner which contained a character from the Russian alphabet and a number.

Michael stopped at each door and perceived. The first two were empty, but the third had a collection of minds, he estimated to be three individuals, all thinking in Russian. None of them were Doctor Lucas.

They walked on to the next door, and the next, and the next. Julie stood by him impatiently each time like a dog owner waiting for the animal to pee up a lamppost before they could keep moving.

Michael's heart raced as, further along the corridor, a door was opened. He willed himself to look calm, at least from the outside, as a woman emerged. Her thoughts were in Russian and her emotions were unremarkable. She wore civilian clothes —a skirt and a plain brown jumper over the top of a white blouse — and he assumed she must be one of the scientists who worked there. As she turned back to close the door behind her, it revealed the bump of a pregnancy under her clothes. Michael was no expert in pregnant women, but the bump was clearly visible and she couldn't be any more than a couple of months away from giving birth.

Julie and Michael had to resort to single file to allow her to pass. She gave them a brief smile and continued on her way.

Michael stopped at the door she had come out of. There were more minds behind it. Not only could he perceive them, but he could also hear them chattering in Russian — all the voices belonged to women.

Julie listened. 'Pregnant women,' she mouthed with surprise.

Michael nodded. He perceived for a moment longer, but Lucas clearly wasn't inside and he shook his head.

Another corridor branched off to the right. They turned down it to find more doors with more Russian numbers written on small plaques screwed into them.

It was the second door that Michael stopped at which caused him to pause. There was a singular presence inside, loud and confused — and thinking in English.

For a moment he thought he had found Lucas. There was something familiar about the mind, but different. It had been a long time since he had perceived the scientist and it took a moment for him to be sure.

"Sarah."

"The girl?" whispered Julie.

Michael nodded. He tried the door handle, but it was locked.

"What are you doing?" said Julie in an urgent whisper. "We can leave her here while we go look for Lucas."

"We can't leave her!" said Michael.

Julie pulled his arm away from the handle which refused to turn even when he forced it. "Remember the mission priority."

"Screw the priority! I came here for Sarah."

"We can come back for her," said Julie.

"No way."

"Do I have to order you?"

"Do what you like, but I'm getting Sarah out of there. I know what it's like to be Lucas's lab rat and I'm not letting it happen to her."

He perceived Julie's frustration, but other than threatening to shoot him, she had no option but to reluctantly go along with him.

Michael's perception of Sarah behind the door had changed. The rattling of the handle had alerted her and she was afraid of it.

Not wanting to shout to her through the door, he knocked as quietly as he could.

"Bugger off!" came Sarah's voice behind it.

He leant close to the door, hoping his voice would carry through it and not down the corridor. "Sarah, it's me."

"Who's me?"

"Michael."

A wave of joy and disbelief rolled out of the room along with the sound of movement. Her mind was suddenly closer to his perception — she'd moved closer to the door? — and random thoughts were bursting from it like someone had dropped a match into a box of fireworks.

"Michael?" came her voice, much clearer now.

"The door's locked." He tried the handle again to make double sure, but all it did was rattle. "Can you get out of the window?"

"No window in here," came the reply.

When they had turned into the second corridor, they must have walked into the middle of the building. It was likely none of the rooms in that row had windows.

Michael reached beneath his coat and put his hand on the hilt of his side arm. Its power to fire a destructive bullet through whatever he pointed it at was unquestionable, but that also made it dangerously noisy.

"Stand back from the door," he told her.

Julie's arm grabbed his as he pulled the pistol from under his coat. "No!"

He shook free of her grip. "I promised her." He felt the weight of the metal in his hand, unclipped the safety and stood back from the door.

Julie, obviously horrified at what he was going to do, but unable to stop him, got out a last minute communication over the radio to warn the others that they were about to draw attention to themselves.

If they replied, then Michael didn't hear them.

He pulled the trigger and all other sound was killed by the explosion that blasted from his hands. His arms shuddered at the recoil and the pressure pained his eardrums.

The shot died, leaving behind it a ringing echo in his ears and the smell of spent gunpowder.

The door swung ajar, its lock shot to pieces. Around the hole where the bullet had entered, splinters of its painted surface had been blasted from the entry point to reveal fragments of bare wood underneath.

He pushed it open and walked into a drab square room of grubby white walls. The only furniture was a camp bed. Next to it was a plastic bucket that smelled of stale urine.

Sarah ran out from behind the door and threw her arms around him, grabbing him tight. "Michael!"

As he returned the hug, her stick-thin body under the baggy jumper that she wore felt even more skeletal than he remembered. "Thank God you're all right," he said.

But even as she trembled in his arms, he perceived a troubled mind that was not all right. Memories twirled inside, all of them from different times and apparently unconnected. She remembered Michael standing helpless at gunpoint outside Ivanov's nightclub, a Labrador dog bounding across a field towards her and looking in a mirror as she applied make-up to her eyelids. Some of her emotions were in the present, as she clung onto the soft warmth of her rescuer, but the rest were a tumble of thoughts without order or control.

Julie dashed in from the corridor and leant back against the door to keep it closed behind her. "There's no way no one heard that," she said. "We have to get out of here."

"Yes, please take me home," said Sarah, her vulnerability showing in her words as well as in her mind.

"Quiet!" Julie's irritated whisper caused Sarah to recoil into Michael's chest, but it did the job and she didn't say another word.

Julie turned to the door and put her ear against it. The grimace on her face showed she didn't like what she heard and, a moment later, Michael heard it too. Concerned voices, talking in Russian, and the footsteps of up to a dozen people in the corridors around them. Not close enough for Michael to perceive clearly, but enough to feel their confusion.

A set of footsteps, sounding more like women's shoes than army boots, click-clacked in the corridor. Michael reached out to perceive the mind of their owner, fearing they would see the bullet hole and raise the alarm. But the footsteps hurried straight past and took the mind of the person away.

Julie sighed. "From what I can hear of their conversations, they seem to think it might be some military exercise. Fortunately for us, it's not unusual to hear gunshots and explosions around a military base."

Michael relaxed just a little. He'd lived on a military base for several years and he understood how people got used to the sound of ordnance being set off as troops practised their fighting skills. Although the gunfire was not normally inside the building.

"We still need to move," said Julie. She looked back at Sarah, who appeared small and fragile at Michael's side. "I still think it's best to leave her here for now so she doesn't get in the way or attract attention. We can come back for her later."

"No!" Sarah wailed, as quietly as she could, but still too loud for Julie's nerves. "I'm not staying here. I'm not!"

She clawed at the material of Michael's coat. He looked across at Julie. "If we find Lucas, we might not have time to come back."

"Lucas?" Sarah let go of Michael suddenly as if she had just found out he was diseased. The mess in her mind turned to fear.

Julie looked Sarah directly in the eye. "You know Lucas?"

"He …" Sarah stuttered. "He gives me the serum. He makes me read the minds of the pregnant women, but it's all in Russian. He says he wants to see when it will turn me mad. I know it's soon. Maybe it's already."

"This could be useful," said Julie.

Michael gave the Russian agent a reproachful glance, even though he agreed with her. She was, it seemed, as cold as the winter weather in her home country. When he turned back to Sarah, he made sure there was a sympathetic expression and a smile on his face. Whenever she had last taken the serum, it was long enough for the perceiver power to have worn off and he hoped her norm's five senses were enough to tell her that she could trust him.

"Do you know where Lucas is?" said Michael.

Sarah nodded. "He works on the middle floor."

"Is that where he keeps his research?"

"I think so."

"Can you show us?" said Michael.

"I want to go home," said Sarah.

"You can go home after you show us. Can you do that?"

Sarah seemed to trust Michael, but she looked warily across at Julie. With a slight reticence, she nodded.

Julie placed her ear to the door again and listened. "Okay, here we go," she said.

They stepped back out into the corridor and resumed their hunt for Doctor Lucas.

THIRTY-TWO

WALKING like they had every right to be in the building, but breathing like three people who feared they would be caught any second, they walked into the corridor and back the way they had come.

Michael led the way, with Sarah in the middle and Julie at the rear. He had told Sarah not to say a word, but to think of the route that would take them to Doctor Lucas. Her thoughts, on the edge of madness, jumped around randomly, but she maintained enough concentration for Michael to follow.

Julie relayed their progress into the microphone of her communicator on her collar. "Got a lead on Lucas. He's on the middle floor."

Patterson acknowledged her. Nothing came back from Pauline and Alex. But that wasn't unexpected. If they were in danger of being overheard, they might not be able to respond.

Michael led them up the stairs one level to the first floor of the building and they were greeted by a copy of the layout below. The only difference was the numbers on the doors.

Sarah directed them to take the corridor on the right.

Michael stopped as he perceived the thoughts of another person in English, so suddenly that Sarah almost walked into the back of him. He raised his hand as a signal for the others to wait as he filtered out Sarah's jumbled thoughts and concentrated on the new mind.

To be, or not to be. That is the question, came the thoughts. Whoever it was, was quoting Shakespeare! *Whether it is nobler in the mind to suffer the slings and arrows of outrageous fortune, or … something, something … Now is the winter of our discontent, made glorious summer …*

Their knowledge of the Bard left something to be desired as their mind skipped through a series of half-remembered speeches.

Michael stepped forward, getting closer to the mind, struggling to remember his old perceptions of Lucas and trying to fit them to the amateur dramatics in his head.

Sarah tugged at the back of his coat as they neared a door. She pointed to it.

Her thoughts told him that Lucas worked on the other side.

So it was Lucas's mind which was quoting Shakespeare. The only mind, according to his perception, that was behind the door.

Michael pulled his gun again from its holster. He glanced behind at Julie who did the same.

He reached out for the door handle and took a preparatory breath. In one movement, he turned the handle, opened the door and walked straight into the room.

Michael stopped two steps from the carnage that greeted him. Upturned stools littered the floor of the laboratory, among the broken glass of shattered scientific vessels.

Romeo, Romeo, wherefore art thou—

The Shakespeare stopped. At the front of the lab, surrounded by the pieces of a smashed computer, stood Lucas: a gun in his hand with his finger poised on the trigger as he held the barrel at Pauline's head. His other arm gripped her tightly round the waist.

With the mask of poetry fallen from Lucas's mind, his true personality revealed itself to Michael's perception. It left him in no doubt that Lucas was prepared to kill Pauline to save himself and his research.

I'm sorry, Michael, Pauline's thoughts desperately spilled out from her. *He made me block my thoughts, he made me—*

Lucas pushed the barrel of the pistol harder against her head.

Pauline let out an audible gasp.

"No thought-speaking!" said Lucas.

It was then that Michael realised what was different about Lucas's mind. He was a perceiver.

At least, it felt like he was. A relatively strong, but unpractised one.

Strong enough, it seemed, to detect Michael's thoughts. "I took the serum," said Lucas. "This perception thing is rather fun, isn't it?"

It didn't feel fun to Michael. He wondered where Alex was. Perhaps they could somehow warn him and he could come to help.

"Sorry about your friend," said Lucas, glancing to the side of the room.

There, half-hidden by a computer monitor on its side, lay Alex. He was face down on the floor next to a smear of blood, almost certainly his own. Michael perceived him and sensed enough to know he was alive, if unconscious.

"Lower your weapons," said Lucas.

Michael, reluctantly, did as he was told.

"Don't!" said Julie. "There's two of us and one of him."

"But can you shoot me before I kill this perceiver?" Lucas squeezed Pauline's waist tighter and her fear spiked.

"Julie, *please*," said Michael.

Julie lowered her weapon with a palpable resentment.

"I see you found Sarah," said Lucas. "I don't know why you are bothering with her."

Sarah, already half hidden behind Michael, tucked herself further behind him.

"Ah," said Lucas. "I perceive that you feel responsible."

In all the shock, Michael had forgotten to raise his blocks. He pulled them up as fast as he could, hiding the rest of his feelings behind a mental barrier that an unpractised man on serum would be unable to breach.

"What do you feel about this one?" He squeezed Pauline again.

To lose her would be to lose his best friend, thought Michael. To lose her would be to lose the only person he'd got close enough to love. But those thoughts were hidden to everyone but himself behind his blocks.

"I understand if you don't want to tell me," said Lucas. "She means nothing to me, although it might be interesting to observe a real perceiver for a change. The thing is, I've put a lot of effort into studying Sarah and it would be a shame if she was to leave before my research is complete. How about a swap?"

Sarah's fear spiked to join Pauline's.

"A swap?" said Michael.

"Yes, you give me Sarah back. I give you back…" He paused as his perception picked up the name from the mind of someone in the room. "… Pauline."

"We don't negotiate!" said Julie.

Lucas ignored her. "What do you think, Michael? If you give me Sarah, I will give you Pauline."

"No!" cried Sarah.

Michael felt the pull of her desperate hands as she grabbed onto the back of his coat. "I can't."

"Never mind. I'm happy to take this one if you don't want her." Lucas stepped backwards, yanking Pauline back with him. "Don't struggle, girl, you can perceive I won't hesitate to shoot you."

"Michael!" cried Pauline, as Lucas continued to back away with his gun to her head.

Michael wanted to run towards her and pull her away from Lucas, but he daren't. He wanted to use his telekinesis to will the gun from her head and throw it across the room, but he remembered how Ivanov had pulled the trigger when he had tried it with him. So he stood, impotent, while Lucas threw open a door at the far end of the lab.

"Don't try to follow me," said Lucas. "I've already raised the alarm. A group of soldiers will be here to capture you in a matter of seconds."

Lucas pulled Pauline through the door and Michael perceived her terrified mind and her sense of betrayal as she was dragged down the corridor away from him.

He was left only with Sarah's bittersweet gratitude and Julie's concern that they would be descended upon by Russians with guns at any moment. Neither of them had perceived Lucas's lie. Not that it mattered a great deal because, although he had not yet been able to raise the alarm, it wouldn't be long before he did so.

Julie spoke into the communicator. "Emergency protocol. Acknowledge!"

Patterson's startled voice came back over the radio. "Emergency? What's going on?"

"Follow the protocol!"

"Acknowledged," said Patterson's disembodied voice. "Jesus Chri—" and he turned off the transmission.

A groan rose from the floor. Alex was regaining consciousness. Michael perceived a growing confusion and a pain in his head.

"Alex!" Sarah was the first one to run over to him. She crouched at his side, brushing strands of bloodied hair from his face.

Michael went round to his other side. "Alex, are you okay?"

"Lucas," Alex mumbled.

"Yes, we found him." Michael decided that perceiving his friend would be quicker than getting him to answer questions. Alex was dazed, but seemed largely unhurt.

Michael grabbed him by the arm. "Come on, you need to get up."

"Pauline?" said Alex.

"She's already gone," said Michael, hoping Alex was still woozy enough not to perceive his lie wrapped in a truth.

Julie was at the door and peering out into the corridor. "We need to go," she said.

"Coming," said Michael. He had pulled Alex to his feet. He managed to stand, but only because he was resting half his weight on Michael.

"The corridor's clear," said Julie. "But I don't know for how much longer."

After a few steps Alex was almost capable of walking on his own.

Julie looked at them. She said nothing, but her thoughts betrayed her doubts that they could make it out with a wounded man and a civilian. When they had walked in, a casual observer would have believed they were soldiers. Walking out, they were going to look like fugitives.

"Pretend you've captured us," said Michael.

"What?" said Julie.

"March us out at gunpoint," he said. "Like we're your prisoners."

It did little to allay her doubts, but with no better idea on the table, she raised her pistol and indicated towards the door.

Michael did his best to block out the anxiety of the others as he stepped out into the corridor, and kept his perception open to watch for approaching soldiers.

They made it along the corridor, down the stairs and into the modest entrance.

Stepping out of the door, they saw an army jeep bouncing over the grass towards them.

"Have they come for us?" said Sarah.

"Probably," said Michael.

"Keep marching," said Julie. She held out her pistol even further so it was clearly visible. "And try to look defeated."

We need to run, but Alex's thoughts were more a wish than a suggestion. He was only just about managing to walk.

If they've got guns, their bullets will outrun us, thought Michael.

The jeep pulled up to block their path with its diesel engine rumbling in the cold.

Two young soldiers jumped out and aimed their rifles directly at them. They were both clean shaven, one with two prominent scabs on his cheek where his razor had taken off the tops of acne spots. Michael perceived that the soldiers had no intention of shooting them, but it didn't mean they wouldn't if they had to.

"Nazovite sebya!" said the clear-skinned soldier.

Julie stepped to the side of her 'captives', keeping her gun aimed at them. Kapitan Irina Zharkova. Ya zakhvatila predateley."

"Spasibo, Kapitan Zharkova," the soldier replied. "Teper' predostav'te eto delo nam."

"Nyet, nyet! Ya zakhvatila ikh. Eto moya zasluga."

Michael tried to perceive what was going on, but he could make as much sense of their Russian thoughts as he could of their Russian language.

This doesn't look good, thought Alex.

I'm getting that impression, thought Michael. He looked down the road towards the entrance. It was a short distance to run, but a long way if they were getting shot at. Making a break for it would be suicide.

He looked at the rifles pointing in their direction. Even though the young men held them casually, he could see each had released the safety catch and their fingers were rested on the triggers.

Get ready, thought Michael.

He focussed on the rifle in the hands of the acne scab soldier. He felt its weight, he felt its shape. Just like he had done with Ivanov, he willed it out of the soldier's hands and across the grass.

The soldier let out a Russian-sounding shriek and grabbed tighter hold of his gun as it swung round towards the one who had done all the talking. A shot blasted from the barrel, striking his comrade in the shoulder.

The clear-skinned one cried out and clasped a hand to the bloody hole in his body.

"In the jeep!" screamed Michael. "Julie, you drive."

They were stunned for a second, but Alex had been half expecting it and jumped into the back of the jeep as Michael jumped in the front. The women realised what was going on and jumped in afterwards.

"Ty vystrelil v menya!"

"Ya ne khotel."

Julie put the jeep into first gear and stamped on the accelerator.

The jeep lurched forward.

"What did you do?" shouted Julie after the guttural surge of the engine.

"Bought us some time."

Michael looked back through the rear window. The soldiers were already raising their rifles to fire. "Get down!" he yelled as a bullet shattered the glass.

Sarah screamed.

Alex swore.

Julie kept driving.

Michael peered up over the dashboard at the barrier across the entrance. It was firmly closed and the guards they had passed using mind control had regained their free will and had emerged from the booth with their rifles drawn.

"What do I do?" said Julie.

"Ram it," said Michael.

"It's a solid metal gate, hitting it will be like crashing into a tree."

A bullet from behind took a chunk out of Julie's arm and splattered a bloody mess on the window. She yelled and swore in Russian, but kept driving.

As the barrier rushed towards them, the guards began to fire. A shot shattered the windscreen. The jeep swerved. Julie looked out of the side window to see where they were going.

"He's there! Slava Bogu!" she cried.

Michael looked out of the other side window. The four-by-four they had used to drive to the secluded lane was parked at an angle next to the booth. Inside the booth was a third soldier. For a moment, Michael thought it was another guard, but then he perceived it was Patterson. Dressed — like them — in military fatigues.

The barrier began to rise. Slowly and steadily with no acknowledgement that they were in a hurry.

Julie aimed the jeep at its widest gap and Michael perceived her praying that, by the time she got there, it would be high enough to drive through.

THIRTY-THREE

JULIE sat on the table at the apartment as Patterson bandaged her wound. She was still bleeding and, as he wound the white bandages around her arm, red oozed into them.

The others were left to tend to themselves using a collection of first aid supplies that Julie had pulled out of a cupboard and scattered onto the table. Only Sarah had escaped with little more than cuts from breaking glass. Michael, it turned out, had been hit by a bullet which had grazed his leg. With the adrenaline of the escape, he only realised that he was bleeding when he was sitting in the back of the car. Alex's head wound, where Lucas had struck him with the butt of his gun during a struggle, looked like it was superficial. Back in England, he would have seen a doctor to make sure he was not suffering from concussion. In Russia, they would have to cross their fingers that there was no internal damage.

Patterson secured Julie's bandage with a safety pin.

"Spasibo," she said.

"I'll need to put a fresh dressing on it at some point," he said. He stepped back and looked at the others. "Do you want to tell me what happened now?"

"We got caught," said Michael.

"And Pauline?"

"Alive the last time we saw her."

"What do you think Lucas will do to her?" said Patterson.

Michael closed his eyes and tried not to think of all the horrors which had been running through his mind since he had climbed safely into the four-by-four and left Pauline behind. "I don't know."

"He'll test her," said Sarah, leaning across the table where she had been pulling a ball of cotton wall into half over and over again until the small, fluffy pieces lay like snow in front of her. "Study her. Give her a bucket to pee in. I want some blueberries."

Patterson was taken aback. "Blueberries?"

"She doesn't want blueberries," Michael told him. Sarah's mind was still confused. Who knew if she would ever regain full control over her own thoughts, or if the serum had damaged her brain permanently.

"You still haven't told me what happened," said Patterson.

"We found Lucas," said Alex. "He wasn't pleased to see us." He winced as he pulled a disinfectant-soaked pad from the gash in his head. He frowned at the amount of blood on it and pressed it back against his scalp.

"Did you confirm he's the one behind the serum?" said Patterson.

"Oh yes," said Alex. "From what I perceived before he whacked me over the head. I think he might have used it on himself one too many times. He wasn't mad, but ... he was trying hard not to lose control."

"Did you plant the computer bugs?" asked Julie.

"Yeah, but I don't know how much data they could have transmitted before he discovered us."

"Hopefully you will have been enough of a distraction that he didn't notice," she said. "Although, I'm sure they will have swept the labs after our escape. I'll have to check the data stream."

"Pauline could tell you more if she were here," said Alex. "I don't know what she perceived while I was unconscious."

"We have to get Pauline out," said Michael, his fingers nervously playing with a roll of micropore tape which he twirled round and round his index finger.

"We'll never get back in there, not the same way," said Julie.

"We can't leave her!" said Alex.

"The base will be locked down tighter than tight after today's breach," said Julie. "We can't just walk in and get her. That's assuming she's still there and they haven't moved her to another facility."

"What about diplomatic channels?" said Patterson. "Can't we do a prisoner exchange or something."

"Diplomatic channels?!" Michael was furious. "We have to act now, before Lucas does to her what he did to Sarah."

"I'm sorry about your friend," said Julie. "But we knew it was a dangerous mission. The three of us did well to come out of there alive and with the intelligence that we have."

"You're happy to lose Pauline to that maniac?" said Michael. "You people are unbelievable!" He stood up from the table and threw the micropore tape back among the rest of the first aid kit. It bounced off a tube of antiseptic cream and rolled onto the floor.

"Where are you going?" Patterson called after him.

"Bed," said Michael, as he went through the kitchen door. He had nowhere else to go.

MICHAEL couldn't sleep. He lay in the single bed of the twin room of the apartment, feeling the lack of warmth from Pauline's absent body beside him. The only thoughts in the room were his own, turning the events of the day over and over, looking for an opportunity he had missed to get Pauline away from Lucas and take her with him.

There was a knock at the door. He was going to tell Patterson or Julie, or whoever it was, to go away, but then he perceived it was Alex.

Alex opened the door, allowing light from a bulb hanging from the ceiling outside to come in with him. He had changed out of the Russian army fatigues Julie had given him, but wasn't ready for bed. He wore civilian clothes.

Alex closed the door behind him and the darkness returned. *Are you asleep?*

You can perceive I'm not.

Yeah, sorry.

Alex approached Michael's bed and perched on the edge. "What—?"

Don't speak, thought Alex. *The norms might hear.*

Hear what?

We can't leave Pauline with Lucas.

I know that, but you heard what Julie said, we can't just walk in and get her.

I have sort of a plan, thought Alex.

What's 'sort of' a plan?

When I was in Lucas's lab, I found something I didn't tell Julie about.

Alex reached into the pocket of his trousers and pulled out two unmarked glass vials.

Perceiver serum? asked Michael.

Yeah, thought Alex. *I saw a syringe in the first aid kit. I thought we could put the two together.*

Are you serious? thought Michael.

Never more so.

We don't know what effect the serum has on people who are already perceivers.

No.

We don't know if it'll send us mad.

No.

We don't know if it'll even do anything.

No, thought Alex. *But are you up for it? For Pauline?*

Michael didn't even have to think about it. *Yeah. Absolutely.*

THIRTY-FOUR

ALEX said he had driven a car before, but that driving experience turned out to have been a year ago and only around the grounds of the base back home and in the daylight. Driving at night in Russia in an unfamiliar vehicle on unfamiliar roads was hairy to say the least. They took one wrong turning and ended up down a farm track. But, a combination of their memories of the route Patterson took during the day and the help of a satnav app on Michael's phone, they got as close as they dare to the Russian military facility and stopped.

Alex pulled the vials from his pocket. "Are you sure about this?" he asked.

"No," said Michael, remembering the disorder in Sarah's brain. "But let's do it."

Alex had wanted them to take the serum together, at the same time, but there was only one syringe and they were forced to take it in turns.

Michael filled the syringe with the contents of the first vial and tapped the top to get rid of any air bubbles. "Roll up your sleeve," he said.

"God, I hate needles," said Alex, as he pushed up the left sleeve of his jacket, and the shirt underneath, and turned his face away from his bare arm.

Michael used a bandage from the first aid kit back at the apartment to tie a tourniquet on Alex's arm and make his veins stand out. Then, in the dimness of the car's interior light, he found a suitable spot near the bend in Alex's arm. He sterilised the skin with an alcohol wipe, just as he had seen on an internet video. He blocked out Alex's increasing anxiety and pressed the needle into his vein.

Alex winced, but the needle went in. Michael pushed the drug into his system.

"Okay?" he asked, dropping his blocks and perceiving Alex's brain, hoping to hell it wouldn't start to scramble.

"I think so," said Alex.

Michael withdrew the needle from Alex's arm, pressed on the puncture point with a ball of cotton wool and secured the pad with a strip of micropore tape. "How do you feel?"

"The same. I think," said Alex. "You'd tell me if I was going mad, wouldn't you?"

"No," said Michael, knowing Alex would perceive his lie. It was a sort of perceivers' joke.

It was also a test.

Alex smiled at the joke. He passed.

Then it was Michael's turn.

Alex sterilised the needle as best he could with disinfectant from the first aid kit and some bottled water. He then filled it with the contents of the second vial.

Alex's nerves and inexperience meant he missed Michael's vein the first time, but found it on the second attempt. It hurt, but it was nothing like the pain of a gunshot wound and he bore it without complaint.

The serum was cold as it entered his vein and it made him shiver as he felt it mix with his blood. Whatever effect the serum was going to have on them, it was now too late to stop it.

Alex took in a gasp of breath. "Oh! Oh, can you *perceive* that?"

"What?"

"The birds! I think I can perceive the birds. And the people. So many people. Thinking in Russian."

Michael looked around, there were no houses in the dark lane where they had stopped and the military base was only visible as lights on the hill in the distance.

"Can you perceive it too?" asked Alex.

Michael felt normal. He could perceive Alex — high on the effects of the drug — but that was all.

Until …

It rolled over him like an angry wave, drowning him in the perceptions of anything and everything around him. The scurrying of night creatures in the trees searching for food, the drowsy thoughts of a woman trying to find the bathroom in the middle of the night, images from the dreams of sleeping Russians far away.

It reminded him of having the cure reversed three years ago, when he had become a perceiver again. The sudden flood of thoughts and emotions was overwhelming. Back then, his father had taught him to block them out. That's what he did now. He shut down every single perception outside of his mind. The serum had strengthened his ability to perceive, but it had also enhanced his ability to control it.

Alex, however, was having a hard time. Still sitting in the driver's seat, his hands gripped the steering wheel like it was the only thing stopping him floating away from the Earth. "Oh God, oh God, oh

God," he was saying, breathing rapid and shallow as he struggled to cope with all the things flying unbidden into his brain.

"Block them," said Michael.

Alex barely heard him.

Block them!

Alex turned towards him, staring with wide bloodshot eyes.

It's like being back at the base with all the other perceivers. Remember how you had to block them before you could sleep? Remember how you had to block your own thoughts so no one else could read them?

Alex nodded.

Then that's all you have to do now. The perceptions might be stronger, but so are you. Shut them down one at a time if you have to. Start with the birds.

Alex closed his eyes and concentrated. He sat for more than a minute like that, frozen in his position in the driver's seat. Then his grip on the steering wheel lessened and he opened his eyes again. They no longer had that panicked stare.

"God, this stuff!" he said. "It's like spending your whole life drinking water, then suddenly downing a pint of whiskey!"

Michael laughed. "That's one way of putting it. Are you ready to try telekinesis?"

"Why don't you go first?"

"Okay."

They got out of the car.

Inside, the only objects they had to move with their minds were small things that they could have moved before taking the serum. Outside, they had the car itself.

The interior light of the car was the only thing that made it visible in the dark lane.

Michael took a step back from the vehicle and imagined it was as easy as an empty Coke can. He looked at the shape of it until it was imprinted on his mind. Then he willed it to rise from the ground.

The car obeyed. He watched, astonished, as the tyres lifted from the road below. It was easy! Like the steel, rubber and plastic were feathers in disguise.

Alex grabbed Michael's arm in excitement. "Amazing!"

It caused Michael to lose concentration and the car dropped the short distance back down to the road and bounced, unharmed, on its suspension.

"Your turn," said Michael.

Alex took a deep breath and nodded.

It took him longer to master the technique, but soon the car was hovering above the ground, just as it had done with Michael. Encouraged by his achievement, he took it higher.

"Put it down!" said Michael as it drew level with their eyes, fearing Alex would drop it and their getaway vehicle would be mess of crashed metal.

Alex lowered the car to the road. The smile on his face was so wide it almost sliced his head in half. "Unbelievable!"

"We need to get going," said Michael. "There's no telling how long this stuff will last with perceivers."

"You're right," said Alex. "Let's go get Pauline."

THIRTY-FIVE

IT was possible they could have got past the main gate into the Russian base using their enhanced powers. With the serum pumping through his veins, Michael felt he could pull the guards' guns clean from their hands and toss them far away. He could toss their whole bodies away if he had to. But the gate was too exposed for them to do it cleanly. It risked being noisy, and if one of the guards was able to raise the alarm, it could bring a whole army of Russian soldiers down on top of them.

Michael and Alex realised they needed a more clandestine route into the military facility, one that they could breach under the cover of darkness. They would have to go over the electric fence.

The fence was lit by floodlights stationed all around the perimeter. But at the point exactly in between each light, there were patches of gloom. Not dark enough to guarantee that they could slip in unnoticed, but dim enough to give them some cover. At the rear of the facility, the fence passed close enough to woodland which they could use to disguise their approach. Parking in the shadow of the trees they could walk to the scrubland which lay outside of the perimeter. From there, it was a case of crawling on their stomachs to get close to the fence, just as they had done in those hideous army training exercises they were forced to endure back when they had first been under the command of Sergeant Norman Macaulay.

Michael remembered getting covered in mud while Norm the Norm shouted at him as he scrabbled under rope netting in the middle of a damp and churned up English field. The hard Russian ground was too cold for slimy mud. Only thistles tried to deter them with their sharp thorns which pierced their clothes and pricked their skin.

As they crawled, Michael and Alex kept their minds open for Russian patrols. It was Michael who perceived the dog first.

He reached out a hand to Alex. *Dog.*

Alex stopped. *I perceive it.*

Michael listened to the wind racing above them. *We're down wind of it, it won't smell our scent.*

It's getting closer, thought Alex.

That's when they saw the two soldiers walking along the inside of the fence. One held a rifle close to his torso and the other kept his gun slung over his back while his hands were busy shining the light of a torch in front of him and holding on to the dog's lead. The Alsatian walked ahead of the soldiers at a steady pace, no more threatening than if it had been going for a walk in the park. Occasionally it stopped to sniff the ground. The handler allowed the animal to investigate for a moment before encouraging it with a few Russian words to resume walking.

Michael and Alex ducked their heads as close to the earth as they could. The dirt tasted gritty on Michael's lips as he kept his breath shallow, and his body totally still, except for the pounding of his heart.

The patrol passed by their position without a hint of suspicion entering their minds.

Once they had gone, Michael tapped Alex on the arm and they resumed crawling the last stretch of hard ground to the fence.

The metal cage that contained the military facility reached two metres into the air in a mesh of chain-linked steel that hummed with electricity. A spiral of razor wire ran all the way along the top of it. The wire had already snagged a passing bird, judging by a feather which had caught on one of the blades and was flapping in the wind.

Ready? thought Michael.

Yes, Alex replied.

Alex brought his feet up from behind him and crouched into a squatting position by the fence with his arms around his knees to turn him into a little ball.

Michael wrapped his thoughts around his friend's body and willed him to lift into the air. Shutting out the perceptions of Alex's amazement, Michael pushed him higher and higher until he was clear of the barbed wire, then he floated him across as easy as a balloon filled with helium. Still holding him in the palm of his thoughts, Michael lowered Alex to the other side until he touched down gently on the grass.

As Michael released him, Alex's ball-like body rolled sideways, but he put out a hand to stop himself falling. *We've so got to try that when we get home*, thought Alex.

Let's get home in one piece first, thought Michael. *Are you ready?*

When you are, thought Alex.

Michael squatted by the fence and hugged his knees as Alex had done. He took a deep breath. *Okay.*

Michael felt himself lift into the air. It was so weird, it didn't feel like he was being pulled up or carried by anything. It was more like gravity had stopped working. His body floated over the top of the barbed wire, then tilted backwards a few degrees as he came down to join Alex on the other side. He landed on his bum and rolled backwards as Alex let go, but it was a gentle landing and he only needed to put a hand out to the side to steady himself.

They waited for a moment, crouched inside of the fence and perceived the immediate area for the minds of Russian soldiers. There were none; the patrol had gone.

Standing up, dressed in the same uniforms they had used during the day, they looked enough like Russian soldiers to walk with confidence to the research building where they had encountered Lucas.

Halfway there, Alex stopped. *She's not in there*, he thought.

Michael perceived the building. It was so much easier on the serum. No longer did he need to get close to someone to sense them. He could feel them through thick, concrete walls — or he could have if anyone was there.

Alex was right, he couldn't detect Pauline's presence. In fact, he sensed no minds at all in the building.

"Do you think they've taken her away?" Alex said out loud.

"They better bloody not have," said Michael.

"Can you perceive her anywhere?"

Michael perceived the whole of the military facility. There were so many Russian minds — so many thoughts, dreams, emotions — it was like listening to a whole orchestra of instruments playing different tunes. "If she's asleep, it's going to be difficult to find her, even with the serum."

"If you'd been captured by Lucas, would you be able to sleep?" said Alex.

He was probably right. And, if she was awake, Michael could probably project his thoughts towards her. *Pauline?* he called in his mind.

No response. He called again, broadcasting as loud as he could: *Pauline?*

Michael? Her reply was faint, but it was definitely her.

Pauline, where are you?

Michael is that you?

He focussed his perception on her thoughts, trying to push away his own excitement of sensing she was alive and within reach. *Tell me where you are.*

I don't know. Still in the Russian base, I think.

Don't worry, we'll find you, came Alex's thoughts.

Alex! You're so clear, you must be really close.

We need to get closer, thought Alex, fudging the answer to her implied question. *Can you describe your surroundings?*

No. I'm in a locked room. There's a window, but it's high up, I can only see the night sky. And it's guarded. I can perceive the guard outside my door and there are others in the building.

Don't worry, thought Michael. *We're coming for you.*

But how…?

It doesn't matter, just keep your mind open so we can find you.

She was in a building nearer to the entrance. Just like the others, it was a concrete block, but this time the regimentally spaced windows were narrower, like they were almost an afterthought in the giant grey wall. Floodlights on each side of the flat roof shone down its grey sides and illuminated the grass that surrounded it.

Michael and Alex stopped just outside the illuminated zone. "Which one is she in?" said Michael, looking up at the windows that rose up to five storeys.

Alex steadied his perception and pointed to a window three floors up in the middle of the row.

Michael perceived Pauline was somewhere in that area, but he wasn't sure Alex had got the right window. "I think she might be in the next one along, to the left."

"Difficult to tell," said Alex. "Perhaps she's standing next to the dividing wall."

Pauline, thought Michael. *I know you can't get to the window, but can you hold something up to it?*

There's nothing in here.

A pillow or something?

There's nothing… but I could take my sock off.

Perfect.

Michael and Alex watched the windows. The one on the left remained dark, but at the one on the right, the white of Pauline's sock could be seen waving behind it.

"Three floors up in the middle of a guarded building?" said Alex. "We'll never get her out."

"What about the window?"

Alex immediately knew what Michael was asking, even though he hadn't said it in so many words. He nodded to Michael and sent his thoughts up to Pauline: *Do you think your body is small enough to fit through the window?*

I can't reach it.

If you could reach it, could you climb through it?

Yes… I suppose… yes, I'm sure I could. Have you got a ladder or something?

Something like that, thought Michael. "Are we sure we can lift her?"

"She's lighter than the car," said Alex.

Except the car had been sitting right in front of them. Pauline was hidden from sight and further away. Michael had never tried lifting objects he couldn't see before. But they had no other plan and not much time.

Smashing the window risked drawing attention, so they decided to remove the whole thing — frame and all.

Fingers could not have grasped around the window frame where it sat sealed into the wall, but thoughts were able to think themselves into the invisible gap.

They wrapped their minds around the window frame until they held it tight, and then they pulled. Just like they had pulled at the fence.

Concrete crumbled from around the window, sprinkling fragments down the wall like pebbles tumbling down a hill. They rocked the window back and forth with their minds until it broke free — so suddenly, their thoughts almost dropped it.

They brought the window slowly and safely down to the ground. As easy as floating an empty Coke can into a rubbish bin.

Pauline's astonishment entered their perception.

Pauline, can you stand by the window for me? thought Michael. *Wave your sock again so we can see you. We're going to do with you what we did with the window.*

Michael reached across and took Alex's hand. He wasn't sure why he did it, but somehow, it made their connection feel stronger.

The two of them looked up at the white of Pauline's sock, waving like a flag of surrender at the window.

Michael felt her body in his mind. Not sexually. Only enough to be sure he could carry her. Like with the car, he evaluated her size, her weight, her skeleton and how her body tissues were framed around it. *Put your arms out above you as if you were going to dive into a swimming pool, okay?*

Done it, she thought.

But he knew that. He perceived it.

One, two, three…

With their minds in unison, Michael and Alex imagined Pauline's body lifting into the air.

Ignoring her surprise and her disbelief, they willed her body to become horizontal and then, gently, they willed it through the window.

Michael's heart raced as he saw the tips of Pauline's fingers appear through the hole where the window used to be. After her hands came through, her arms followed, then her head, her body and finally her legs and feet. She was suspended above them, flying like Superman.

The barking of a dog sounded across the darkness.

They lowered Pauline down to the ground, tipping her back up the right way as she descended so that her feet touched the ground first.

They let go with their minds and their hands parted. Pauline stood in front of them. She looked pale, haggard and bemused as she shivered in only T-shirt and trousers.

Pauline threw her arms around Alex in relief. "I thought you were dead!" she said.

Michael longed to hug her too. "We'll all be dead if we don't get a move on," he said.

The dog's bark was closer. There were voices, too, reaching up into the night.

"The dog's found our scent," said Alex.

"You can perceive dogs now?" said Pauline, half joking.

"Yeah," said Alex. Distracted: perceiving.

Michael could perceive the animal too. The alarm had been raised and the thoughts of a whole lot of alerted soldiers were getting louder.

"Can we get to the fence?" asked Michael.

Alex shook his head. "We'd have to get past the dog."

"Out the front gate, then." But down the slope, Michael saw that the guards were out of their booth and standing with their rifles ready to fire.

"We're never going to make it out that way," said Alex. "Even if we did, the entrance is nowhere near the car."

Behind him, Michael perceived two soldiers emerging from the five storey building.

"We need to run!" said Pauline.

"Not yet," said Michael.

The soldiers marched forward with their rifles drawn. Michael stepped out to face them.

He focussed on the rifle in the hands of the first solider and willed it away. The gun wrenched from his grasp and up into the air. The startled man looked up aghast as his weapon flew far from reach and fell back to the ground.

The second soldier aimed, but Michael already held his gun in his thoughts and sent it sailing off in the other direction.

The pair of them stopped: fear and uncertainty playing in their minds. Michael's thoughts wrapped themselves around the body of the first soldier and lifted him into the air. The soldier cried out — screaming frantically in Russian — as his arms and legs thrashed uselessly against air. Michael threw his body like a bowling bowl into the path of his companion and let go. He landed on top of the second soldier and the pair of them collapsed to the ground in a heap of green camouflage.

"Wow," said Pauline.

"I can't do that with the whole army," said Michael. "We need to get over the fence."

But the noise of the dog was louder and, as they turned, they saw the Alsatian running towards them, bringing with it its handler on the other end of a lead. His comrade from the perimeter patrol struggled to keep pace with them as he held his rifle tight in both hands.

Michael grabbed the gun with his mind and tossed it aside.

It flew right past the dog handler's eyes. The soldier was so startled he let go of the dog lead and grabbed his own rifle from off his shoulder. But, before he could even aim it, Michael had ripped it from his hands and thrown it onto the grass.

The dog — now free of the human — bounded towards them, barking wildly and revealing the white of its sharp teeth.

Alex crouched down at dog level.

"Alex!" called Pauline, but Michael held her back.

They watched as the fearsome animal slowed to a walk. It's barking became snarling and then quiet wailing before it stopped an arm's length away from Alex's face. It looked at him with wide, curious eyes. Alex glared back and the two became locked in eye to eye contact.

After a moment, the trance was broken. The dog turned around to face its Russian master.

It leapt towards him like a domestic pet, pleased to see its owner come home. The dog's master said something encouraging and put out his hand to stroke the dog.

The animal opened its mouth. The soldier pulled his hand away, but not quick enough. The dog snapped his jaw shut onto the ends of his fingers. He screamed and let out a stream of Russian swear words.

"Run now!" Alex yelled.

Michael and Pauline obeyed as Alex got to his feet and followed.

You mind controlled the dog? thought Pauline as they ran.

It's trained to attack us, I just reversed its target so it would attack the soldiers, thought Alex.

Michael — in front — kept sprinting towards the fence, hoping he had remembered correctly where the hole was.

A gunshot pierced the air behind him and hot pain stabbed through his thigh. He stumbled and clasped his leg, feeling the warm blood ooze out of his wound.

He looked back: the second soldier had pulled out his pistol and aimed it at them. As he fired a second shot, the dog leapt up at him. It bit into his gun arm and held it tight. The man screamed and wrestled to get free of the animal's jaws. But the bullet had already done its damage.

Alex fell forward onto the ground.

"Alex!" screamed Pauline.

Alex's pain seared through Michael's perception. It was so loud in his serum-enhanced brain that he felt how it burned through his chest at the same time as perishing cold advanced up from his hands and feet.

Pauline turned back and rushed to Alex's side. She tugged at his arm to get him to stand up. "Alex! Alex!"

Alex's body shook as she pulled him, but he didn't move of his own accord.

Michael hobbled over to join her, keeping one eye on the soldier fighting to free his arm from the jaws of the Alsatian.

Alex's mind was cloudy. The only two emotions inside of it were fear and pain. *I can't, I can't…* he thought.

"Alex, *please*. Get up!" Pauline continued to tug at his arm. "We have to go."

Michael could see the pool of blood soaking into the back of Alex's jacket where the bullet had passed through. Michael had experienced being in the minds of people as they died, twice before, and he remembered how they clung desperately to every last second of life.

Alex's mind was trying not to let go, but his body was weakening with every moment.

Michael turned to Pauline and he felt her reluctance as she perceived what he was about to do.

"No!" she cried.

But he already held her body in his thoughts. He lifted her off of the grass. Her arms and legs flailed uselessly against the air.

"Michael, put me down!" she cried.

We can't all three of us get caught, he thought as he sent Pauline over the top of the fence to safety on the other side. Still fighting it, she landed awkwardly on her hands and knees with a cry of frustration and pain. At least she was out.

But Alex was in a bad way. Michael considered enveloping his body in his thoughts and carrying him over the fence. Even if it meant leaving himself inside to face the Russians, Pauline could perhaps get Alex to the car and then to a doctor.

Michael knelt next to Alex and brushed aside the hair from his fringe which was covering his face. Alex's nose was a mess of blood: he must have smashed it on the ground. There was very little life left in his eyes which stared glassy and unseeing at nothing. He began to doubt that even a doctor could help.

You have to go, Michael, Alex thought.

"No."

You have a chance, but I …

He couldn't bring himself to say that he was dying. Instead, he reached out a hand to touch Michael's arm. He patted it gently.

As he did so, Michael perceived the minds of many more Russian soldiers closing in on them. There was a chance for only one of them to get out of there alive, and it wasn't Alex.

Reluctantly, Michael crouched into a squatting position as he had done before.

Alex took a breath, closed his eyes and gathered his strength. Michael felt his body lift from the ground. Unsteadily, like an aircraft in turbulent conditions, Alex carried him on his thoughts over the fence – so close to the razor wire that it caught the leg of his trousers. It snagged Michael for a moment, but Alex pushed through, the material ripped with an ugly tearing noise and Michael made it to the other side.

Alex's thoughts faltered and he let go. Michael plummeted the last couple of metres and landed hard on the earth. He took a moment to sit up and feel his bruises, but it appeared no bones had been broken.

Pauline was suddenly at his side. "What the hell are you doing?"

"Alex isn't going to make it," said Michael.

He stood and approached the fence, wanting to press his face against the wire to see his friend on the other side, but he knew he couldn't without sending an electric shock through his body. So he stood as close as he could and perceived.

There was barely anything left of Alex. He had used up his final strength to get Michael over the fence and his presence felt as distant as a whisper on the wind.

Alex's thoughts drifted over to them. It was fun, he thought. I loved being a perceiver. I don't regret—

Then stopped.

His mind was empty.

"No!" screamed Pauline. "Alex, get up! Get up!"

Michael said nothing. This was death, just as he had perceived it before.

"We have to go, Pauline."

"We can't leave Alex!"

"He used the last of his strength to get me over the fence," said Michael. "If we get caught, it will be for nothing."

Inside the military compound, he could see Russian soldiers emerging from the dark and advancing on their position. The fence would only stop them for a while.

Michael pulled at Pauline's sleeve. "Let's survive, for Alex's sake."

She took one last look at Alex's body, then turned away. "Okay," she said.

Michael limped off towards the woods, with Pauline beside him, hoping that the car was still where they left it.

THIRTY-SIX

MICHAEL hadn't driven a car before, but he had watched other people drive and he had some understanding of what to do. In theory.

Every time he changed gear, he crunched the gearbox. It didn't help that it hurt to press his leg on the clutch pedal. He should have stopped to wrap some sort of bandage around his wound, but there had been no time. Even though he realised, the longer he left it, the more blood he would feel oozing down his trousers and the more light-headed he would get. Continually fighting the wooziness, he forced himself to focus on the road ahead. There were no street lights, only the headlights of the four-by-four which allowed him to see a little way ahead of him as he bombed down rural Russian roads with barely half an idea of where he was going.

Pauline sat in the passenger seat, traumatised.

"Get the mobile phone out of my coat pocket," said Michael.

"What?" she said.

"There's a mobile phone in the pocket of my coat nearest to you. Take it out and call Patterson."

"We shouldn't have left Alex," she said.

"He's dead, Pauline, there was nothing we could have done. If we get caught, Alex will have died for nothing. Please, we need to call Patterson!"

Pauline fumbled in his coat pocket and found his phone. He told her the passcode to get into his phone's address book and she clicked on Patterson's name.

Their conversation over speaker-phone was short and Michael was glad he couldn't perceive Patterson's anger. Patterson told them he was going to have to wake Julie and find a way to get out to them somehow. He said he would text a location for them to put into the phone's satnav. Then he hung up.

Michael kept driving and praying he was going roughly in the right direction for several minutes before Pauline said what was on her mind.

"Why did you choose Sarah over me?"

"What?" said Michael. The road was bumpy and seeing the way ahead was getting harder. His only consolation was he could perceive no one was following them. Yet.

"Lucas gave you a choice: Sarah or me. Why did you choose Sarah?"

"I didn't choose Sarah. We were rescuing her, I couldn't simply hand her over to Lucas."

"But you left me."

Michael's phone bleeped. It was the text from Patterson. Pauline copied the location details and programmed them into the phone. The phone's artificial voice told Michael to take a left turn at the next junction.

"Lucas had a gun to your head, he was going to shoot you," said Michael. "We did what we had to do to get away. So we could come back for you."

"And look at what happened."

Michael perceived the image in her mind of Alex lying dead on the ground. The image was in his mind too, but he was trying not to think about it.

The car jolted as its front wheel drove up the verge on the side of the road. Michael turned the steering wheel the other way and the car lurched across to the other side. He hadn't realised he was driving so close to the edge. He braked and aimed for the centre of the road, but the way ahead looked misty. He blinked to focus, but when he opened his eyes, all he could see was the black of the night they were driving into.

He must have lost too much blood.

The thumping of his heart, pushing the blood out of the hole in his body, thumped even louder in his head. A pain worse than a headache. A fire, smouldering in the corner of his mind. He tried to hold back the flames, but they were burning hotter and hotter.

The car juddered again. He didn't know what he had done. Whether he had hit the verge again or if he had struck a wild animal running out from the trees.

"Michael!" Pauline grabbed the dashboard in front of her to stop herself being thrown forward.

Michael pressed his foot on the brake — so sharply that the car skidded sideways. He turned the steering wheel in the other direction, but that only made it worse and the car spun round with the tyres screeching beneath them. He braked harder and the car stopped dead in the middle of the road.

Michael's head was still spinning. He freed himself from the seatbelt and threw open the driver's door. He stepped out into the road and his wounded leg gave way underneath him.

Collapsed on the floor, he knew he should get up. He knew he should drive faster and further away from the Russians. He knew he needed to get Pauline safely to Patterson.

But he couldn't move. Not because of the damage to his leg. The pain inside him was coming from his mind.

Red hot flames burned through his neural pathways.

His power shrank. He couldn't perceive the wild creatures of the forest anymore. He couldn't perceive the minds of the Russians living miles away. He couldn't even perceive Pauline. His perception was empty.

He only knew Pauline was suddenly at his side because he heard her. "Michael, what's the matter? We can't stay here."

"I think the serum's wearing off."

"You can still drive, can't you?"

He looked up at her face. Even though the interior light from the car shone out through the open door, all his eyes would allow him to see was a blur.

"We need to stop the bleeding," she said. She grabbed his leg and squeezed, but it was his brain that was burning.

He reached out for her arm and held onto it to get her attention. "It's not the bullet wound that's killing me, it's the serum. It makes norms go mad. We don't know what it does to a perceiver brain."

He cried out as a stab of pain spiked through his mind.

The blur of Pauline's face morphed into darkness and he knew no more.

THIRTY-SEVEN

IT took a long time to chase away the black of the Russian night. Time that Michael wasn't aware of. All he knew was that it was replaced with the white of a hospital room. A room without personality, only plain walls and ceiling and a vinyl floor upon which sat standard-issue furniture. There were two wooden chairs with padded seats covered in black plastic for guests, a bedside table for his possessions and a plastic cup of water, and a tray on wheels that could be moved up the bed for when he needed it and down the bed for when he didn't.

Winter had arrived in England, but that day the clouds were few and sunshine shone through the window where it landed on Michael's bedclothes and lit up the bluey whiteness of the sheets. He'd asked for the window to be open a little so he could smell the freshness of the air. It made the tip of his nose feel cold, but at least he could feel something in the cocooned atmosphere of medical care.

Michael dialled Pauline's number on his mobile phone and listened to it ring. His disappointment swelled as the rings continued and it went to voicemail. Pauline's recorded cheerful voice played in his ear: "Hello, it's me! If you leave a message I'll call you back as soon as I can. Promise."

Michael waited for the phone to bleep. "Hi, Pauline, it's Michael again. I know you're upset about Alex. Me too, I just … will you call me back? Please?" He hung up, wishing he had thought of something better to say.

The door to his room opened. He expected it to be a nurse checking up on him as part of the ward rounds, but it turned out to be Agent Cooper.

Cooper wore the same black suit with open-necked white shirt that he always wore. At least, his clothes looked the same as they always did. Perhaps he had a whole wardrobe full of black suits and white shirts back at home and they weren't the same ones at all. Despite the clothes, he seemed different somehow. Perhaps it was the way he crept into the room like he was approaching a sleeping baby. Michael wanted to perceive him to understand what had changed, but he couldn't.

"Hello, Michael," said Cooper. "The nurse said you were probably awake, but she wasn't sure."

"I'm awake," said Michael.

Cooper closed the door behind him. He reached into the inside of his jacket and pulled out an envelope. Not a letter-sized one, but a larger rectangular-sized one with the word 'Michael' written in swirly writing on the cover. He handed it over. "The kids back at the base got you a card."

Michael ran his finger under the flap of the envelope. It wasn't stuck down very well and he prised it open without tearing it. He took out the card which had a cartoon drawing on the front of a man lying in a hospital bed with his leg in plaster. The man was grinning with a thermometer in his mouth while he played some sort of game on his phone. 'Get well soon' said the writing above his head. Inside, the card was full of signatures and messages from his fellow perceivers. There was even a message from Norm the Norm: 'Get back here — double quick march — and that's an order!' it read, followed by a little hand-drawn smiley face to show he was making a joke. He'd signed it: 'Sergeant Macaulay ("Norm the Norm")'.

He looked for Pauline's message among the different handwriting in different inks and at different angles. At first he thought she had not signed the card, then he saw her name in the bottom right hand corner. Just her name, no message or flourish of the pen. He looked at it for a moment, trying to work out if it meant she hadn't really wanted to sign the card or if she didn't know what to say.

He reached over to put the card on his bedside table. It was a bit too much of a stretch without shifting closer to it.

"Let me do that for you," said Cooper. He took it from Michael's hand and placed it on the table so the picture faced out to the room. Michael had been going to turn the picture towards himself so he could see it from the bed. As it was, the open halves of the card were facing him so he was looking at the signatures. He turned away from them.

"How are you?" said Cooper.

"I still can't perceive anything, if that's what you mean," said Michael.

"I actually meant 'how are you?' generally. But I was also going to ask you about your perception. Has anything come back at all?"

Michael shook his head. It was strange having to live inside his own mind without the awareness of others about him.

"We'll get some tests done," said Cooper. "Find out what's going on in that brain of yours. I've been speaking to the doctors, they think an MRI scan first, some blood tests and cognitive tests, that sort of thing."

"Was it worth it?" said Michael.

"You mean the mission?"

"I mean getting Alex killed."

Cooper avoided looking directly at Michael like norms do when they are embarrassed about something. Not as if Michael could perceive what Cooper's real emotion was.

"We got some good intelligence," said Cooper. "The reports I'm getting back from the data are provisional, but we think the Russians want to make a perceiver army. Lucas is experimenting with perceiver genes, implanting them in embryos, and then implanting them in women. The pregnant women you saw in the Russian military base are carrying what the Russians hope will be perceiver children."

"Do you think he could have got the perceiver genes from me?"

"He was studying several perceivers in Britain before he fled to Russia, wasn't he?" said Cooper. "I know he took your blood, but my understanding is that he had blood samples from several people. I wouldn't be concerned."

"It's just that …" Michael took a breath. "It's just that, when Lucas captured me that time, when he made me unconscious and took me away for a few hours, I don't know what he did to me. I thought he might have taken genetic material."

"I don't know," said Cooper. "Our intelligence is not complete, but we know from what I've seen so far that Lucas was using frozen sperm."

"Sperm?" Michael felt suddenly hot, despite the cold draught from the window. All the pregnant women he perceived behind the closed door and the two pregnant women he saw in the corridors — could they be carrying *his* children?

He was only eighteen. Too young to be a father. Too young to be a father of multiple babies.

Michael reached over for the cup of water on the bedside table. But his hand was too shaky and he mis-judged his grip. The end of his fingers pushed the cup instead of picking it up and it tipped sideways, spilling water all over the table.

As Cooper rushed to rescue the cup, his arm knocked the card over into the pool of water. He grabbed the card and held it out in front of him as water dripped from the edges. But it was too late and some of the signatures had started to run.

There was a little bit of water left in the cup. Cooper handed it to Michael and he drank what there was. It did little to calm his shock.

"The Russians won't know if they have bred any perceiver children until the babies reach puberty, of course," Cooper went on. "That's a long time to wait for a country that's jealous of Britain's perceiver programme. That's almost certainly what the serum trial was about. If Lucas was able to find a treatment which could be injected into fully grown soldiers and special agents, then the Russians wouldn't have to wait for the babies to grow up and get trained: they would have a fully-formed perceiver army overnight."

It all made a horrible kind of sense. "Then testing the serum on Sarah was a way of killing two birds with one stone — find out more about the British perceiver programme while, at the same time, test the serum."

"That's a reasonable assumption," said Cooper.

Just like Michael's theory about sending spies high on the serum into the energy industry.

He still didn't think it was worth Alex dying for.

"So," said Michael. "What happens now?"

"You concentrate on getting better, then we can talk about it."

"I don't know if I want to go back to the Perceiver Corps."

"We can talk about that when you're well," said Cooper.

Michael wondered if he really wanted to fully recover. He might be better off if the serum had destroyed his perception, then Cooper would have no hold on him.

Silence followed and Cooper looked uncomfortable. "I should let you rest," he said eventually. "We'll get those tests underway and see what's what. But I'm sure you will be fine."

"Yeah," said Michael, for want of something better to say.

Cooper edged towards the door. "I'll come back later in the week, then. Get well soon."

He left the room and Michael felt a tension fall from his body.

He imagined a Russian military parade ground full of perceiver children being turned into super soldiers. But then fatigue overtook him and he drifted off to sleep.

THE Peace Garden lay at the centre of the hospital. It was a courtyard formed by four wings of the building which ran round the edge and provided a little oasis where visitors and recovering patients could get some air. Because of the high walls, very little sunlight reached the ground, but somehow a tree planted in the centre was able to survive. Surrounding it were paths wide enough to take wheelchairs and there were small gravelled areas where stone boulders with an interesting or angled shape provided a focal point.

Four wooden benches were placed along each wall of the courtyard. The one Michael sat on had a plaque screwed to the back which said the bench was bought in memory of a girl called Andrea who had sadly died from cancer at the age of five.

Michael pulled his phone from the pocket of the dressing gown he had been given to wear. He went to the list of recently dialled numbers and touched Pauline's name. The phone connected and played out a ring tone. Michael counted the usual eleven rings before it went to voicemail. He listened to all of Pauline's cheery recording which asked him to leave a message and promised to call him back, then he hung up. There was no point leaving any more messages. She obviously wasn't going to call him back.

The sound of an opening door somewhere behind his right ear made him jump.

He still wasn't used to how norms could get up close to him without being able to perceive them. It made him on edge all the time.

"Michael?" said the person.

Michael turned to look and saw Patterson had walked into the courtyard. "Inspector Patterson!" he said.

The wiry-haired policeman was out of his usual working day garb and was wearing a casual jacket over a blue polo shirt and jeans. Perhaps it was Saturday. Or maybe Sunday. He had lost track of the days.

"Call me Tony," said Patterson.

Michael tested the name in his head. It didn't seem right.

It was then that he saw Patterson was carrying a bunch of flowers. They were red, purple, yellow and white daisy-like blooms called chrysanthemums, according to the label stuck on the cellophane in which they were wrapped.

Patterson seemed to notice that Michael had seen them. "I didn't know whether to get flowers or grapes and then the shop had run out of grapes, so …" he trailed off. "I'll put them on the bench, shall I?"

"You can sit on it too if you like," said Michael.

Patterson did as was suggested and laid the flowers on the seat beside him.

Michael suddenly realised how good it was to see him. With Alex gone and Pauline ignoring his calls, Patterson was the closest thing he had to a friend.

"What's this I'm sitting on?" said Patterson, shuffling his bottom on the bench. He reached underneath his leg and pulled out Michael's mobile phone.

"Oh, that's mine."

Patterson handed it back to him.

"I was trying to call Pauline," said Michael.

"Oh, how is she?" said Patterson.

"I don't know. She's not talking to me."

"Give her time," said Patterson.

"I don't know if time will be enough," said Michael. "She blames me for Alex."

"No one is to blame for Alex apart from Alex. It was his idea to go back to get Pauline."

"Who told you that?"

"You did," said Patterson. "After myself and Julie got you out of Russia."

"I did? I don't remember."

"You were pretty out of it."

Michael couldn't remember anything after passing out on the road outside the military facility until waking up in a hospital bed in England.

"How are you?" asked Patterson.

"Okay," said Michael. "My leg was not much more than a flesh wound. They think I'll have a scar, but no lasting damage."

"That's not what I meant."

"If you mean the perception thing, then no change. I've had a scan and tests and I hear the doctors whispering about me, but no one's told me anything. I get the feeling they don't know what the problem is, let alone how to fix it."

"Your system was overloaded," said Patterson. "It will come back." He reached over and put a reassuring warm hand on Michael's cool fingers.

"You don't know that. No other perceiver has ever taken the serum before. Apart from Alex."

"I thought I lost my hearing once," said Patterson.

It seemed an odd thing to say. Michael's instinct was to perceive him to get an idea of the point he was making, but he forgot that he couldn't do that anymore.

"I did, really," he continued. "I went to this rock concert when I was in my early twenties. The band was called The Boiled Eggs and I thought they were amazing. I wanted to stand at the front, right next to the speaker so I could feel the boom of the base through my body. The band played all my favourite tracks and did two encores. I had such a great time. By the next morning, I could barely hear anything. It was like walking around with a bucket of water on my head. My hearing came back, eventually."

"Nice story," said Michael. "But you didn't get injected with an experimental drug that turns people mad."

"Except, it didn't turn you mad, did it?"

Michael changed the subject. "Do you know how Sarah is?"

"She came into the police station to give a statement, not as if I can put much of it into the police file. She seemed the same. I understand she's having treatment and it's too early to say if her mind is permanently damaged."

"Did she say anything about going to Manchester to set up a hair salon?"

Patterson smiled at that. "She did, actually. She kept talking about it like it really was going to happen. She also talked a lot about blueberries. Personally, I don't think I'd trust her with a pair of scissors."

Good. It meant Cooper was honouring his deal with her. Or, at least, she believed he was.

"Look, Michael, there's something that I came to tell you."

Michael's stomach tightened. He didn't like the way Patterson said it. It was so frustrating not to perceive him to understand what that tone of voice meant. "Tell me what?"

"I've enjoyed working with you over the past year or so. Really, I have. But I think it's time to move on. That whole thing with going to Russia made me realise that I don't want to be dealing with this complicated perceivers stuff anymore. I miss normal police work. The sort where there is a crime, there is a police investigation, a trial and then the scumbag is sent to jail. There are rules to follow: simple, important rules. I feel like I've been breaking too many of those rules recently."

"So what are you going to do?" said Michael.

"I've put in for a transfer to the Homicide and Serious Crime Command. I could do with a good murder. Something with a simple motive — like revenge or money or jealousy — definitely nothing involving mind reading."

"So you've come to say goodbye?"

"I suppose I have," he said. "What about you? What are you going to do?"

Michael shrugged. "It depends if I get my perception back."

"And if you do?"

"I don't think I want to go back to working for Agent Cooper. It's like you said, the place where we live is more like a prison camp than a home. And I've seen too many of my friends die: Alex, Peter…"

"Don't stay there if you don't want to. Life's too short."

"It's not that easy," said Michael. He'd more or less made a deal to join the Perceiver Corps to avoid jail. He didn't think Cooper would just let him leave.

"Not everything we want in life is easy. It doesn't mean we shouldn't try to have it."

Patterson stood up from the bench. "Well, I should be going. You need your rest and all that."

"Thanks for coming to see me," said Michael.

"Good luck in whatever it is you decide to do." He held out his hand for Michael to shake.

Michael obliged. It felt odd to shake hands with a man standing up while he was sitting down. It felt odd altogether to shake hands with someone who had come to be his friend.

"Don't forget to put those in water," said Patterson, pointing down at the bunch of flowers on the bench.

"Oh yes," said Michael.

"And next time you have a perceiver adventure…"

"Yes?"

"Don't hesitate *not* to drag me into it."

Michael laughed. "I'll try to do that."

"Good," said Patterson. "Look after yourself, won't you? And give my best to Pauline — I'm sure she'll come round soon."

"I will," said Michael.

Patterson waved as he walked out of the courtyard and back through the door that led into the hospital.

Michael waved back as he watched him leave.

After only a moment, Patterson was gone.

Acknowledgements

I would like to thank Valentina Kingsolver for translating the Russian dialogue for me.

As always, a big thank you to July Daly for her help and encouragement with this novel and the whole *Perceivers* series.

As peace between perceivers and norms unravels, Michael gets drawn into a world of politics where he faces his most dangerous mission yet.

Mind Power: Perceivers #4

The Perceivers series:

Mind Secrets
Mind Control
Mind Evolution
Mind Power